The
BREAD *of*
ANGELS

Amber Albee Swenson

WESTBOW
PRESS®
A DIVISION OF THOMAS NELSON
& ZONDERVAN

WestBow Press books may be ordered through booksellers or by contacting:

WestBow Press
A Division of Thomas Nelson & Zondervan
1663 Liberty Drive
Bloomington, IN 47403
www.westbowpress.com
1 (866) 928-1240

ISBN: 978-1-5127-2574-2 (sc)
ISBN: 978-1-5127-2575-9 (hc)
ISBN: 978-1-5127-2573-5 (e)

Library of Congress Control Number: 2015921449

Print information available on the last page.

WestBow Press rev. date: 01/21/2016

For those without a voice who have experienced
the cruelties of man and the horrors of hell:
God, who is in heaven, sees you, hears you, knows you.

To help end human trafficking consider sponsoring a
child through Compassion International. Sponsored
children are rescued from poverty and educated, fed,
given medical care, and taught about Jesus. This keeps
them out of the high risk group of children that is
preyed upon by traffickers. Compassion ranks in the
top 1 percent of charities for financial accountability
and integrity. That means for about one dollar a day,
you can keep a child safe. Visit www.compassion.com

Chapter One

WHEN THE CUT
GOES DEEP

It only took a second for my life to change. It was the second I stepped into the hair salon on an otherwise ordinary August day, never imagining it could pull the thread to unravel my existence.

Laminate wood floors and an open floor plan met me as I opened the door to Hair Nation, a training school for cosmetologists. A student at the reception desk offered a welcome, and after taking my name, she sent me to a row of chairs. I grabbed a magazine from the rack on the wall, hunkered into a seat, and started perusing.

The hair on the models was perfectly styled, of course, and their smiles lied that it would be just as easy for me to do. Page after page, I considered my options. My face was too round for a pixie; I wasn't sophisticated enough for an inverted bob; I didn't have enough inner turmoil for a spike, and, hopefully, I was fifty years from the short, curled grandma do.

I pushed the magazine back onto the rack as students dispersed from their huddle. At the reception desk, each student picked up her assignment card and, after calling the name, led the client to her station.

One by one, people were escorted back, and the waiting area cleared. My girl was fumbling with something in her pockets while staring at the sheet. When she finally came toward me, I realized her hesitation.

"Meghan?"

She didn't call my name. She asked, as if to say, "Are you sure you want to do this?"

I wasn't.

"Are you ready?" she asked flatly, as if I had purposely planned this meeting.

"Becky?" I asked pensively.

"You're Ben's wife, I assume."

For all of my married life, and for a few months before I was married, Becky was a name and a person to be avoided. She was the only other human to have known my husband in the biblical sense. It was a cruel joke, one that left me wrestling with God. He, working through the powers that be, had assigned my newly pastored husband to her hometown, the only town that had in its clutch the leverage to make his ministry ineffective.

She led me to her chair, shook out a folded black cape, and wrapped it around my neck, no doubt considering how long of a prison sentence she might face if she strangled the life out of me.

It had been nearly five years since I saw her briefly in a restaurant in Ben's arms. She had been slender then, with long, dark hair and glasses. She was heavier now.

Her hair was short with sideburns and a whole lot of rebellion on top.

"What were you thinking?" she asked matter-of-factly.

Did she not realize I had no say in our destination, that if it were up to me, we'd be at least a thousand miles from here in any direction?

"Your hair," she said, pulling me from my thoughts.

"I'm not sure," ... *I want to be here,* I confessed. In truth, I was very sure I did not want to be there. "I was hoping for something easy that looks halfway decent."

"Do you want to keep your length?" She was all business now.

"I like to put it up when I run." Not that she cared.

"What color highlights did you want?"

"Just a shade or two lighter than my natural color."

"Caramel," she clarified.

"I guess."

She motioned, and her instructor, a middle-aged woman with chin-length, curly red hair, came over. Becky explained what we were going to do because she apparently knew something I didn't.

The instructor marked the assignment sheet, she and Becky discussed the color combination, and Becky disappeared.

I closed my eyes and said a desperate prayer that Becky would not color my hair green. I could live with red, black, even blonde, but not an "accidental" chemical overload that made my hair fall out. She wouldn't do that, would she?

Had I done anything that would make her hate me? I married Ben—"her" Ben—but only after her parents broke them up and she said she was dating someone else, so no. She had no reason to hate me.

Still, what were the odds of Ben being assigned to Oronoco, Minnesota, or of me having coffee with another pastor's wife, who recommended Hair Nation—which wasn't even in Oronoco, but seven miles south in Rochester—and then making an appointment and being assigned Becky as my stylist? Probably a bazillion to one.

This was no coincidence. I was divinely appointed to this moment, which meant I had absolutely nothing to fear.

I opened my eyes to see Becky returning, coloring paraphernalia in tow.

"Do you want a lot of thin highlights, or do you like the chunky look?"

"I don't care for the chunky look."

She nodded and worked silently. The other students smiled and chatted with their customers.

"When do you finish school?" I asked at last.

"December."

More than four months away. How long was this program? Did she know what she was doing? "Do you have a job lined up?"

"You don't apply until you finish."

I nodded and waited for her to talk. She didn't.

"When I found out we were moving here, I wondered if you were still around," I admitted.

Her head tilted slightly, as if it were strange for me to say that.

"Are you dating anyone?"

"It's not easy with a child."

Ah, she had a baby, maybe from the relationship after Ben? How could she let that happen, when the negative pregnancy test was the impetus for her parents breaking her and Ben up? "When did you have a baby?"

She snorted. "Are you kidding?"

"What do you mean?"

She stopped midbrush stroke and stared at me. "Do you expect me to believe you don't know about my son?"

"Should I?"

She brushed a few strands of my hair, put the brush down, and wrapped the hair in foil.

I noticed now her mirror and the pictures around it: a baby lying on his back, standing next to a one, with a fishing pole, on a rocking horse next to a two, running with a balloon, beside a four.

"You're kidding, right?" she asked again.

"I'm starting to wish I were."

Four years. The child was four years old. We had been married almost four years. It couldn't be Ben's child, could it? I worked on the math—pregnancy lasted nine months.

She lowered her voice to a whisper. "You really didn't know that Caleb is Ben's son?"

"Caleb?" I asked, pointing to her mirror.

"Yes," she said matter-of-factly. She scooped the brush in the dye and tugged it through a chunk of my hair.

"Does Ben know?"

She chuckled again, this time shaking her head. "Ben's known since Caleb was a baby."

"But I was there when we came to see you. You weren't pregnant."

"Caleb had already been born. I was three months pregnant when I got home from school."

"You told him the test was negative. You said you were dating someone else. He didn't know about a baby."

"Not then, no. When you guys came to the restaurant and I saw Matt with you and another girl, I knew you and Ben were together. I told him I was dating because I didn't want him to know I hadn't moved on."

"I wasn't dating Ben. I was in love with someone else at the time."

My hair was an afterthought now. She reloaded her brush and plopped it on my hair, caramel oozing down the strands and spilling onto other strands not meant to be highlighted. *I definitely won't walk out of here looking like one of the models in the magazine.* "When did you tell him?"

"I sent him an e-mail right around Christmas. He never replied."

He never opened the e-mail.

"So I sent another e-mail, and then I called. He said he was getting married and starting the seminary."

"But you told him about—"

"Caleb," she said hastily. "Yes. He said he couldn't do much, but he'd support me."

"As in child support?"

She scowled. "Yes."

"I didn't mean he shouldn't."

"I can't imagine why he didn't tell you."

"Especially once he found out we were moving here. Had you heard he was here?"

She took a piece of foil, parted the hair, and continued working until I realized. "You've seen him since he's been back?" It was more of a statement than a question.

"We met at the park a week ago Tuesday."

"Who watches Caleb while you're here?"

I half expected her to answer, *Ben.* "My parents."

"They're still in Oronoco?"

She nodded. "I live with them."

I exhaled. "I need to go. Here," I said, reaching for my purse and getting a twenty-dollar bill. "Will this cover it?"

"It will, but you're going to need to wash the highlights out or you'll have a mess. You might have one anyway. I've only done one side."

I handed her the cape. "My hair is the least of my concerns right now."

I pulled the tinfoil out of my hair as I drove, throwing it on the floor mat. Child support, a clandestine meeting with Becky at the park—what else was Ben hiding?

As soon as my hair was washed, I retrieved the suitcase from the spare bedroom and began to fill it with clothes.

"Meghan?" Ben called. "I thought it would be hours."

"I ran into Becky."

He bounded up the steps and into the room. "Becky?"

"Yes, Caleb's mother. The one you've been sending money to. The one you saw last week. The one that slipped your mind every time you talked to me for the past four years." I brushed past him into the bathroom to grab my toothbrush, makeup bag, and brush.

He was sitting on the bed when I returned and dropped my load haphazardly in the open suitcase. "I didn't know how to tell you."

"Oh, let's see, something like, 'Meghan, remember when you wondered if Becky was pregnant and we went to see her? I got an e-mail yesterday, and it turns out there is a baby. It's a boy. His name is Caleb.'"

"Where are you going?"

"I don't know." He touched my arm, but I wriggled away. "Don't touch me. I don't even know who you are. This whole marriage is a lie."

"I didn't want to hurt you."

"Swell plan, Ben," I said, grabbing shorts from the closet. "Where did the money for child support come from?"

"I tutored, gave guitar lessons."

"But I have the checkbook."

"I have a checking account from before we got married."

"A secret son. A secret bank account. Anything else you want to tell me while we're at it?"

"I don't want you to leave."

"I don't care what you want."

"Listen, Meghan. You aren't in any condition to drive. I'll leave. You stay here. I'll go somewhere for a while."

"I *won't* stay here."

I scanned the room before shutting the suitcase and taking my purse. "This is not a marriage, Ben."

"Meghan—"

"Save it."

If only a tornado would swoop in and take me away. The tears came so heavy at times I could hardly see. Ben was right. I was in no condition to drive. But I drove. I depleted the supply of napkins in the glove box and tried to stay in my lane. I couldn't listen to my CDs, because they were the CDs Ben and I listened to together. Christian radio wasn't any better. When I finally pulled into my parents' driveway, I wanted nothing but a couch, or a bed, or the living room carpet to soften the landing when my feet fell out from under me.

The doors were locked and the lights were off. *Where are they?*

I put my head on the steering wheel as my ringtone echoed from the backseat. The third time Ben had texted, I'd sent my phone flying.

When I arrived at Ben's parents' farm, his sister Katie answered the door.

"Meghan!"

"Katie, are your parents here?"

"Mom's in the garden, and I think Dad's in the pasture fixing the fence."

Most weekends the four summers prior had been spent there, in part because of Millie's gardens. Fruit trees and plants, perennial and annual flowers and vegetables all needed weeding and staking and watering. I was happy to help and equally happy to leave with buckets of strawberries, raspberries, green beans, or tomatoes. The gardens had been a solace after a long week at work. It was as if I'd married into English royalty and this was the manor.

I darted through the lilac bushes on the side of the house and called for Millie.

She was in the raspberry patch. She put down her pint container and stepped over the bushes to where I was crisscrossing the gardens. Upon reaching me, she put her hands on my tear-swollen face.

"Ben's got a son. He's known since before we were married." It spilled out of me.

She pulled me into her and held me.

"I'm so sorry we didn't tell you. It seemed—"

"Wait," I said, pulling back. *"You knew?"*

"We were afraid you wouldn't handle it well. I remember what you looked like the first time I met you. You weren't eating. You weren't sleeping."

"You thought it would be best if he lied to me? Since when do you build a marriage on lies?"

"At the time, you were working so much."

"No!" I cried, stepping back. "You are all *so* messed up. And tell Ben to quit calling. I hate him!"

I ran to the car, jumped in, and spun it around.

Ben's dad was driving his pickup truck full of post and wire up the drive. He waved and stopped the truck. I sped past.

I didn't know where to go, but I knew it had to be away from Ben, so I got on I-94 heading toward Chicago. Should I have known Ben was too good to be true when he showed up just in time to walk me through the carnage in the aftermath of Jeff? Hadn't I fasted and prayed before agreeing to marry him? *What did I miss?*

The Evanston exit was unplanned but habitual. In another week, this place would be crowded with college students, but for now, the beach belonged to the locals.

Not far from the parking lot, a pier jutted into Lake Michigan. A stout lady, probably in her sixties or early seventies, with a worn-looking face, large, dark sunglasses and a floppy blue sunhat leaned against the wood railing at the end of the pier. She might have donned the pages of Eddie Bauer with her khaki capris, her striped blue-and-white blouse, tan sandals, and distant gaze.

She smiled as I approached, noting, I supposed, my swollen face long devoid of makeup, my half-highlighted head, blue shorts, and gray shirt.

I'm not sure whether fright or empathy motivated her to saunter away.

I slumped onto the pier, resting my head against the wooden railing. *Where could I go? Without Ben, I didn't have a house or a job. I had a car, a credit card, and one suitcase full of clothes.*

It was after seven when I pulled into Margaret's drive.

Lily Menteen opened the door. Another day, I might have noted she looked more thin and feeble than even two months prior. For now, her hair was carefully folded into a bun, and that was enough for me.

"Meghan!"

"Lily, something's happened, and I don't know what to do."

"Come in," she said, grabbing my arm and leading me to the dining room. She pulled out a wood chair with a lilac cushion and motioned for me to sit.

"Margaret is outside weeding in the back," she said, nodding toward the French doors as she eased into a chair. "It's therapeutic, you know."

"Maybe I should join her."

"What's going on?"

I recalled the events of the day.

"Oh, dear."

"If he lied to me about this, what else is he lying about?"

"Maybe nothing," Lily suggested hopefully. "I like Ben. He's a decent young man who got himself in some trouble early on. Hopefully now that this is out, you can deal with it and move on."

"I don't see how I can stay married to him."

The porch door opened and shut, and Margaret came through the French doors into the dining room. Her graying hair was pulled into a ponytail, but wet wisps around her forehead clung to her face.

"Well, hello," she said. "I didn't know you'd be in town tonight. Do you want some iced tea?"

"Yes, get her some tea," Lily said. "Meghan's had a rough day."

"Oh?" She brought the glasses of tea to the table and sat down.

She seemed guarded to me, and why shouldn't she be? Her ex-husband was in prison.

I told her what I told Lily, watching for signs that she wasn't interested. Instead, her face fell, and she shook her head in a knowing nod.

"You'll see the signs as you look back," she said. "No one lives a double life without leaving clues. You were too busy, just like I was too busy to notice. Even what I did notice didn't cause me to slow down long enough to say, 'Wait a second. This isn't right.'"

"How can I be in a marriage with a man I don't trust?"

"You have to forgive him either way," she reminded me, wiping her forehead. "You do that for your sake."

"I can't go back. I'm sure everyone in town knows."

"Meghan, if I can face my neighbors and coworkers, then anyone can. My husband murdered a woman because her husband murdered his mistress. His picture was on TV, in the papers. Don't think for a minute I didn't want to crawl into a hole, or pack up and disappear. If it weren't for the apartment building, I would have, and it would have been the worst thing. I had to go on. Some people treated me like *I* had done it. A whole lot of others have reached out, held me up, prayed for me, and encouraged me. Because of them, I went on," Margaret finished.

"If anything, I'd think people would feel sorry for you," Lily said to me.

"Or think I'm incredibly stupid," I said.

Margaret nodded. "I got letters from people telling me if I had been a better wife and hadn't been so consumed with my own life, that woman would still be alive. And maybe that's true. I tried to change Earl for years, and when I couldn't, I gave up."

"It isn't your fault, Meghan," Lily said.

"Ben made a terrible choice," Margaret decided. "And once he decided to keep it from you, he knew there was no good way out, because it would always come back to 'Why didn't you tell me sooner?'"

"I don't know what to do," I said at last.

"You can stay here as long as you want," Margaret offered.

She picked up her glass and stood. "Have you told anyone where you are?"

I shook my head. "I don't want to talk to Ben."

"This affects more than Ben. His parents, your parents, the friends he's called are all probably worried."

"I'm not sure I care."

"But they do," she maintained.

"I'll get a pillow and blanket for the futon in the sunroom," Lily offered. "You look tired."

"I am."

I pulled my suitcase out of the trunk and dug my phone out of the backseat.

"Just so you know," Margaret said, lowering the bamboo blinds, "these blinds are great at blocking the midafternoon sun and offering a little privacy, but when it's dark, anyone can see through, especially if there's a light on in here."

"Thanks," I said.

We said our good-nights, and I sat on the futon. I had twenty-four messages. Margaret was right. My parents, Amanda, Ben, even the pastor's wife from Rochester, Tonya, left messages asking me to call.

I texted my parents: I'm in Evanston with Lily. I'll call tomorrow.

Ten seconds later, I got a text back: Thank you for telling us. We love you.

I started to undress, unconcerned about who could see. Message after message came to my phone.

I turned it off and opened up my Bible. After two verses, I shut it and turned off the light.

For the first time in a long time, I didn't know what to pray, so I just said, "I'm here."

Chapter Two

BACK-DOOR VISITORS

I awoke to the rattling doorknob. It took a minute to remember I was on Margaret's sunporch. Reaching for the lamp, I stopped short of screaming at the face on the other side of the door.

"What are you doing?" I rebuked, checking to make sure the door wouldn't lock before stepping outside and shutting it.

"Ben called," Jeff explained.

"What?"

He nodded. "He wondered if I knew where you were."

"How would you know I was here?"

"There are two places in Evanston you would be: at the Harbachs' or with Lily. It took a bit to get Margaret's address. Thankfully, she used to be my landlady, and I'm slow to empty my phone of old info. So, do you want to tell me what happened? It must have been pretty epic if Ben is calling *me*."

I sat on the step and looked up to where he was standing. "Did I ever tell you about our trip to Minnesota?"

"I don't think so."

"I'm sure I wouldn't have. It was about the time you decided to sleep with Carol and break my heart."

"Oh, brother."

"Well, it was."

"I did that for you."

"That's twisted."

"I did."

"You slept with my best friend for my sake?"

"I knew you wouldn't move on unless I made you move on. Sleeping with Carol was a guarantee you wouldn't come back."

"You thought you were doing me a favor by sleeping with Carol?"

Jeff waved his hand to dismiss the subject.

"I don't think I want to talk to you anymore."

"Meghan, I'm getting annoyed. Either tell me what's going on or I'm going home to bed."

I sighed.

He shrugged. "Your call."

I told him about our trip to Minnesota, seeing Becky at the salon, my conversation with Ben, what I'd said to Ben's parents.

"I think Ben did the right thing," Jeff concluded when I finished.

"How can living a lie be the right thing?"

"I wouldn't have told you."

"Why?"

"Ben knew if he told you, World War III would break out and you'd run away, or stop eating, or go into some cataclysmic spell and blow it out of proportion, and that's exactly what you did."

"You're a jerk."

"Think about it, Meghan. Who knows what the e-mails said? Maybe she threatened him if he didn't pay X amount in child support. Maybe she threatened to tell the seminary or send letters to you about their past. You have no idea what the guy's been through. I kind of feel sorry for him."

"I should have known better than to tell to you."

"You realize you have a tendency to run, right? Remember after we broke up—"

"You mean after you slept with Carol—"

"We broke up, remember? You broke up with me. Then, afterward—"

"After I found out you slept with Carol when you knew I loved you—"

"You ran everywhere. You were a hundred pounds and went through a pair of sneakers every other week."

"I was not a hundred pounds, and I didn't wear out any shoes."

"Well, you could have. You don't handle stress well."

"I worked at a newspaper for four years."

"I bet you were a basket case."

"I was not."

"Would you say you enjoyed the job?"

"For the most part."

"Liar."

"I didn't enjoy it, but only because of the perverts I worked with. I couldn't bend down without a whistle. If I looked tired, there were comments."

"There you have it," Jeff said with a celebratory nod. "You can't handle a lot, Meghan. That's just your DNA. I love you. Ben loves you. I'm sure Ben's parents love you, but you need to be coddled."

"That's *not* true."

"Emotionally, you're on the higher end of the maintenance scale. If I were to tell Carol tonight that I had a son living in Michigan, she'd ask when I wanted to go see him. Not handling things well makes you an unlikely candidate to be told much."

He read the deflation on my face. "Honestly, this is the best thing to happen to you. Ben is going to have to deal with a lot of crappy situations. If you learn to cope, then you'll be able to help carry the load. As it is, you're too … combustible. He can't have you skipping town every other week."

"I hate you."

"The list of people you hate is getting pretty long, Meghan."

I put my head in my hands. Jeff sat next to me and put an arm around my shoulder.

"Because I love you, I will always tell you the truth."

"Your version of the truth."

"Well, yeah."

"I'm not seeing the value in that just now."

"Ben is the best thing that's happened to you. The guy screwed up. He didn't handle this the best, or even well. It's not the end, Meghan."

"I'd expect something like this from you, but not Ben."

"Come on," Jeff said, standing up and grabbing my hand.

"I'm not dressed."

"Let's go to the beach."

"I can't leave. What if Lily wakes up and I'm gone?"

"We'll be back in an hour. Bring your phone. If anyone wants to know where you are, they'll be able to get a hold of you."

"I'm tired."

"So am I. Quit whining and come on."

Jeff parked under the lights. The warmth retained by the sand during the day retreated with the sun. As sand permeated my sandals, shivers ran up my legs.

I slid my shoes off and dipped my toe in Lake Michigan. "How did we swim in this? It's freezing."

"We were young and had plenty of hormones."

"I wish I could dive in and disappear."

"Pain is a liar. It doesn't let you see clearly."

"Where did you read that?"

Jeff scooped me into his arms and started into the water.

"Jeff, put me down."

"I'm going to."

"I don't want to get wet," I said, wriggling.

"I don't particularly either, but we're going to."

He held me until he was in up to his waist and then he fell forward, sending both of us into the lake.

"I'm cold and I'm wet. Are you happy?" I screamed, finding the lake bottom and standing up.

"Not really," Jeff said. "Honestly, right now, I'm wondering if you're more work than you're worth."

"Great," I said, starting back to the beach.

He put his hand out to stop me. "Tell me how you feel."

"I feel like killing you."

"This can take as long as you want, but we're not leaving until you tell the truth."

"Unloved."

"It's a lie."

"Ben would not have lied to me if he loved me."

"That's the pain talking. My mother lied to me all the time *because* she loved me. She said we had plenty of money. She said I never had to worry. She lied to keep me from worrying while she bore the brunt of the worry."

"I can't trust someone who lies to me."

"Did you ever ask him if there was anything he was keeping from you? Did you ask him why he was afraid to go back to Oronoco?"

"I shouldn't have to ask those questions. We're married. He shouldn't be keeping things from me."

"Have you lied to him?"

"Never."

"You told him about the perverts at the paper in Milwaukee and about the comments they made and the whistles when you bent down?"

"No."

"Why?"

"He would have made me quit, and we needed the money."

"Why do you think he would he have made you quit?"

"He wouldn't have wanted me to be treated like that."

"So you lied to him for four years?"

"I didn't lie to him."

"Right. He never asked. You just kept it from him, for his own good, right?"

"My job paid off his college debt. It paid for the seminary."

"And let's not forget how much he had on his plate. He was going to school. How could you bother him with more?"

"Jeff—"

"You were working two jobs, Meghan. Sixty hours a week."

"I could have handled it, Jeff."

"What would you have done if he told you he had a son?"

"I would have asked when we could drive to Oronoco to see him."

Jeff lunged at me, catching me off guard. I toppled backward into the water.

"What was that for?" I gasped, standing up and catching my breath.

He grabbed my arms. "This isn't a joke. What would you have done?"

"I don't know."

"How badly do you want a baby?"

My shoulders slumped. "I've wanted Ben's baby for years. It's not fair she had his baby first."

He pushed me away from him. "Oh, shut up. When has life been fair? Your husband kept something from you. Let him explain why. Get over the hurt feelings about trust and lies and all the other crap. Ben loves you, and other than this, he's a decent guy. He's human. He doesn't walk on water and make infallible choices. I know he knows how much you want a baby. Becky had Ben's baby first. That wasn't a decision you got to make. And you don't get to decide when you'll have a baby. What if you are pregnant and you don't even know it? You're off speeding around and wanting to disappear. And you aren't even thinking about the four-year-old boy who finally has a chance to have a dad. Don't deprive him of that. I'd give my left leg to get my dad back."

"I didn't think about that."

Jeff turned toward shore. "I know you didn't. You're being a selfish brat. Now that we've figured that out, I'm getting out of this lake before all hopes of *me* having children someday are lost."

"You want children?"

"Someone is going to need to knock some sense into you when you're old and I'm no longer around."

Stepping out of the water was devastatingly cold, and the realization there was no towel, and therefore no relief in the immediate future, was equally disconcerting.

"You're going to have to take off your clothes," Jeff said, slipping off his shirt as I retrieved my shoes and phone. "I have leather seats."

"I'll walk."

He popped the trunk and threw a shirt and pair of shorts to me and kept another pair for himself.

"Change on the beach, away from the lights in the parking lot."

"Jeff."

"You're all but naked now, but you might note where my eyes have been."

I walked to the beach obediently and returned carrying my pajamas.

"There's a plastic bag on the floor," he instructed.

I deposited my pajamas, noting Jeff and Ben could not be more different.

When he parked the car in front of Lily's, I turned to him.

"Jeff—"

"I know. You're welcome. I love you too."

"I was going to ask why you keep extra clothes in the trunk and say it's pretty sad they fit me."

"I may not have bulging muscles like Ben, but as you saw tonight, I'm still stronger than you. And, to answer your question, I play softball. I don't like to go to the bar afterward in my uniform."

"You change to go to the bar? Are you looking for women?"

"I don't want everyone to know I work for the paper. You'd be surprised how annoying some people can be about that."

He leaned in to give me a hug and then pulled his face to mine and brushed his lips against my cheek, giving me a prolonged peck. I hesitated and then backed away.

"Do you want me to walk you to the porch?"

"I'll be fine."

Once inside, I locked the door.

I was just falling asleep when I heard the door rattling again. *What does Jeff want now?*

"What did you forget?" I whispered as I opened the door.

"What?"

"Ben?"

"What do you mean, what did I forget?"

"I thought you were Jeff."

"Jeff's been here?"

"What time is it?"

"A little after one."

I stepped outside and closed the door. "What are you doing here?"

"I took the bus to Madison. I thought you'd be at your parents', and I didn't want two cars there. Your Mom texted that you were with Lily, so Dad brought me here. He's out front. Can I put my things in the car so he can go home?"

I didn't want to make his dad wait, but if his things were in my car, then we'd be together.

"Meghan, I know you're hurt and your head is spinning, but I want a chance to explain."

Did I have an option? I turned on the light and dug through my purse for the keys. I handed them to him and sat on the steps twirling a piece of still-wet hair through my fingers.

Car doors slammed, and there were voices and the sound of a car leaving before Ben emerged through the gate.

"I talked to one of my seminary professors," he said, stopping in front of me. "He said we could use his bungalow in Port Washington."

"A sem prof has a bungalow?"

"It's tiny, he said, but we can use it a few days to work things out."

"Port Washington is two hours away."

"I know. Could you get your things?"

"I can't just leave. What about Margaret and Lily?"

"Leave them a note."

"Ben, I don't even know who you are."

"I'm the same person I've always been."

"That's a not a good thing right now."

"I'll explain everything, but it's late and we're both tired. I'd like to get to Port Washington."

I hesitated.

"Meghan, please."

I reluctantly threw everything in my suitcase, closed it, and gave it to Ben. In my purse, I found a receipt, turned it over, and used it to explain to Lily and Margaret that Ben had come and we were going to Port Washington and thanked them for their hospitality and prayers. I straightened the futon, took my wet pajamas and purse, turned off the light, and shut the door.

"Ready?" Ben asked.

"Almost," I said, throwing the plastic bag in the backseat.

"What's that?"

"My pajamas."

Ben waited until I had my seatbelt on and he started the car before asking, "How'd they get wet?"

"Jeff took me to the beach."

I felt him bristle.

"We talked," I explained.

"While swimming in your pajamas?"

I resented that he asked. *He* had broken trust with me. *He* had called Jeff. How dare he question my integrity?

"He carried me until he was in up to his waist, and then he dropped me."

"Sounds romantic."

"He may as well have slapped me. The water was frigid. Neither of us was comfortable. He was trying to make me understand that pain is a liar. He wanted me to face the truth of the issues instead of getting caught up in the emotions and hurt of the situation."

"So what truths came out of it?"

"It doesn't matter, but if our marriage doesn't work, you can't blame Jeff."

"What do you mean 'if it doesn't work?' We agreed to never bring up divorce."

"We also agreed to face our troubles together. You broke every promise you've made to me."

"That's not true. This wasn't *our* trouble, Meghan. This was my issue."

"I was good enough to inherit your debt. That wasn't my issue. I thought everything, good or bad, from the past was part of the marriage."

"I can't believe you just brought up divorce," Ben huffed.

"I can't believe you expect me to just overlook the fact that you've kept so much from me. Did you think you were picking me up for a romantic getaway?"

"I thought I was picking my wife up to work things out. I never thought I'd hear those words come from your mouth."

"Don't get me started on the 'I can't believes,' Ben, because I have a list a mile long."

"What do you mean?"

"I can't believe you didn't use birth control with Becky. You've always made sure we do. I can't believe you've never found a good time to tell me about Caleb. I can't believe you brought me to Oronoco, a place where seemingly everyone else knew, and kept me in the dark. I can't believe—"

"You know what? Just stop."

"Fine. I just can't believe you came down here and thought everything was okay. Nothing is okay."

"I get that, Meghan."

"I don't think you do."

"You've made your point loud and clear."

He turned the music up.

"You've got to be kidding. Did you put in this CD hoping to summon nostalgia?" I accused.

"I grabbed a CD out of the glove box while you were leaving your note. I'm not trying to fool you into anything, Meghan. Pick another if you want."

We entered Wisconsin and drove through the heart of Milwaukee, our home for the first four years of our marriage. Familiar sights whizzed by. It occurred to me to tell Ben about my job at the journal, but I was angry and I didn't want to give him anything he could hold against me. I put my head against the window.

"Jeff made me realize I kept something from you," I said at last, testing Ben's reaction.

"What?"

I had a sudden and desperate yearning to say something hurtful, something like "Jeff and I did have sex," or "I have ties to the Chicago mafia and your parents are in grave danger." The truth seemed underwhelming.

"I didn't tell you certain things about at my job at the *Milwaukee Journal* because I was afraid of how you'd react."

"What didn't you tell me?"

"If I came in looking tired, someone would ask if you kept me up all night. If I bent down, someone would whistle or—"

"Why would you stay there?"

He was more horrified than I imagined he would be.

"It paid off your college loans."

"I never would have wanted that for you."

"I never participated or led them on, Ben. I knew it was a four-year assignment, and as much as possible, I went, did what I needed to do, and got out."

I shifted in my seat, suddenly afraid I had lost ground. "Jeff excused you from telling me about Caleb because he said I don't react well to things. He says I'm putting too much weight on one situation. To say you don't love me is overkill in his book."

His eyes shifted from the road to me. "You don't think I love you? Nothing is farther from the truth."

"Jeff thinks the deepest hurt comes from the fact that I want to have your baby and someone else already has."

I knew Ben's demeanor enough to know my words hurt because they were a truth he couldn't change.

"Why wouldn't you tell me, especially once you knew we were going to Oronoco?" I continued.

"What would you have done if I had told you about Caleb before we got married? Would you have told me to go back to Becky?"

"Would you have? She had your baby. When we went to Oronoco to see her, weren't you still in love with her? If it weren't for her parents, you wouldn't have broken up, right?"

"After what her parents did, I didn't want anything to do with her. I always felt that if she really wanted to be with me, she would have found a way. So what if her parents told her not to e-mail or call me? She knew she was pregnant. I didn't know that."

"But you didn't call her."

"I was told not to."

"And you didn't. How is it different?"

"They lied to me."

"And you felt you couldn't trust them after that?"

"I couldn't."

"Then why should I trust you?"

Ben didn't respond. I looked out the window until I finally fell asleep. I awoke when Ben stopped the car. He found the key while I retrieved my suitcase.

Tiny was an accurate adjective. The kitchen, dining room, living room, and bedroom were all one and the same room. Only the bathroom had its own walls and door.

I dropped my suitcase at the foot of the double bed, crawled under the thin blanket, and fell asleep.

Chapter Three

THE TRUTH, THE WHOLE TRUTH, AND NOTHING BUT THE TRUTH

The light sneaking through the slats in the wood blinds registered as home invasion in my just-waking state, as the events of the previous day hurricane their way into my conscience.

The incense offered by the cedar boards on the ceiling would be pleasant, I supposed, if you weren't going through the trauma of realizing your husband was a creep. Ben was hunched over his Bible near his laptop on the kitchen table. I stood to go to the bathroom and locked the door. When I came back, he was sitting on the end of the bed.

"How did you sleep?"

Is that timidity in his voice?

"It doesn't feel like I did," I grumbled. I pulled my legs to my chest and propped the pillow behind me before wrapping the blanket around me. The chill from the lake the night before had seemingly burrowed its way into my core.

"I'm sorry you found out the way you did."

"Everyone thinks I'm the problem, that if I handled things better, you would have been able to tell me."

He shook his head aggressively. "No."

"Then what?"

"I'm fairly certain Becky systematically seduced me. I'm just not sure why," he said.

"You were probably one of the better-looking guys on campus. Isn't that reason enough?"

Ben shrugged. "I don't know if she realized the year was almost over, or if she had fallen in love. For some reason, she became sexually aggressive."

"Why were you alone with her in a place where that could happen?" *You certainly didn't let that happen with me.*

He shook his head. "Stupidity. Overconfidence. I thought I could handle it. We were just kissing—"

"Please don't say, 'And the next thing you know.' There's a lot that happens between a kiss and 'next thing you know.'"

"Not for a twenty-year-old whose girlfriend unbuttons her shirt."

"Seriously? You see her shirtless and pull down your pants?"

"Pretty much."

Does he know his answers are making it impossible for me to respect him? "Then what?"

"About thirty seconds passed before it occurred to me what we'd done. She kept telling me it was okay, and I kept saying, 'It is *not* okay.'"

"But then you had sex with her again?"

"Eventually, yes, but not for a while."

"Why?"

"Why did I do it again or why did it take awhile?"

"Pick."

"She was there and willing, that's why it happened again. It's like standing at a buffet when you're starving and telling yourself you don't need to eat."

"That's a ridiculous and flawed analogy, especially for a pastor who will be training youth."

"I had gotten a taste. Before I had sex, I thought about it some, but afterward, it was consuming."

"What about birth control?"

"It wasn't a thought the first time."

"And yet you've always made sure we use birth control, even though, I might add, it would have been fine for us to be pregnant because we are married and should be having sex and babies."

Ben rubbed his face. "This experience has all but obliterated my desire to have a baby."

"Were you planning on telling me that, or was the idea to string me along with excuse after excuse until I was too old to get pregnant?"

"I needed to deal with this before we had a baby."

"But you did nothing to make that happen."

"What I went through at my parents' dining room table the day Becky's parents called to inform my parents that Becky had taken a pregnancy test and admitted we'd been having sex ..." He let his words drop. I imagined them falling into a deep canyon and making the tiniest whisper of a splash. "Until yesterday, that was the worst day of my life. I had all summer to regurgitate the way our

THE BREAD OF ANGELS

relationship went down and the way she pushed me to go further sexually. I felt stupid. When we went to Tilly's and she said she had moved on and I knew for certain there wasn't a baby, I never wanted to hear her name again. Finding out there was a baby and she lied to me again ..." He shook his head. "I didn't want anything to do with her."

"Maybe she was scared."

"Scared that I'd take care of her and Caleb?"

"Would you have?"

"If I found out right away and had not been banned from seeing her, I would have asked her to get married so we could raise Caleb together."

"But you found out about Caleb before you and I started dating, didn't you?"

"It was too late."

"Why?"

"I fell in love with you on our trip to see Becky. I saw you were repentant about your relationship with Jeff. I saw you reading your Bible. That's what I wanted in a wife. Becky wasn't spiritually mature."

"You could have led her. Don't you think she was different after all she'd gone through? You didn't give her a chance."

"She had a chance to come clean when I went to Tilly's. She lied. As far as I was concerned, she wasn't trustworthy."

"Yet you consistently lied to me."

"I loved you. Don't you see? That was the problem. I didn't want to be with her."

"Don't you think she loved you, despite her lies? She still does. You must have seen that when you were with her."

When he didn't answer, I continued. "Jeff told me to think about Caleb. Didn't you think he needed a dad?"

"If I was in his life, it would tie me to Becky. I didn't want you to have to deal with that."

"Your parents didn't think you should make an effort to be part of Caleb's life?"

"The situation with Becky's parents left us all with a bitter taste in our mouths. If they hadn't forbid me to talk to her, it would have been different."

"When did it occur to you that you might have done the wrong thing?"

"When they announced my name and Oronoco, Minnesota, on call day. I knew it would all come out."

"And the district president, what did he say when you called him to ask for a different assignment since you'd had a sexual relationship with Becky?"

"I never called him. *He called me* a few days before we moved and said there was a rumor going around that I had an ex-girlfriend and she and I had a son together. He wanted to know if it was true."

"Another lie. You said you'd talk to him."

"It's all the same lie, Meghan."

"It's not the same lie, Ben. Each time, you deliberately chose to keep something from me. Can't you see that?"

"No. The decision to keep it from you was made. Everything else was about sticking to that plan."

"So if a person decides to rob three banks and move to South America for the rest of his life, then it isn't a sin each time he robs a bank because it's part of a plan? Don't you see, Ben? Each lie was deliberate. Each time you lied to me, you had a choice to tell me the truth instead."

"Okay. I deliberately lied. I didn't know how to tell you, and I was afraid of how you'd feel about me when you found out."

"I *don't* know how to feel about a man who can hold his wife in his arms and lie to her after finding out they'd be moving to the town where his ex and son live. I asked about Becky! I said 'What do I do if I run into her in the grocery store? Isn't that going to be awkward?' And you said nothing! You all but put me in a situation to be devoured."

"I froze."

"You chose to cover yourself instead of protecting me."

"You're right. I'm to blame. Just leave my parents out of it. It's not their fault."

"It *is* their fault! When you came to them, they should have told you to tell me. They should have encouraged us to work it out. You and me. They should have had nothing to do with it."

"My mom is crushed over the way you talked to her yesterday."

"She should be crushed. Our relationship will never be the same. My parents would never let me do this to you. I don't think you can begin to understand what it feels like to find out your spouse is keeping something like this from you. It means you don't trust me, and it's fairly hard to imagine ever trusting you again, or even staying together, for that matter."

"And yet, you've forgiven Jeff for cheating on you."

"He didn't cheat on me. I had broken up with him," I recited, thanks to Jeff. "He slept with Carol in part to get me away from him because he wanted me to be with someone like you."

Ben considered this. "So he's a hero now?"

"Look, Ben. Jeff isn't part of this equation."

"I think he is. I think there's a part of you that still loves him. If you didn't, you would have changed out of his clothes when you got home from the beach. You're still wearing them now."

"Why did you call him in the first place?"

"Believe me, it was one of the harder things I've done."

"Well, you shouldn't have. I felt safe in his arms last night, and then, suddenly, I felt very unsafe because I realized I *was* capable of cheating on you. I didn't care about much at the time, and it didn't seem like you put too much value on our marriage either."

"I knew when I got there you hoped it was Jeff coming back."

"That's not true! I hadn't thought of Jeff in years. I never would have if you hadn't brought him into the situation or hurt me so bad."

Ben stood. "So far, we've established that you don't plan on trusting me again, you are going to hold a grudge against my parents, and, at least momentarily, you were willing to throw away all we have on your ex-boyfriend."

"You were willing to throw away everything we had every time you lied to me!"

His footsteps were deliberate. The timidity I'd presumed earlier announced its departure when he walked out, slamming the door behind him.

I took Jeff's clothes off and threw them on the floor. I hadn't been in the bathtub long when I heard Ben return, walk across the room, and lie down on the bed. When the heat from the water subsided, I dressed in my clothes and, for lack of anything better to do, went and fell asleep next to him.

When I awoke, the car was gone. The clock on the stove said 4:48.

Ben's laptop was on the table, the Microsoft emblem darting across the screen. I hesitated. When I pressed the space bar to unlock the screen, his Facebook account showed he had been chatting with Matt an hour earlier.

I scrolled to the start of their conversation. Matt asked Ben what was going on. Ben replied that we were in Port Washington. I had found out about Caleb and ran away to Chicago, where Jeff took me to the beach.

Matt wrote back, "Why would she go to the beach with Jeff?"

"Obviously she has feelings for him. She wore his clothes half the day."

"Did you tell her about Alyssa?"

"No," Ben responded.

"I suppose she'd freak out."

"She doesn't need to know."

As if I'm not already freaking out? Who is Alyssa, and why would knowing about her make me freak out more?

I shut the laptop and put on my shoes, furious Ben was trying to keep me in a marriage that obviously was nothing more than a scam. I'd made it clear earlier that I needed the whole truth, nothing left out, but he deliberately left out Alyssa, whoever that was. In my book, that sealed everything. He could not be trusted.

My stomach was well beyond the growling phase. It was in a full-blown temper tantrum, and I had no means of calming it.

The driveway curved onto a two-lane road. At the bottom of the drive, I scanned my surroundings. The road ahead curved to the right. The road to the left looked to be swallowed by dense expanses of pine. I sighed. Unless one of the scurrying squirrels led me to his stash of acorns or walnuts, there was no hope of food here.

Across the road, sand and pines scattered across the terrain. Once there, I could see water at the bottom of a long, sloping hill.

I had just slouched beneath a pine when my phone rang.

"Where are you?"

"Port Washington. Let me move away from these trees and see if I can get better reception."

I shimmied a ways down the hill. "Are you still there?"

"Where are my clothes?"

"Sorry, Jeff. Ben came shortly after you left and brought me apparently to the middle of nowhere. I can barely get reception out here."

"Is he planning to kill you?"

"I can only wonder. Your clothes have gotten me into a whole lot of trouble, that's for sure. Ben seems to think we had some sort of romantic rendezvous, and that's what he's dwelling on."

"Cause he's afraid he's losing you, and that's his biggest fear. It's why he didn't tell you to begin with."

"You think?"

"Burn the clothes. It isn't worth it."

"I'm not going to burn your clothes. Ben has to get over it. I told him we didn't do anything."

"It doesn't matter. Alone with a guy on a beach at night is alone with a guy on a beach at night."

"Then why did you take me there?"

"Why did you go?"

"I don't know why I've ever done anything you've wanted me to. It's never turned out good. I suppose if this marriage does work, I won't be able to see you again."

His pause made me wonder if I'd lost him.

"I never saw you as someone who'd get divorced," Jeff said at last.

"Don't pin your hopes for marriage on me, Jeff. Ben's hiding more, and I don't know if I'm prepared for what it is."

"How do you know?"

"I saw a message from Ben's friend asking if he'd told me about Alyssa."

"Who's Alyssa?"

"No idea. Maybe she's the daughter he had with someone else or the woman he had an affair with at seminary, or some chick he murdered and buried behind our apartment building."

"I didn't think Ben had it in him."

"I don't know what to think anymore. I go from thinking he's despicable to almost feeling sorry for him to thinking he's repulsive. How much more is there?"

"When you deep clean a closet, you take everything out so you can wipe the shelves. That way you see everything, so you know what to keep and what to throw away."

"This will get messy is what you're saying."

"It will probably get worse before it gets better."

I stared at the waves. "All these years, I knew you were struggling with a pain deeper than I'd known. I thought I experienced it when you and Carol got together, but this—"

"Pain is a liar, Meghan. It will always tell you the worst. Hold onto what you know until proven differently. For now, Ben loves you. He doesn't want to lose you. He thought he might lose you if he told you. Now he knows it's a real threat. He's fragile."

"What about me? I'm fragile."

He sighed. "We all are, Meghan."

"I wish someone would think about me. All I hear is Ben, Ben, Ben."

"I relate to Ben. Like him, I went to great lengths to do what I thought was best for you, only to watch the only woman I've loved be crushed by my actions."

"You don't love Carol?"

"My relationship with Carol is what it is. We both know and understand it."

"Do you still love me?"

He didn't answer.

"If I would have kissed you last night when we were saying good-bye, what would you have done?"

He hesitated. "Do you want me to come get you?"

I pulled my head into my knees. "That can't happen."

"Go sort out your life. You know where to find me."

"Delete my number, Jeff."

"Good-bye, Meghan."

I cursed and threw my phone on the ground.

When I finally walked back to the road, my car was in the driveway. Another was behind it.

Two men were getting in the second car as I approached.

"Oh, hello," one said, noticing me.

"Hi, James," I said, recognizing him as Ben's drummer friend from seminary. The other man seemed vaguely familiar.

"We drove Ben home," James explained.

"From?"

"Pat's Saloon."

"He's drunk?"

He winced. "We met for a beer, and we," he pointed to himself and the other man, "had a beer. Ben started with Jack Daniels."

Jack Daniels sounded pretty good right about now, not that I'd ever had it.

"We left the car keys on the table."

"Thank you."

I started toward the house and then turned around. "Where can I get some food? Is there anything around here?"

"You're five miles out of town. If you head down this road, you'll run into a bunch of fast food places," James explained.

"Got it."

"Would you like us to get you something?" the other man offered.

"That's okay."

"No, Meghan. Todd is right. You stay with Ben," James urged.

I started to protest, only to realize the futility of it. I was weak and hungry. I gave them my first and second choices and went inside.

Ben was on the bed. I unfastened his sandals and put them on the floor, more for the sake of the professor than for Ben. Two days earlier, I was happy to follow and content to spend my days with Ben. Now I looked at his arms and wondered how many other women they had held. What had been beautiful and safe now sent shivers down my spine. How many lies had he convinced himself to tell me for my own good?

When we were first married, I often noticed women looking at him. Each time he didn't respond to the stares, my paranoia faded. When women approached, he was quick to introduce me as his wife. His demeanor was matter-of-fact with a touch of friendly, not flirty with a touch of "check me out." During our first year of marriage, I learned to trust him. *For what?*

When James returned with my sandwich, I asked the name of the professor who owned the house.

"Ambrose."

"Do you have his phone number?"

He took his phone from his pocket. "I have a school directory somewhere in an e-mail."

"You don't have to look for it now," I assured him. I handed him a piece of paper with my cell number on it. "When you find it, could you text me?"

"I'd be happy to," he said.

I summoned the courage to ask if Ben had told him what was going on.

James gave a sympathetic smile and affirmed. "He said his marriage was probably over."

"Really?"

"I told him you wouldn't just walk away."

"Did you ever hear him talk about another woman?"

"Not Ben. He's one of the most decent guys I know."

"I keep hearing that ..." Apparently, my face objected.

"He taught me more about integrity than anyone. He lives by a pretty high standard. It's why he married you."

I nodded, deciding not to ask James to envision the man he obviously looked up to as capable of falling farther than either of us knew.

"If you could just text me the professor's number."

"I will," James said.

"I appreciate it."

When I received his text, I stepped outside, sat on the steps, and dialed the number.

"Professor Ambrose?" I started when he answered the phone. "This is Meghan Martins, Ben Martins's wife."

"Oh, yes. Hello, Meghan."

"We need your help."

Ben was in the shower by 6:30 the next morning. When he emerged, I went to the bathroom. He was sitting on the bed when I came out.

"I'm going to town. I forgot my razor and need coffee. Do you want something for breakfast?"

I weighed the feeling of being trapped when I woke up and he was gone the day before against implying I wanted to spend time with him. Being trapped trumped. "Do you mind if I go with you?"

We picked up breakfast and then Ben stopped at a superstore to buy a razor. I stayed in the car sipping my tea. Once back at the house, Ben went to the bathroom to shave. When he emerged, he sat down and looked at the bagels.

"How do you feel?" I asked.

"Like a pile."

"I asked Professor Ambrose to come. He'll be here in an hour."

"Why would you do that?" Ben sneered.

"Because right now, I don't want to be married to you. I don't know how to get through this, and it's obvious that you don't either."

Ben exhaled. "Whatever."

I ate and then went to the bathroom to get ready. I'd had all night to consider and had come to the conclusion that if Alyssa was a woman Ben had dated or been intimate with on any level, or was the result of a relationship like that, our marriage was over. In the meantime, I'd take the steps so no one could accuse me of not trying.

Professor Ambrose was a short, petite man with a thick, brown mustache and a full head of hair. His hands were slender, and when he shook my hand, his touch was gentle. He took off his suit coat and put it on the back of his chair before he sat down.

"Fill me in," he said. "Ben called me Wednesday, so I know his version of what was going on. Meghan, I'd like you to tell me about Wednesday."

I started with the encounter with Becky at the hair studio and what I'd said to Ben, going to my parents' house and Ben's parents'. I told him what Lily and Margaret said, about Jeff showing up at the door and then taking me to the beach, throwing me in the water, tackling me when I was facetious, telling me to change my clothes, getting back and going to sleep, only to be woken by Ben, our argument on the way to Port Washington, the events of the previous day.

"Okay, Ben. Let's hear your version."

"Meghan's is accurate. I hadn't heard of her conversation with Jeff at the beach. I didn't know she read the message from Matt, or about her conversation with Jeff last night."

"How do you feel about that conversation?"

"I'm a little surprised. And yet I'm not. I've always known he has feelings for her."

"Care to tell us about Alyssa?"

"She's Becky's sister. She's been showing up since she found out we were in Oronoco."

Not a daughter. Not a lover.

"Showing up how?" Professor Ambrose nudged.

"She's come to the church a couple times. Once, she came to my office."

"In our house?" I gasped.

"What does she want?" Professor Ambrose asked.

"She wants me to help Becky."

"What did you tell her?" Professor Ambrose asked.

"I told her I have been sending Becky money. She thinks I ruined Becky's life."

"What else could she want?" I asked.

"Becky wants to go to nursing school. She ended up in cosmetology school because she had to do something, but back when we were at Wheaton, she was in the nursing program. I suggested to Becky that Meghan and I might watch Caleb so she could do that."

"So you had plans to tell Meghan?"

"I always wanted to tell Meghan. Before we got married, I was afraid Meghan would call off the wedding and tell me to go back to Becky, and afterward, I've both wanted to spare her from the nightmare that it is and I've been ashamed that I hadn't told her. I didn't want her to lose respect for me."

Which I have.

Professor Ambrose looked at me.

On cue, I spoke. "By shielding me from what you knew would be painful for me, you've hurt me as badly as anyone could or would."

"I know," Ben said, sitting back in his chair. "I wish I could go back and do it over. But I can't, and I don't know what to do."

"First of all, Meghan, I applaud the decision you made in regards to Jeff," Professor Ambrose stated. "If your marriage is going to work, Jeff has to be out of the picture. Jeff's ability to bring clarity to the situation by reading both you and Ben is admirable, but clearly, it's important that he isn't around, and you took it upon yourself to make that happen. So, Ben, your insecurities about Meghan being faithful to you can be put to rest. As far as Alyssa, now that the whole thing is in the open, she should lose most of the power to terrorize you. If it continues, on any level, I'd go straight to the police. You've let her know of your intentions to do what you can to help Becky get her life on track, and that should be enough. Let me say, though, that watching Caleb is the extent of the help I would give her concerning school. It is not your job to pay for her schooling, or tutor her, or to be involved in her life in any capacity other than as a parent to your child."

Ben nodded.

Professor Ambrose turned to me. "That puts your fears about Alyssa to rest."

I nodded.

"Ben has made some horrible decisions, and the fallout from these decisions is going to be long-lasting and will require work to get through. Are you prepared to stay in the marriage?"

His bluntness caught me off guard. "I don't know what to think," I admitted. "Until a few minutes ago, I thought he might have been having an affair with a woman while at the seminary. Last night, seeing his arms repulsed me. I didn't know how many women those arms had held. I'm blown away by his ability to lie to me so easily. On call day, we were on our bed talking about going to Oronoco. How could he stay quiet, or lead me to believe he hadn't talked to Becky when he knew otherwise?"

Professor Ambrose looked at Ben.

"That day was tragic on so many levels," Ben said. "I knew it would all come out, and I was doing damage control to buy time to make it come out on my terms."

"What were you hoping that would look like?" Professor Ambrose asked.

"The only thing I could come up with was to ask Meghan to imagine the worst possible thing I could do to her. I was hoping it was something so horrid that this would pale in comparison. I knew it would hurt her, but I wanted a chance to tell her why I did what I did and how it had played out."

"How did you think she'd react?"

"I thought she'd be angry and disappointed in me for not telling her sooner, but I thought she'd probably understand why I did it, even if it was a poor choice."

"What do you think about what she said about being confused in knowing who you are?"

"I don't think it's possible to feel worse than I feel. She doesn't trust me, and that's an awful feeling."

I was thinking of a few ways to make him feel worse. "What do you want her to know about you?"

"I've never touched another woman or looked at another woman since the day I fell in love with you. I lied to you repeatedly, but only about one subject. Everything else I said to you was truth."

I shook my head. "I thought you wanted a baby like I've wanted a baby. You didn't tell me the truth about that."

"Because of Becky! The only reason I didn't want a baby is because of the situation with Becky."

Professor Ambrose leaned forward. "I'm going to be blunt, Ben. Rebuilding is harder than building the first time because now there's a wound, and wounds require extra attention and care or the scar will be ugly. You did this, and it's your job to make it right."

"I know."

"Meghan, you're confused and angry, and rightfully so. When you search the scriptures, you'll see that God calls us to forgive whatever grievances we have against each other. That's going to take time, but I'll be praying for you, and I know a lot of others will be too. I think you two should plan to meet with Pastor Gibbons for a while until you get this straightened out."

I looked at Ben. I couldn't read what he was thinking, so I looked away.

"As for the implications concerning being a pastor, I assume you talked to someone from the church before leaving town."

"I called the president of the congregation and the head elder."

Professor Ambrose sighed his relief. "You can't effectively lead anyone else until your own house is in order. It might take two weeks. It may take two months. You can stay here as long as you want, or you can go back home and work it out. I'm going to call Pastor Gibbons and recommend you do nothing but work this out for a while.

"When you return to the pulpit, you can determine it isn't anyone's business but yours, Becky's, and Meghan's and wait for things to settle down. Hopefully, your congregation would see you taking responsibility for Caleb and find that respectable, and over time, you'd earn their respect. Or, you could go back and be upfront about the way you handled it, why you handled it that way, and let them know you are repentant, and ask for your congregation's support as you start over with Meghan and Caleb. One way isn't more right than the other. It's a private family matter that doesn't have any bearing on the congregation, other than that they might not take you seriously when they know you've lied to your wife for four years. Unless they see you repentant, they may see you as a hypocrite."

"I've thought of that," Ben said, crossing his arms.

"When it comes to church matters, it's not important for you to tell Meghan everything. In fact, I'd advise against it. People come to you in confidence, and you need to keep their confidence. But when it comes to your relationship, honesty is important. True repentance always results in a changed life. Your friends and parents shouldn't know much, if anything, about you that your wife doesn't. And you're going to get a lot farther with Caleb if you work together."

Ben agreed.

Professor Ambrose said a prayer. We thanked him for coming and for the privilege of staying in his house.

Ben walked Professor Ambrose to his car, and the two of them talked for a few minutes. When he returned, Ben asked if I wanted to take a walk.

We sauntered down the drive and across the street. The morning coolness had been overtaken by debilitating heat and humidity.

We went down the embankment to Lake Michigan. I slipped off my sandals and carefully navigated around the rocks to find a perch where I could sit on dry rocks, yet dip my feet in the cool water lapping the shore.

"I'm sorry," Ben said, coming up behind me.

"Sorry for lying about Caleb, or sorry because you are about to hold me under the water until I quit breathing, somehow make it look like an accident, and go back to Oronoco as an object of everyone's sympathy?"

He laughed.

"One never knows," I said.

"I'm glad it's finally out."

Lake Michigan was on its best behavior. Modest waves twinkled in the sun. I'd seen it as a monster, lashing out, holding me down, but now it was begging me to forget.

Truth would never be found on these shores, I realized, because Lake Michigan was as fickle as the rest of us.

Hold on to what you know until proven differently, Jeff had said about Ben. *Ben loves you. He doesn't want to lose you. He thought he might lose you if he told you. Now he knows it's a real threat. He's fragile.*

I am the man you fell in love with, Ben said. *I've never touched another woman or looked at another woman since the day I fell in love with you. I lied to you repeatedly, but only about one subject. Everything else I said to you was truth.*

"Want to get in?" I asked.

"Huh?" Ben murmured, obviously shaken from his own monologue.

I maneuvered around the rocks and into the water, only stopping once I was knee deep.

"I'm not sure how deep this is, or if there are currents," I said, turning back to Ben.

I held my breath and dove in, coming up to catch my breath before disappearing again. The third time I surfaced, I put my legs down but couldn't touch.

"It's deep," I called to Ben. He hadn't moved. "Take your phone and your wallet out of your pocket!"

"I don't think so," he called back.

I dove beneath the water again, relishing the weightlessness. If only there were a way to live beneath the surface, beneath the noise.

When I resurfaced, Ben still only had his feet in the water. Yesterday, I was Ben, content to dip my toes, and Jeff was the one carrying me into the water. I wanted Ben to be Jeff, fearlessly facing Michigan. But he was cringing in ankle-deep water.

"How was it?" he asked as I returned.

"Refreshing," I said.

"You're crazy. It's freezing."

I sat on the rocks, letting the heat of the sun and the warmth of the rocks dry me. Eventually, we meandered back to the house.

I peeled the damp clothes off as I made my way to the bathroom to hang them over the shower curtain. As I scrounged through the suitcase, I wondered if we'd be getting something to eat.

"This is where the problem occurs when you swim with people you aren't married to," Ben observed from the edge of the bed.

"I'm well aware of that. I changed on the beach with Jeff last night."

"You changed in front of him, like you are in front of me?"

"He changed behind the car. I went to the beach."

He raised his eyebrows.

"Are we going to get something to eat?"

"Are you hungry?"

"Starved, aren't you?"

He shook his head. "Not in the least."

Chapter Four

FACING THE MUSIC

"Meg."

I opened my eyes. Ben was sitting beside me on the bed.

"We should decide what we're going to do."

"What are the options?" I asked, yawning.

"Are we going back today, or are we staying here?"

I rubbed my eyes, forcing myself to wake up. "What do you want to do?"

"We can stay here as long as you want."

I sat up and pulled the blanket to cover me. There was so much damage. I felt like we were standing at the edge of a city devastated by a tornado and Ben was asking where I wanted to eat.

"I don't know where to start," I said; then, noticing his rigidity, I asked, "Did you want to go back?"

"It's Friday afternoon. I need to get the bulletin to Pastor Gibbons and make sure he knows who will open the church."

"Can't you do that from here? You've got your laptop, right? I don't want to go back. Not now. We've barely scratched the surface."

"I'll give him a call."

While Ben went outside to make the call, I got dressed and combed my hair. The circles under my eyes were nothing short of catastrophic. If my face were any paler, I might disappear altogether. I amused myself with the idea that putting on makeup could be chalked up as a step in being willing to repair what was damaged.

When Ben flopped on the bed, I realized the futility of my efforts.

"This is so degrading."

"What is degrading?"

"Hello, Pastor Gibbons. This is Ben Martins, the new pastor in Oronoco that's been nothing but trouble. Yeah, hey, I'm sure Professor Ambrose told you that I didn't tell my wife about my son and when she found out, she left. I'm here in Port Washington, and it looks like I'm not going to be preaching for a couple weeks, so what do you need?"

He sighed.

"Are you mad at me?" I asked.

He didn't respond.

"Oh, I get it," I said at last. "If I would have stayed, no one would have known. We could have pretended nothing was wrong, and that we didn't have four years' worth of debris to deal with."

"What is there to deal with? I've never lied to you about anything except Caleb."

"Yesterday, when I read about Alyssa—"

"Alyssa is nothing to worry about."

"I know that now, but I'm struggling to figure out who you are."

"There's nothing else. I've never been with anyone but you and Becky. I didn't cheat my way through the seminary. I didn't leave a string of unsolved murders in Milwaukee."

"Not that you'd tell me if you had."

He didn't try to hide his disgust.

I sat down on the bed. "Could you forgive me if Jeff and I had sex on Wednesday night?"

"Does it matter?" he snarled.

"Of course it matters."

"Why?"

"How can you even ask?"

He rubbed his face with his hands. When he finally let his hands fall, the hatred was gone. "Yes. I could forgive you. I was with someone before we were together. I hurt you and you were in a desperate situation."

"So the next time you hurt me, it would be okay if I ran to Jeff and slept with him again?"

"What are you getting at?"

"I'm sensing some holes in the wall of your integrity. It would not have been okay for me to sleep with Jeff on Wednesday night, even if I would later find out you'd been with eight other women. I'm still married to you, and as tempting as it is to run away from the mess we're in, being with someone else doesn't make this mess go away."

"You didn't ask if it was okay if you slept with someone else. You asked if I could forgive you. My answer was, and still is, yes. I wouldn't like it. I wouldn't get over it very quickly, but I think our marriage is worth saving, don't you?"

"It is, but—"

"And why does that matter?"

"I didn't have sex with Jeff, and if I had, we'd have much bigger issues to deal with than saving face with the district president."

The slightest smirk betrayed his poker face. "It must be nice to be you."

I laughed. "I doubt many people are thinking that just at the moment."

"It was pretty hard to walk into the sanctuary on Sunday knowing what Ben was about to do," I told Tonya Fredin, before taking a sip of my tea.

"Did you sit in the front or the back?" she asked, clutching her coffee mug.

Pastor Scott Fredin made a point to be home to watch Elijah, their one-year-old son who usually joined us for coffee, so she could meet me alone.

"Front. Two rows back. Same side as Ben."

She exhaled and nodded.

"Shortly after he started the sermon, I was wishing I had sat in the back, but I knew if I got up and left, it would look very bad for Ben."

"I couldn't have done it."

"It had to come out or we'd have to lie our way through, and thanks, but no thanks; I've had all the lying I can handle for a while."

"How many people from the congregation knew before this?"

"Some heard rumors about Ben having a son with Becky, but I'm sure they assumed I knew. Pastor Gibbons told the congregation we had a family emergency and needed time to ourselves. He asked the congregation not to call or stop by until after Ben's return on Sunday."

"What happened when Ben explained the situation?"

"After the services, Ben and I walked out together and stood in the narthex. Some people came over and gave us a pat on the shoulder or a 'You'll get through this,' but just as many walked right out of the church. A group of them got together and called Pastor Larimer and asked him to return to his former position."

"That was nice of them."

I nodded.

"What did he say?"

"He thanked them for thinking of him and encouraged them to lead the effort to forgive Ben. Then he called Ben to let him know. Within a couple hours, four families notified Ben they'd be transferring."

Tonya nodded knowingly. "They don't realize they'll be going through a counseling session on forgiveness. If they refuse to forgive Ben, they're being hard-hearted. They can understandably not agree with his actions and decisions. None of us do. I can't fathom how he could think that was the best plan for you guys."

"His parents knew and encouraged him to keep it from me. I'm having a hard time getting over it. He told them six months after we were married."

"Have you talked to them?"

"I stopped at their house."

"How'd that go?"

"In hindsight, it wasn't the best time, but they were able to see the raw pain, and maybe that was good. I told them I was the laughingstock of Oronoco. Considering my hair was highlighted on only one side of my head, that probably wasn't hard to imagine."

Tonya smiled. "When did you get that fixed?"

"I found a nice hair salon at the mall when we got back. For a hundred dollars, they highlighted the rest of my head and put lowlights in too."

"It looks good."

"I'd like to thank you for suggesting Hair Nation in the first place. Super affordable."

She laughed. "Happy to help. So what happened with Ben's mom?"

"I asked her when they decided that building a marriage on lies was a good thing. And I told her I hated Ben."

"Uh-oh."

"At the time, I did."

"Have you talked to them since?"

"Ben has."

"Why on earth would they come up with that solution in the first place?"

I took a drink. "When I first met Ben's mom, I'd just gotten out of a relationship, and my ex slept with my best friend. I spent the ten days before Christmas break in a daze. I hardly ate, couldn't sleep. Ben's mom remembers the girl who didn't deal well with a breakup."

"I'd think him sleeping with someone else would make you happy to be rid of him."

"Jeff and I are … oh, I don't know. Some people have something; you know what I'm saying?"

"You mean you have feelings for him even now?"

"I hadn't thought about him in a long time. This happened, and—"

"Tell me you didn't run to him."

"I didn't run to him. Ben called him and he came to me."

"Why would Ben do that?"

"He must have been desperate. Honestly though, Jeff gives good advice, and he's able to read situations. Even Professor Ambrose saw it."

"You're talking about him like you love him."

"We agreed not to see or talk to each other again."

"Well, Ben has a lot of ground to make up, but there's only room in your heart for one person, and it needs to be Ben."

"I know. I don't know how Jeff and I got so close."

"You trusted him for advice, which would be appealing to a guy who wants respect. I'm guessing Ben's relationship with Becky was mostly physical and didn't have the same depth."

I nodded. "Ben was attracted to my 'spiritual maturity.'"

"There you have it."

"I kind of wish he'd have added, 'And looking at you made my head spin.'"

Tonya guffawed.

As much as I tried to forget, I kept ruminating over the fact that Ben said when Becky had taken off her shirt, he'd lost all moral sense. Obviously, she was better endowed in the breast department than I was. *But*, I reasoned, *you can only talk to a breast for so long. At some point, an intelligent man wants a brain, and a moral man wants a moral compass.*

I sighed and took the last sip of my chai. That analysis didn't make me feel as good as I'd hoped it would. "Before I go, I have to ask if you're expecting. Last time we met you mentioned it was time to start trying again."

"As a matter of fact—" Tonya replied.

"You are! Congratulations! When are you due?"

"April."

"That's awesome."

"There's still time for us to be pregnant together."

"Regretfully, I think that's a ways off for us."

"I'm sorry, Meghan."

I shrugged. "I figure I have at least fifteen years' worth of eggs left, so another year or two isn't going to matter in the whole scheme of things."

"Right," she said. "Babies don't fix marriages. Best to work that out first."

I nodded, threw my cup away, and gave Tonya a hug.

One more person checked off who knew the details, who I could look in the eye next time we met. One down, about a hundred left.

"So?" Lexie asked as I dropped into my blue chair in the back of The Strange Brew, Oronoco's one and only coffee shop.

"Is it just me or is everyone watching me?" I asked, scooting my chair closer to hers so I could speak softly.

"There are exactly four people in the coffee shop including you and me, so you probably don't have to be paranoid."

"I meant in general."

"There are more people watching, but you also have a heightened sense of awareness now."

"Which means?"

"This is Oronoco, Minnesota. We're a small town. You and I go to a tiny church. Relatively speaking, there aren't that many people interested in your life, but you notice the ones who are and it makes you uncomfortable," Lexie explained.

"I could have used your investigative journalism skills a couple years ago. You might have pointed some things out before this became the scandal it is."

"Wannabe investigative journalism skills," she corrected. "The marketing director doesn't really participate in any investigations, real or imagined. Anyway, I didn't see it in Ben," she admitted. "I've only known him two months, but he doesn't seem deceptive to me. I'm a bit baffled by it all. I have to think you're here for something bigger than this."

"Like?"

She shrugged. "Obviously, Ben's supposed to be in Caleb's life. Whatever else God is brewing is his business. He has a way of working things out."

"An older lady told me the same thing the day of Ben's installation. I, on the other hand, had an ominous feeling about Oronoco from the start."

"You're going to blame all that's happened on the town?"

"Yes. Oronoco is my scapegoat."

"You might want to remember that some people live here by choice. It doesn't bother me, but ..." She dropped her words, content I could fill in the blanks.

"I feel like a contestant on one of those survival shows where they plop you in the middle of a foreign land and you have to find your way out."

"Obstacle one: your husband isn't who you thought he was."

"Obstacle two is expected to landfall tomorrow night."

"Oh?"

"Becky and Caleb are coming for supper."

Lexie considered. "No one wins when families are broken."

"Yeah, well, I wasn't planning on having my husband's ex over for supper."

"Are you worried about Becky?"

"Yes. She acts like she hates Ben, but I think she still loves him. She's definitely annoyed we're together and quite possibly sinister enough to do something about it."

"You've picked this up from meeting her once?"

"Yes."

"Well, you're observant."

"I know she's going to be in our life, but I worry she'll talk Ben into things."

"Like?"

"I don't know. I just get a bad feeling with her."

"Like the ominous feelings you had about Oronoco?"

"Yes! See!"

Lexie considered. "Ben won't let her talk him into anything."

"He has some blind spots, and I think she may be one of them. Even more worrisome is why she'd be a blind spot."

"You mean ..."

"Yes. Obviously, something about her is spellbinding to him. It keeps me up at night."

"For Pete's sake, just ask him!"

"Ask him for details about their sex life?"

"If you're concerned, yes."

"What if he likes her body better than mine?"

She shrugged. "At least you'd know."

"I already do. It's got to be her ... you know ..." I held my hands to my chest.

"Are you telling me Ben has a fascination with Becky's breasts, and that somehow, five years later, they have him in a hypnotic trance that makes him obey her every whim?"

"When you put it like that—"

"It sounds ridiculous because it is. Becky is not a threat. Caleb, on the other hand, might be."

I scrunched my face. "Caleb?"

"When it comes to a spouse's child from another relationship, the tendency is to blame all the bad traits on the ex instead of overlooking them or dealing with them."

"You mean when he misbehaves, I'll blame it on Becky?"

"Or her family."

"Well, in this case, they are to blame, right? It's not like Ben's corrupted him."

"Children misbehave. At some point, they make their own choices. He may even misbehave because of you."

"*Me?*"

"Think about it. Caleb just met his dad. Why should he like you? For all Caleb knows, you're the reason his dad hasn't been around. He's got a mom who's been emotionally messed up, grandparents who've made some questionable decisions ..." She bugged out her eyes. "The kid's been dealt a bad hand, that's all. I'm not implying he's a rotten kid. I just wouldn't expect him to be totally stable, all things considered, and I wouldn't be surprised if you are his scapegoat."

"I didn't expect him to be stable; after all, he's spent his first almost five years of life in Oronoco. He probably needs therapy."

"I need to find me a scapegoat."

"I never imagined Caleb might not like me."

"Expect him to hate you."

"Why would anyone *hate* me?"

"Right, it's impossible not to love you, since you're so perfect."

Jeff, you've been replaced by a woman every bit as sassy as you.

I sighed. "So should I just avoid him?"

"Heavens no. I'd slather him in grace, especially at first. Overlook a lot."

"You might want to start doing something other than reading. It's ridiculous that you're what, twenty-nine, unmarried, no children, and you're teaching me about stepchildren."

"It's probably because I grew up in Oronoco."

"What does that have to do with anything?"

She waved her hand, like a model on *The Price Is Right* showing a new car, presenting her argument for no connection between Oronoco and bad behavior or thinking.

"If I didn't blame everything on Oronoco, I'd blame Ben, and for the sake of my marriage, it's best to stick with Oronoco."

"How *is* the marriage?"

"We're going through some pretty heavy counseling with Pastor Gibbons right now. I'm working through trust issues—"

"You don't have trust issues. You have a husband who lied to you for four years."

"Yeah, well, apparently that doesn't mean I can interrogate him every time he says he's going to the gas station. I've taken up smoking, by the way."

"What?"

I nodded. "I tried it back in college, but it burned all the way down my esophagus and I just couldn't get the hang of it. I'm on my second pack now, and I think I've got it this time."

"Tell me you're joking."

"Dead serious."

"Okay. You need to stop. Smoking is not the answer. Have you told Pastor Gibbons?"

I shook my head.

"What about Ben? Does he know?"

"He hates the smell of smoke."

"You're doing it for revenge?"

"Not so much. More for survival."

"The irony in that statement is monumental."

"Have you ever had a broken heart?"

"Yes. My dog died. I'd had Bandit for fifteen years, and since I was an only child, he was my best friend."

I leaned forward. "The Ben I thought I was married to is dead, and he is never coming back. You can get another dog, but it's not the same."

"Are you sure you shouldn't be in counseling? I mean, just you?"

I sat back again. "We talk about the new family I need to get used to with Caleb and Becky, the ideations I had for marriage. No secrets. Pastor Gibbons knows *everything*."

"He doesn't know about the smoking, and you realize you are going to need to quit before you have a baby. Last I knew, that was one of your main objectives."

"There won't be any babies for Ben and me for a long time. In fact, one of the things I learned through all of this is that Ben didn't really want a baby. It's probably a good thing I didn't have one, don't you think?"

Lexie's hand flew to her mouth. "Oh, Meghan. I'm sorry."

"The puddle is very deep, Lexie." I had come to love that analogy.

"I may have to find a habit just to get through this with you. It won't be smoking though."

"I don't expect you to get on this ride."

"I'm already on," Lexie said. "And besides, I'm twenty-nine years old and single. The marketing department isn't really all the excitement you'd imagine. Until I find a man, you are my entertainment." She picked at one of her manicured nails. "You and my nails, that is."

"I can't compete with those. What's up with the pink and gold, by the way? Is there symbolism in that?"

"I was thinking of dyeing my bangs pink, but I thought I'd try it on my nails first to see if I like the blonde/pink combination."

"And?"

"I'm going to try purple next time. I'm not totally sold on pink."

"Well, I'm done dyeing my hair." I shuddered as I thought back to my day in the salon with Becky.

"I'd have paid good money to see that."

"I kept it in a ponytail, so I don't think many people noticed."

"See, *that* is a better way to deal with the pain and frustration, and money much better spent than on cigarettes."

I shrugged.

"Have you ever been around people when they try to quit? It's like heroin. They're moody and angry and they gain weight."

"I forgot about the weight."

"I've dealt with my weight most of my life. You know, the only child who goes home from school and eats? Yeah. It's not as fun as it may look."

"I think being an only child is your scapegoat."

"Oh, good! Now I don't have to wrack my brain looking for one. Let's go dye our hair and celebrate."

I smiled. "Anything else new?"

"With me? Nothing. That's why I'm living vicariously through you," she replied.

"This silly situation is the only newsworthy thing in all of Rochester?"

"For the moment."

I cradled my chin in my hands. "Perfect."

Chapter Five

OPENING A DOOR

Although I didn't have the desire to see Becky in the same room with my husband, I was intrigued as to how Ben would act around her, and how many cigarettes I would need after she left to return to sanity.

I took one last look in the mirror before shutting my makeup bag. Maybe the mascara was too much. Hopefully I wouldn't get an eye infection. It was probably severely outdated.

The table was set with a plastic car plate and cup. The potato fries were ready to go in the oven, and the salad and the coleslaw were made. A new ball was on the couch.

"Don't worry," Ben told me. "He'll love you."

"I appreciate the sentiment of that lie, but it is a lie. He's not going to love me, Ben. I'm a stranger and I live with his dad. Anyway, I'm more worried about Becky."

"How do you think she feels? This has to be awkward for her too."

So good of you to think of her. "At what point do we realize this is a horrible idea?"

"At the point of forgetting there's a four-year old boy involved."

"Right."

Caleb and Becky arrived eight minutes late. Caleb's hair was brown and short and his skin tan. His petite head, pointy chin, and oversized ears screamed "elf" to me.

"Hey, Caleb, this is Meghan," Ben said to Caleb.

Caleb hugged Becky's leg, looking as if Ben was speaking Russian.

"Once he warms up, you'll wish he was always this shy," she said.

I smiled. *So when he warms up, he will be a terror?*

He looked at Ben. "Are you my dad?"

Ben nodded.

"Are you going to live with my mom?"

Ben shook his head. "I live with Meghan. She's my wife." He paused to let that sink in. "I thought maybe you and I could cook some burgers and hot dogs. I've got the grill going out back. Wanna come with me?"

Ben grabbed the meat from the fridge, and Caleb followed him outside.

"Would you like something to drink?" I asked Becky. "Iced tea, lemonade, soda?"

"I'll have tea."

I poured two cups of tea and handed her one, noting her jean shorts were similar to mine, though a bit shorter and tighter. She wore a red V-neck, and I, a navy T-shirt. She filled her shirt a bit more, not just in the chest, but in the stomach too. She was definitely wearing mascara.

"Do you want to go outside or stay in?"

"As long as Ben has Caleb, I'll stay here. My life stopped the minute I found out I was pregnant."

"How old were you?"

"Twenty-one."

"What were you going to school for?"

"Nursing."

"You must have been almost done, weren't you?"

"I finished my junior year."

"What about cosmetology?"

"Another waitress at Tilly's talked me into it so she didn't have to go alone. I thought it would be fun to figure out how to do hair. That's a skill you can use your whole life."

I nodded. "I can see that."

"It won't pay anything compared to Tilly's."

"You make good money there?"

"People who drink tip well."

"Why didn't you go back to nursing school?"

"It's been four and a half years. I'm not sure which credits are still good."

"There's only one way to find out."

"My parents would be thrilled if I quit cosmetology school. I've been one letdown after another."

"You kept your baby. That's admirable."

"Most of my friends are married. They've got careers. I'm twenty-six and have nothing."

"Have you dated anyone since Ben?"

"I've never wanted to."

Is she telling me she's still in love with him?

"What do you mean?"

"I loved Ben," she said. "After what he's done—"

"I think it would have been different if your parents handled the situation differently," I said, surprised at feeling myself getting defensive.

"They did what they thought was for my good."

"How could lying to the father of your child be for your good? Or keeping you from the guy who you loved and who loved you? You probably would have gotten married and Ben would have taken care of you. You could have gone to school after he was done, or finished school with Caleb."

"I've always wondered what Ben would have done if I had hopped on a bus and showed up on his doorstep."

"If Ben wouldn't have been lied to initially, or even if you told him when he came to Tilly's, things might have been different."

"How's it going in here?" Ben asked, peering through the door.

I smiled. "How's Caleb?"

"He's on the neighbor's swing. Did you put the fries in?"

"I will now."

He shut the door again.

"I think I'll head outside," Becky said.

I put the fries in the oven, set the salad on the table, and grabbed a clean plate for the meat before going outside.

Walking from the air conditioning to the humidity nearly took my breath away. *What a night to stand in front of a grill.* But Ben wasn't standing in front of the grill. I set the plate on his lawn chair and walked behind the garage.

He and Becky were standing next to the neighbor's swingset. It seemed impossible they weren't married as they watched Caleb go down the slide and run to climb back up again. I felt like an intruder as I approached—more so when Becky quit talking.

"I brought a clean plate for the meat," I explained.

"I better make sure the burgers aren't burning," Ben remembered.

I turned to follow him.

"Dad!" Caleb cried. "Wait for me!"

Ben held out his hand and waited for Caleb.

"You want to check them?" Ben asked.

It occurred to me at that instant that Becky and I both had hearts that were breaking: hers for what could have been, and mine to watch Ben be the father I was hoping he'd be, but with a child that wasn't mine.

"That went well," Ben said, as I loaded the dishwasher.

"What were you and Becky talking about by the swingset?"

"Nursing school."

"She mentioned that to me too."

"I feel sorry for her," Ben said. "My not dealing with the situation left her without a lot of choices."

"I think she could go to nursing school if she wanted. She's in school now. How would it be different?"

"We should pray she figures it out."

"And that she finds a husband."

"Oh?"

"I can see in the way she looks at you that she wishes you were hers."

"Well, that bed has been made. She's got to move on. We all have to."

He went to his study, and I sat outside the door on the opposite side of the house sucking in the comfort of my cigarette and pondering Ben's words. I'd have to remember to bring that up with Pastor Gibbons. Who was at fault: me for needing more, Ben for not offering it, or me for not telling Ben I needed more? At the end of the night, I was hoping for more than, "We all have to move on." Those words hinted at regrets. Was the new relationship with Becky and Caleb making him second-guess his relationship with me?

As I looked up to exhale, I caught a glimpse of the moon. Only a sliver was noticeable.

There's always so much more than what we see.

I had a hard time falling asleep, and when I finally did, it was restless. I woke often, looked at the clock, repositioned myself, thought about Becky, and tried to get back to sleep. I must have finally entered a deep sleep sometime in the early morning. When I woke, it was already ten o'clock.

There were several bags and a suitcase at the bottom of the steps.

"Ben?"

"In the office," he called.

Caleb was on the chair racing a matchbox car around Ben's desk while Ben tried to work on his laptop.

"What's going on?" I asked, surprised to see Caleb.

"I'll be right back," Ben told Caleb. "Play here for a minute while I talk to Meghan."

Ben followed me out of the office and shut the door most of the way. He led me to the kitchen.

"Becky and her parents got into a pretty nasty fight last night. She spent the night packing and left this morning. She asked us to keep Caleb for a couple days while she tries to figure things out. I told her we would."

"I don't know the first thing about taking care of him."

"Didn't you ever babysit?"

"A couple times when I was twelve. Where's he going to sleep? We don't have a bed for him."

"I thought you could get one today, and some sheets. Maybe you could take him along so I could get some work done."

The required two-week sabbatical for Ben had left him roaring to get back to work. In truth, he'd spent several hours of his "off" time planning Bible studies and sermons.

He pointed to the floor. "Becky left his car seat."

"That was nice of her."

"Meghan, she's struggling."

"How's Caleb going to feel about being left with strangers?"

"He seems fine so far."

Caleb came down the hall. "Dad?"

"Yeah, bud."

"I'm hungry."

"I am too. What should we have for breakfast?"

"Grandma Barb makes me waffles."

Ben looked at me and then at Caleb. "How about toast?"

With Caleb in the backseat, fifty-five miles per hour seemed fast, and the cars in the other lane were enemy weapons to be avoided. I couldn't escape the feeling of being an abductor. Thoughts of Becky's parents showing up at our house and demanding Caleb flooded my mind.

Did we even have a legal right to this child? What if he got hurt? He wasn't covered under our insurance.

The Furniture Superstore was in the same shopping complex as Target. As we looked around, I noticed twin beds weren't a whole lot cheaper than a full size, and the queen wasn't much more than the full. I decided on a bed and matching dresser.

"Is this bed for you?" the salesperson asked.

"It's for him," I said, "but it will double as a guest bed."

"Did you want a protective covering over the mattress, in case he wets it or throws up in it?"

I looked at Caleb and cringed. "Do you ever pee in the bed?"

"Only on accident," he answered.

"It's a good idea," the salesman suggested.

"Okay. And can we get it today?"

"We can deliver it this afternoon."

"What is this?" Ben demanded, walking into the bedroom as the delivery men left.

"A bed."

"I thought you were buying a bed for Caleb."

"I bought *us* a queen-size bed. He's going to sleep in it."

"That was considerate of you. Just what every boy wants."

"It seems ridiculous to buy a twin bed for the few days he'll be here when the queen bed will get used long after he's gone. Anyway, it wasn't much more to buy the queen."

Ben started to say something, stopped, and then went downstairs to get his tools. Caleb and I held as Ben screwed the frame together, and then we slid the box spring and the mattress on.

"Look at this," Ben said, dropping Caleb on the bed. "This bed is big enough for both of us."

I went downstairs to get the mattress pad and the new sheets out of the dryer. We made the bed, and Caleb put the pillow and blanket he brought from home on top.

"How cool is that?" Ben asked.

"Pretty cool," Caleb said.

"What time do you usually go to bed?" I asked Caleb after supper.

"I have to go to bed when the news comes on."

"The six o'clock news?" I asked.

"He doesn't go to bed at six," Ben chided.

"Nine o'clock?"

Caleb shrugged. "After Grandpa's shows."

"He can't mean ten. That's a bit late, isn't it?"

"It is what it is," Ben said.

Shortly after eight, Ben took Caleb upstairs to give him a bath. When they came back down, Caleb was in his pajamas, his wet hair slicked back.

"You don't want his hair to dry like that, do you?"

"What's wrong with it?" Ben asked.

"Is that how your mom does it?" I asked Caleb.

He didn't respond.

Overlook a lot.

"Do you want a snack before bed?" I asked him.

"Grandpa and I eat ice cream."

"Before bed?"

He nodded.

"I think we have some frozen yogurt."

I scooped a dish and put it in front of him at the table.

"We put chocolate on top."

"I don't have any chocolate syrup."

"We eat it by the TV."

"What do you watch on TV?"

"Grandpa's shows."

"Hm. Well, I'm not sure what Grandpa watches, but Dad and I don't watch much TV, and I think it's best if we sit at the table."

I went to Ben's office. Ben was at his desk in front of his laptop.

"It's okay for you to be in the room alone with him, you know," Ben advised.

"I don't feel comfortable being in charge of him."

"I'm sure Becky assumed that you'd take care of him at least part of the time."

"Becky did, or you did?"

He walked past me to the kitchen.

"Done?"

Caleb nodded.

"Okay, let's get you into bed."

"He should brush his teeth first."

"Of course," Ben said.

I sat on the bed, listening as Ben helped Caleb with his teeth.

"Do you want to come in for prayers?" Ben asked as they crossed the hall.

I stood in Caleb's doorway. Ben sat on the bed next to Caleb and thanked God for the day and prayed for us to know and follow God. When he finished, he turned off the light.

"Do you want me to leave the hall light on?" I asked Caleb.

He didn't answer. I wondered if he could. His bed seemed as if it might swallow him.

"How do you usually go to sleep?" Ben asked.

"I get my wooki and lay next to Grandpa."

"What's a wooki?" I asked.

Caleb stepped out of bed, went downstairs to his bags, unzipped a side pocket, and pulled out a pacifier. He stuck it in his mouth and started back up the steps.

"Caleb, you are much too old for that," I asserted.

Ben raised his hand to object.

"Grandpa usually lies next to you?" Ben asked.

Caleb pulled his pacifier out to answer. "I lay next to him, on the couch."

"While he's watching TV," I added.

Caleb put his pacifier back in.

"I'll tell you what. I'll lie next to you tonight," Ben said.

I shut the door on the two of them and went downstairs to put Caleb's bowl in the dishwasher. I wiped the counter and table and tucked in Caleb's chair. Caleb's bags were scattered from us taking things from different bags throughout the day. I lined them up against the wall next to the door, turned off the light, and went upstairs.

Caleb came on Monday. Thursday afternoon, Becky called and asked if she could stop by Friday after work.

We put most of Caleb's things back in his bags when we finished using them. I washed the clothes and pajamas he had worn, folded, and packed them. Friday after dinner, I had him pack his toothbrush and comb and put his car seat by the steps.

Becky arrived shortly before 8:45. We were in the front yard. Caleb and Ben were kicking the ball while I tried to determine where I might want to put a garden next year.

Caleb ran to Becky. She rubbed his back as he hugged her leg.

"How are you doing?" she asked him.

"Good."

"Have you been behaving?"

"Yes."

"Are you having fun?"

Caleb nodded.

"Why don't we play on the swings for a couple minutes," she prompted. "I'll come with you."

Ben and I followed her to the neighbor's yard. She gave Caleb a push on the swing and then stepped over to us.

She wrung her hands and straightened her Tilly's shirt. "One of the girls from the cosmetology school is letting me stay with her. She and her boyfriend have a two-bedroom apartment. They were using the bedroom I'm in as an office. It's not very big, but they moved the desk out to the living area. There isn't much room, and they don't have kids. I was hoping Caleb could stay here."

"Indefinitely?" I asked, noting that she had been looking primarily at Ben as she spoke.

"I saw a counselor at the college. I heard it was all but impossible to get into the nursing program, but miracle of miracles, they let me in, probably because there is such a shortage of nurses and I'm a year from being done. I can start classes next week. If I take eighteen credits, I'll finish the nursing program in the spring."

"Of course Caleb can stay with us," Ben said.

"Are you sure? I know it's a lot to plop on your plate all at once."

"It's not a problem," Ben assured her. "We'll work it out. Do what you need to do."

Ben took Caleb upstairs for a bath. I brought Caleb's bags upstairs, set them down in Caleb's room, and then went to my room and sat on the bed.

Why did I feel like the earth had just opened up and swallowed me alive? Pastor Gibbons's mantra came to me: *Don't wait to call. Let's deal with the issues as they arise.*

"I'm sorry, Pastor Gibbons. I know it's only been a couple days, but—"

"It's not a problem, Meghan. I was expecting your call. Will tomorrow work?"

"He didn't even ask how I felt before he told Becky Caleb could move in," I told Pastor Gibbons when we were all seated in Ben's office. Caleb was in the living room watching The Lego Movie DVD that he had brought with him.

"Because we agreed that we'd help her with Caleb while she went to nursing school," Ben explained.

"There's a difference between watching him a couple nights a week and him moving in," I huffed.

"What did you want me to do?"

"Acknowledge I'm there! Tell Becky we'd take a day or two to talk about it and get back to her. You get by her and it's like you're a puppy waiting for her next command."

"Why are you so angry?" Ben prodded. "You've been begging me for a child."

"You can't possibly think that having Caleb in our house is even remotely the same thing as having a baby of our own."

"Of course it's not the same. But I have a problem with you not being able to do anything for him. For someone who's wanted a baby, you show absolutely no interest in him."

"He's not my child!"

"Okay. We need to bring it down a couple decibels," Pastor Gibbons reminded us.

"What *is* the problem, Meghan?" Ben asked.

"When Caleb and Becky are around, I disappear. You give me commands. You treat me like a child, not your wife."

"I'm sorry, but it would be nice if you'd take some initiative with Caleb."

"He doesn't want to be around me, Ben."

"I know, but I can't do it all."

"Until he warms up to me, you don't have much of a choice."

"I think he'd warm up to you if you tried to be nice to him."

"I don't know a thing about him," I reminded him.

"You know as much as I do."

"I think Meghan needs your permission to mother Caleb, Ben," Pastor Gibbons interjected. "She can start to treat him like her child, but if Caleb decides he doesn't want to do what Meghan asks of him, then you have to make a choice. Are you going to stand by Meghan, or will you give in to Caleb? If Meghan puts herself on the line, she wants to know you'll back her up."

"He's coming from a much different environment than what we would have given him," Ben explained. "We haven't set the rules or been the ones who've told him what to eat. It seems to me we need to ease into it and take it as it comes, measuring how he's been doing it with how we'd do it."

"He needs to know what's expected of him in our house," I asserted. "We can't let him get away with things for a couple weeks or a month, then all the sudden change the rules on him."

"Maybe not, but he doesn't need to know every rule his first day. Break him in slowly, Meg. Pretend he's an orphan boy off the street or something."

"An orphan?" I sneered.

"Whenever you're ready to admit it, your problem is Becky," Ben touted.

"Look at how mad you were at Jeff after I went to the beach with him. You bristled when you saw my wet pajamas. You threw a fit when I hadn't changed out of his clothes. Now, imagine I had slept with him, seen him naked, felt his body inside of mine. Can you see how that would up the ante?"

"How many times do I have to tell you that I love you, not her?"

"I guess until I believe it."

Pastor Gibbons gave Ben a slight shrug and a nod.

He leaned forward. "I'm sorry you have to deal with this. Caleb is my son. Could you find it in your heart to love him because you love me?"

You're assuming that I love you, and right now, I'm not sure I do.

I corrected my slouch and wondered how much longer it would be until I could smoke before realizing they were waiting on an answer from me.

I shrugged, because honestly, I'd forgotten the question. "I'll try."

Ben sighed. "Great. Now, can we talk about the smoking? What you just said made sense. You don't let something go for a month or two and then suddenly change the rules."

"You don't get to make this rule," I stated.

"You don't care how I feel about it?"

"I know how you feel about it."

"And you don't care," Ben huffed.

"It's my body," I declared.

"And mine. The two are one, remember?"

"I need something."

"What about running? Isn't that what you used to do?"

"Now you want me to run? In Milwaukee, you told me to stop."

"Because you were skin and bones."

"Because you were never home. I didn't need much, Ben, but I hated coming home to an empty apartment at eleven o'clock at night and sliding into a cold bed."

"I was tutoring and teaching guitar lessons."

"And I was working sixty hours a week to pay off your debt."

"I didn't ask you to do that," Ben snickered.

"Nor did you come up with your own plan for how to get it done."

"The same way everyone else does it, Meg. Little by little."

"Do you want to know the best part of this?" I asked Pastor Gibbons. "Ben didn't notice I had lost weight until his mom asked him if I was pregnant. She thought I was sick with morning sickness and losing weight. I would have given anything to be pregnant and sick with morning sickness, but Ben kept saying we had to wait until he finished school. So after talking to his mom, Ben asks me if I'm pregnant, as if I wouldn't have told him or shouted it from the rooftops if I was, and when I said no, he went back to his own little world. It took my parents coming and my dad taking Ben out and telling him I was his responsibility for Ben to even care about me."

"What did you do then, Ben?" Pastor Gibbons asked.

"First of all, just to clarify, I knew she was running, and I knew she was losing weight. I'd seen it before when Jeff slept with Carol. There were several months where she did the same thing. She ran everywhere, ran away from the hurt and ran away from the feelings. So when she started doing it with me, I thought it was childish, and I didn't want to acknowledge it."

"Right," I scoffed. "You didn't care why I was hurting then, and you don't care that I am now. You just want me to run till I get over it."

"If it's running or smoking, yeah, I'll pick running."

"How was the running resolved?" Pastor Gibbons prodded.

"I chased her, carried her up three floors, opened the apartment door, plopped her on the couch, and said I wasn't going away—that I was her husband, and she was my responsibility. If she was broken, we were both broken."

"You were never there to listen," I murmured. "I would have told you so much when I got home from work, but you were never there, and I finally figured out that would never change. That's the number-one gripe of pastors' wives. Their husbands are there for everyone else, but when it comes to them … I might as well get cozy with my cigarettes."

The door opened and Caleb peered in. "Dad, the movie's over."

Ben stood up. "All right bud, what do you want to do now?"

Caleb shrugged.

"Want to play with your cars for a while?"

"Okay."

"Why don't you go get them and bring them down? I'll be out in a bit."

Ben sat down and said, "I don't know how to make you happy."

"I didn't know wanting your child or wanting to spend time with you was such a huge thing to ask. I thought, crazy as it was, that you'd want to be with me. I never dreamed I'd cry myself to sleep, or that I could be married and still be lonely. Now, after all these years, you tell me you don't want kids and then you plop your four-year-old on my lap like it's supposed to be this great gift, and I'm supposed to be happy about it. It's like your parents' cat leaving a dead bird on the step and thinking he's done a great thing."

"Caleb is not a dead bird. He's my son, and if you don't want to help me raise him, I'll do it alone."

"Hold on, Ben," Pastor Gibbons interjected. "You're not hearing Meghan. She's wanted a baby. That's usually not something Christian husbands balk at. We know now that you didn't want a baby while you were in school because you were paying child support and felt like you had too much on your plate, but Meghan didn't know that. All she knew was that you were putting her off. You can't expect her to be at the same place as you are when she didn't have the same information. And Meghan," he turned to me, "running isn't the answer, and neither is smoking. You are going to experience all kinds of hurts in your life. Find your solace in God. Pray. Read your Bible. If you're running to get Ben's attention, it doesn't work. It just makes him mad."

A man can smell desperate a million miles away.

"I just don't understand why he's so comforting and reassuring to Becky but matter-of-fact with me."

"She's had no one the last four years," Ben replied.

"You're not the one to comfort her, Ben."

Pastor Gibbons nodded. "You've got to be careful, Ben. She may still have feelings for you. You're married, whether she wants you to be or not."

It was all I could do to not stick my tongue out at Ben. *Why, after three weeks of counseling, does it feel we are farther apart than ever? How does everyone else do this?*

Chapter Six

PULL ME OUT

Matt and Amanda's visit had been planned for weeks. By their estimation, they would arrive around noon.

I glanced at the alarm clock a little before eight. As I prayed, I created a mental list of to-dos.

I slipped on purple wind pants and a gray T-shirt, stripped the sheets off our bed, and crept to Caleb's room. Ben was huddled on the far side of the bed, his arm under his head. Caleb was sprawled across the rest of the bed.

I shut the door gingerly, hoping to cajole the old door into a quiet move. Once the bathroom door was shut, I combed my hair, brushed my teeth, and put on foundation and powder before stopping back in the room for my sheet bundle.

The grocery list was made and sheets were in the washer before I started for Rochester.

The weekend was besotted with nostalgia. Matt and Amanda held the roots of my relationship with Ben. It was on our road trip with them that both our futures were sealed. They would be engaged a few weeks later, and Ben's affections shifted from Becky to me.

I was halfway through my list when my phone rang.

"Where are you?" Ben asked, sounding frazzled.

"Target."

"I have a meeting at church this morning. I was hoping you'd watch Caleb."

"When is your meeting?"

"Ten minutes."

"Can you bring him to church? I'll finish and get him as soon as I can."

I rushed through the remaining food aisles, checked out, and drove to the church. Dora, Ben, and Lara Kenton were in the sanctuary. Caleb was walking through the rows of pews.

"Time to go," I whispered to him.

"I want to stay with Dad!"

"Have you had breakfast?"

"No."

"Let's go get something."

"I want to stay with Dad!"

"It's okay, Meghan," Ben called. "He can stay. He's not bothering us."

I drove home, put the sheets in the dryer, and unpacked the groceries before heading up to make Caleb's bed. Caleb's pajamas were on the floor next to the bed. I folded them and put them next to his pillow. Ben's pajama bottoms were on the floor of our room. I took them to Caleb's room and threw them on the bed.

It was 10:30 before I finished making vegetable lasagna. I covered the pan with foil and went upstairs to change. I was on my way down when Ben and Caleb came in.

"What's for lunch?" Ben asked. "We're starved."

"Vegetable lasagna, but we're not eating until Matt and Amanda get here."

Ben looked at Caleb. "I'll make us a piece of toast."

"I'm going for a run," I said. "Do you have anything else planned today?"

"I need to practice my sermon."

Why do I not feel inclined to help him after he made me rush home, only to send me away without Caleb? I decided against discussing it until after my run.

Nearly every yard on First Street contained pines. As I ran, I was wishing it were called Oak Street with mature oak branches canopying the street.

I spotted Dora a half block ahead. Dora was the first name Ben remembered when we came to Oronoco. He said it was because of Dora the Explorer. I was pretty certain it was Dora's long, bleach-blonde hair and Barbie-like figure.

I was about to call to her when a man opened the door of a house just ahead.

"Where have you been?" he snarled. "Braden's looking for you."

She hurried in, and he shut the door.

The road ahead ended in a dead end. I turned onto Fourth Street and then Minnesota Avenue. If I went to the right, I could go about a mile until it joined a busy highway.

I steered to the left. Two blocks took me back to the church and within a block of home.

Nothing like going in circles.

I ran past my house and went down the block, where the windows to Dora's house were open, giving escape to heavy, screeching music.

She came out the side door with a young boy who ran to a tree swing. She followed him, head down, looking at her phone.

"Hey, Dora!" I called. "I was attempting to go for a run, but apparently, all these streets circle."

She waved timidly.

"How was the praise band meeting?"

She crossed the grass in her black wedge sandals.

"We picked a couple songs."

I smiled. "Do you live here? I didn't realize we were on the same street."

She nodded and looked over her shoulder toward the house. "It's my roommate's music."

"A male roommate? How's that working?"

"I think of moving all the time."

"What's stopping you?"

She glanced over her shoulder at the boy before turning back to me. "It's complicated. He's not mine," she added.

"But you watch him?"

"Part of the living arrangement."

"How old is he?"

"Three and a half. I'd bring him to church, but I'm not interested in the rumors."

This I had not expected. The Barbiesque girls I'd known were all too happy to be the subject of other's conversations, good or bad.

"Gossips would have nothing over us if we were willing to be open and real," I advised.

"I'm curious as to what you'd share that people don't suspect about you."

Whoa. Brains and brawn.

"I have been planning for years to start a family once Ben was done with school. I have a family now, but it's not the family I was hoping for. It's almost more than I can handle to see Ben fathering someone else's child."

"It's horrid to watch a boy who doesn't have a good living situation," she offered.

"Where's Braden's mom?"

"In jail. She was selling heroin."

"That's sad."

"Not what I want for my children, assuming my fiancé and I have children someday."

"You're engaged and your fiancé is okay with you living with another man?"

"He doesn't know I'm living here. He's in the navy," she explained. "As soon as he gets home, we're getting married."

"When will that be?"

"Next August."

"And he doesn't know you're living here?" *Is everyone keeping something from the person they love?*

"He thinks I'm Braden's nanny, which is true. He just doesn't know I'm not getting paid with money, but with a room."

I rubbed my eyes, certain now the running portion of the day was over. "I didn't understand the harm of keeping things from Ben, but now that I do, I wouldn't recommend that route."

"Chris likes to party."

Is Chris her fiancé?

"He usually goes to friends' houses, but the next day, he's a bear." She looked down. "He likes the idea of being a dad more than actually being a dad."

Not the fiancé. Braden's dad.
"Dora, are you safe?"
"Physically, yes, but I worry about Chris watching me."
"Watching you?"
"You know, like in the shower, or when I get undressed. He's the kind of creep who might put a camera somewhere."
Look what she's living through for the sake of one child.
"You know, Dora. Our house is right down the street. If you need a quiet place for Braden to play, you're welcome there. Caleb's going to be with us for a while. We have an extra bedroom upstairs where you could study."
"I doubt very much you need me around."
Swallow your insecurity. "It would be fine. You could even shower at our house. You wouldn't have to worry about anyone spying on you. You could just keep your stuff in a basket at our house so Chris doesn't know."
"That would be a little uncomfortable for Pastor, wouldn't it?"
"We could work something out. He could stay in his study or go to church for a bit."
Her smile thanked me for the empathy but contradicted the idea.

Matt and Amanda pulled in the drive at quarter after.
"How was the trip?" I asked, giving Matt a hug.
"We'll be getting real familiar with Skype after this."
"That bad, huh?"
"I wasn't aware Max's attention span was so short," Amanda lamented. "Abby managed to nap for forty-five minutes, but the other—"
"Ten hours," Matt interrupted.

She gave him a look of consternation. "Were not quite so fun."

"Well, we're glad you're here," Ben said, shaking Matt's hand. "Let me help you unload the car."

"Do you mind if I disappear for a bit?" Amanda asked. "Abby should eat, and I'm going to need to change her."

"There's an empty bedroom upstairs."

"Where are we going with this?" Ben asked, carrying a Pack 'N Play and another bag.

"Take it to our room."

Ben stared in bewilderment.

"I'll sleep on the couch. You haven't slept in our bed for a week."

"What?" Matt cried. "You aren't sleeping with your wife, Ben?"

"I've gotten in the habit of falling asleep with Caleb," Ben admitted, climbing the stairs.

"That is a major no-no. You start that and you'll never get back."

I turned around and noticed the two boys. "Caleb, this is Max. I bet after lunch, you two would have fun playing with your cars."

Caleb walked away and up the stairs. He returned with the men a few minutes later.

"Lunch is ready," I told Matt. "But should we wait for Amanda?"

"No," he said. "She'll be awhile."

After prayers, I passed the food.

"Aren't you going to eat?" Matt asked.

"I'll eat with Amanda."

"You're looking good, Meghan. Ben must be taking care of you."

Ben's eyes met mine. "It's not my doing, Matt. This move hasn't been easy on Meghan."

"Then you better be taking care of her," Matt admonished.

"Dad, I don't like this," Caleb said.

"Just eat the noodles," Ben said.

Amanda came down as the guys were finishing. She put Abby on a blanket on the floor with a pile of squeeze toys and soft books.

"I thought we'd eat at the counter," I said, pulling out a stool.

"Fine with me," she said. "Oh, vegetable lasagna! That's one of my favorites."

"I know."

"You could have made peanut butter and jelly sandwiches and I'd be happy. My favorite meals these days are the ones I don't make."

"Which is a majority of them," Matt poked.

Amanda agreed. "I go in stages. I'll cook like a crazy woman for two or three weeks, and then I putter out and we scrounge for a bit, or Matt will pick something up on the way home from work."

"Is Max a good eater?" I asked.

"He eats what we eat."

"That helps."

Amanda nodded.

"Do you want to take the boys hiking?" Ben asked Matt. "It looks like Whitewater State Park is about a half hour away."

"Have Max go to the bathroom first," Amanda suggested.

"Do you think we can make it without the girls?" Matt teased.

I turned to Matt. "Ben will do just fine with Caleb." Turning to Amanda, I asked, "Do you want to go to town?"

"Fine with me."

"What time do you want us back?" Ben asked.

"No later than 6:00, please!" Amanda answered. "Max goes to bed at 7:30."

"Are you serious?" I asked.

"Oh, yeah. Eight p.m., my sanity starts," she replied.

I eyed Ben and said, "Nice." He smiled and shuffled the boys out the door.

When the dishes were cleared and the counter and table wiped, I started the dishwasher. "Can you drink coffee while you're nursing?"

"I do on occasion."

"I could use a tea today."

"You got it," she said.

We packed Abby's things, put her car seat in my car, and headed to Rochester. Caribou Coffee was in a strip mall across the street from Target.

"Do you want to go in, or should we find a park?"

"Let's find a park," she said. "It's gorgeous outside, and I wouldn't mind walking off some of my baby fat."

"You look great, Amanda."

"For a mother of two, maybe. Look at your flat stomach."

"I'd do anything to be pregnant."

"Isn't it working?"

"Hold that thought. I'll be right back."

I returned with our drinks and put them in the cupholders. "To answer your question, nothing is working."

"How long have you been trying?"

"Ben hasn't touched me since I came back."

"What! It's been awhile."

I nodded. "Three weeks. Not a peck, not a hug, nothing. Now, with Caleb living with us, everything is about Caleb. He sleeps with Caleb, plays with Caleb, talks to Caleb. I get that he lost four and a half years with him, but I feel like I've disappeared."

"Oh, man, Meghan, I'm sorry."

"It's worse around Becky. The two of them talk as if I'm not there. She looks at him. He looks at her. I interject something and Ben talks over me. He's carrying a lot of guilt about not being there for her, so whatever she wants is fine with him. He doesn't seem to care how it affects me."

"I still can't believe he didn't tell you."

"I can't either."

I started the car and drove onto the frontage road. "But in Ben's defense, I knew Ben would make me quit if I told him how terrible it was to work at the journal, so I didn't tell him. I wanted the income."

"Terrible how?"

"The newsroom was full of young, sex-in-the-city types who talked about their sexual exploits pretty consistently and graphically. After awhile, they more or less avoided me because they knew I wouldn't add to the conversation. It was a sexually charged environment, to say the least. I learned a lot; I can tell you that much."

"Ugh. You're right. Ben wouldn't have wanted you there."

"I didn't tell him because I knew I'd be done. I haven't quite figured out why he didn't tell me about Caleb. Both

Ben's parents and Jeff said Ben didn't tell me about Caleb because I've proven that I don't handle tough situations well, like, for instance, when Jeff slept with Carol."

"Who would deal with that well?"

"Apparently not me."

"That is ridiculous. I reject that reasoning. What else do you have?"

"I think it may have been a combination of saving face and not wanting to crush me because he knew I wanted a baby."

"But why not tell you before bringing you here? He knew Becky and Caleb were here. Oronoco is tiny. What are the odds?"

"I didn't hear about them in Oronoco. I found out about them right up the street at Hair Nation."

"Still, it's lame that when you finally found out, you went to people looking for advice and they blamed you. Then Ben cuts off all affection to you, moves his son in, whom he showers with affection, and treats you like dirt in front of his ex-girlfriend."

"I don't think he's willfully doing it, Amanda. I think he's being a good dad to Caleb and figures I'm a big girl."

"That doesn't make it right."

"No. It doesn't. But, this situation makes me wonder if we could handle it if we knew the worst about each other."

"I don't know. What are you hiding?"

I gave her a sideways glance. "Well, for starters, I'm trying to not get nervous about Ben being around Dora."

"Who's Dora?"

"She's a hot blonde who sings in the praise band with him."

"You don't have to worry about Ben."

"I think we have to be careful around everyone. Anyone of the opposite sex who shows any of us empathy or compassion or affection is likely to become an object of our affection."

"You're talking as if you have personal experience."

"I guess."

I turned into the park and we got out of the car. Amanda pulled the stroller out of the back and fastened Abby in.

"Here's another thing I don't feel good about: I don't feel anything for Caleb, Amanda," I said as we started walking.

"Did you think you would?"

"Ben loves him, but he's just a little boy to me."

"I think that's normal."

"I've prayed for years to be a mom—"

"Meghan, stop. If you had known, or if you had seen him over the past four years, or if Ben was including you and talking to you, then things would be different. You just met him, what, a week ago?"

I nodded.

"It would be crazy to love him at this point."

"It's not just that I don't love him, Amanda. He drives me nuts. Until Saturday, he was using a pacifier to go to sleep."

"No!"

"Ben told me to let it go because we thought Becky was taking him back, but the minute she said he'd be staying with us, I threw it away and told him he was way too old. His previous bedtime routine was falling asleep on the couch next to Grandpa while watching TV. Now

Ben sleeps with him, and that drives me crazy too. He picks at everything I make for meals and refuses to eat, so Ben caves and gives him what he wants."

"It's sad, Meghan, but it's not Caleb's fault. He's the result of—"

"A neglectful father. It's divine justice. It's our mess to clean up."

She exhaled. "If Caleb's staying, then it's time to get some things straight. Is he going to school this year?"

I shook my head.

"Hm. You should maybe reconsider that. He could at least go to preschool a couple days a week. That would get him into the routine of getting up early, and you could get him to bed at a decent time. He eats what you make for meals, period. He'll learn to eat the way you guys eat eventually. Ben sleeps with you; Caleb sleeps by himself. Get him a night-light, or keep the hall light on, or stay upstairs while he's falling asleep so he feels secure, but he needs to know that husbands sleep with their wives, not their children."

"Yeeeeppp."

She chuckled. "That doesn't sound too promising. Anyway, what's up with Ben? You'd think he'd want sex."

"You'd think. I don't know. I guess I haven't done anything to let him know I'm interested."

"Are you watching *Burn Notice* again?"Amanda prodded. "It's impossible to watch that show and not lust after Michael. Except when he's eating yogurt. There's something about his face when he eats that is a major turnoff to me."

"What? No. I quit *Burn Notice* after season four. I can't get past the concept of the end justifying the means."

"*Psych?*"

"I quit *Psych* too. Too much foul language. Anyway, what does TV have to do with anything?" I challenged.

She shrugged. "Just trying to get to the bottom of things."

"Do you sit in bed watching TV and lusting after people instead of paying attention to Matt?"

"What makes you think that?"

"Amanda?"

"We were talking about you, remember? You've hinted twice now about leaving the door open for an affair and being uninterested in Ben. Someone else is on your mind. Now, who is it?"

"I love you like a sister, but anything I tell you goes straight to Matt. I don't have a problem with that, but Matt would take it to Ben, and that would only complicate things further."

"So you don't want Ben to know because you're afraid of how he'd react?"

"I guess."

"Where have I heard that before? Oh, yeah. That's why Ben didn't tell you about Caleb."

I stopped walking. "It's all the same, isn't it?"

"Who are you lusting after? I promise I won't tell Matt."

"Ever since I got back, I'm having a hard time getting Jeff out of my head."

"Shut up!"

"I know. I know. It's completely irrational."

"It's completely predictable. Ben hurt you. You ran to Jeff. Jeff comforted you. Your mind sees Ben as the pain and Jeff as the pleasure. It's like a drug, and you just keep going back to your happy place."

"I didn't run to Jeff. Ben called him in desperation looking for me, and Jeff showed up at Margaret's house. The rest is spot-on though."

"I have my own happy place. It's just not a person. It's a place with wide aisles and bright colors, happy people, and wonderful names like Nieman Marcus and Macy's and American Eagle."

"Nieman Marcus has wide aisles?"

"In my mind, it does. My guess is Jeff isn't all you've made him to be either."

"He isn't. In fact, I was disgusted with some of the things he said, and yet I can smell his cologne and I can feel his arms around me, his face next to mine."

"His tail wrapping around your legs, his horns piercing your heart, his fangs draining the blood from your neck."

"Were you going for the devil or a vampire with that imagery?"

"Does it matter? Either way, it's suicide. What can he offer you other than an STD and no commitment?"

"He doesn't have an STD."

"You don't know that. Anyway, he has no spiritual bearings whatsoever, and he's got a cliché problem."

"What?"

"They roll off his tongue."

"You've never even talked to him."

"Well, he seems like the kind of womanizing guy that would use them. The only reason you don't see it is because you've been bitten. He's like a rabid dog. He bit you however many years ago, and you've never got the rabies out of your system."

"But I did. I haven't thought of him in four years, and if I did, it was a fleeting thought. I never lingered."

"Okay. He's like a case of the shingles. Once you've had them, they can flare up again. You get stressed out or your body comes under duress, and it's all over."

"What am I going to do?"

"I think shingles have to run their course. Or, hold on, I think you can use herpes medication if you catch them right away."

"Perfect. I just need to get some herpes meds."

"Seriously, Meg. You've got the hottest husband. Most women are lusting after him. Don't get me wrong; they'll have to answer for that."

"Are you lusting after my husband?

"I may have in the past on one or two occasions, but that's not the point. The point is that it is nothing short of ludicrous for you to lust after anyone else. You can't covet either. You and Ben are financially set. Now, if you were jealous of someone's career, that I could see."

"You aren't seriously suggesting a reasonable sin, are you?"

"Oh, heavens, no. I would never do that. Just suggesting a more rational one."

"I should never have left with Jeff that night. When he brought me home from the beach, he hugged me and kissed me on the cheek. I thought he was going to kiss me on the lips and I remembered the way we used to kiss, and a switch turned on again."

"You're trying to escape because you're unhappy with the way things are, and the temptation is that he could make you happy. It's a lie. He wouldn't. You've been there before."

"I know. I can't believe this is where I'm at. I never thought I was capable of this, or that I'd still be struggling with it three weeks after I told Ben I wouldn't talk to Jeff again."

"That's why. He's forbidden fruit now."

"You're probably right."

"It doesn't help that Ben is elusive. Have you thought about counseling?"

"We're in counseling. Pastor Gibbons is on speed dial."

"Isn't it helping?"

"I think it's made us realize we have more problems than we thought."

"You're worse off now than when you started?"

"Not to bring Jeff up again, but—"

"You are going to."

"He compared sorting out our life to cleaning a closet. You take everything out and wipe the shelves and then go through everything to decide what to keep and what to throw away. It gets messy before it gets better."

"He's good."

I looked at her and nodded. "I've met a girl who sort of reminds me of him. Now I just need to get him out of my head. We're like two magnets with opposite charges who keep getting sucked into each other."

"Well, Matt and I have our share of problems. I think every married couple does. Lots of couples get divorced right around five years."

"When I married Ben, I thought he was the *perfect* guy. If I can't make it work with him, there's a good chance I couldn't make it with anyone."

She laughed. "That's as good a reason as any to keep working at it."

"I guess."

We talked about shopping at a couple secondhand stores, but when we put Abby in the car, she protested. She fell asleep on the way home. Amanda carried her to the Pack 'N Play.

"I don't want to stay in your room," she said, coming down the steps.

"Why?"

"Because I want Ben to stay in there with you. We can set up the air mattress. That's what we were planning to do."

"I was going to put you in Caleb's bed, but I'm not sure he'd adjust well to the couch or a sleeping bag on the floor."

"No. I agree. Why don't you buy him a twin bed? Then you wouldn't have to worry about Ben sleeping with him."

"Yes. Had I done what Ben wanted me to do, that would be settled. I thought he'd only be with us a few days and we could use the bed as a guest bed, so I got the queen."

"Oh, crumb. Well, you're going to have to get Ben back in your bed somehow."

"I never thought I'd have to worry about that."

"Remember how before you got married, you couldn't wait to have sex and it was hard to keep your hands off each other? Run your fingers through his hair, touch his back, hold his hand. It's been three weeks; honestly, at this point, it shouldn't take more than a look."

We laughed.

"And, you know, they're always nicer afterward."

I nodded. "Did I just hear your van?"

Amanda looked at her watch. "It's not even four yet."

Matt opened the door, put a twelve pack of beer on the counter, gave Amanda a peck on the cheek, and went back outside. Ben came in, got himself a glass of water, and stood at the sink looking out the window.

"How did it go?" I asked.

He put his glass next to the sink. "To say Caleb is not a hiker would be the understatement of the year."

"That well?"

"Ben, why don't you and Meghan go out tonight?" Amanda suggested. "Matt and I can watch Caleb."

Ben shook his head. "You didn't come all this way to babysit for us."

"We stood up for you at your wedding. It would be good for you to have some time together."

Ben walked to the couch. "I get that Caleb is a mess, Amanda. But he's my mess."

"And no one wants to take that mess off your hands, Ben. But you're still married, and your wife needs you too."

Ben looked at me. "Do you want to go out?"

"Only if you do," I answered.

"I don't," he said, walking out the door.

"Ouch," Amanda whispered.

I shrugged. "Welcome to my world."

She put a hand on my knee. "It's got to get better."

After Matt and Amanda left, I washed the sheets to our bed. I was putting them on again when Ben came to the doorway.

"I'm sorry I didn't take you out last night."

"It's not a problem."

"It stunk when Amanda confronted me about taking care of you and our marriage."

"She was only trying to help."

"I didn't want to leave Caleb with Matt, because I could see how ticked off Matt was at him. Caleb was a nightmare while we were hiking. It was a total embarrassment. He didn't want to climb and complained constantly, and Matt was more than a little put off. It wasn't that I didn't want to go out with you. I didn't want Matt with Caleb."

"I understand."

"I could see he had one thing on his mind last night."

"When did he start drinking so much?"

"I don't know."

I put one pillow down and reached across the bed to get the other.

"I don't really know what I'm doing," Ben admitted.

"I know you don't. But it shouldn't be either Caleb or me. If this is going to work, it has to be us working together."

"I know. I keep thinking I should have married Becky and let you marry someone without all this ..."

I threw the pillow on the bed. "Do you want to be with Becky?"

"No."

"There were a whole bunch of things that should have been done differently, but they weren't. And this is where we are," I said, turning to him.

"Dad!" Caleb yelled from the bottom of the stairs.

"What?"

"Can you get me a drink?"

"In a bit, Caleb. I'm talking to Meghan."

"That's a start."

"What?"

"You showing him that I mean something to you, too, and he doesn't need to be waited on hand and foot."

"I guess."

"There's no guessing about that. You're going to have to start teaching him some things and letting me teach him some things too."

"Why do I have a feeling you have a list?"

"He just needs a little guidance."

"Thanks for sticking around."

"This time, it was sheer determination. Your good looks had nothing to do with it."

He smirked. "This has been such a nightmare."

"Speaking of nightmares," I sat on the bed, "I bumped into Dora yesterday after praise band when I went for my run. She's in a bad place, living with a guy mostly for the sake of his son."

"She's living with her boyfriend?"

"No. She's not dating the guy she's living with. She's just living there. The mom's in jail on drug charges. Dora takes care of Braden and, in return, lives there free. There's just one problem."

"What's that?"

"The guy she lives with is a drinker, and when he drinks, he's not a very nice person. Besides that, she doesn't trust him."

"Doesn't trust him how?"

"She thinks he watches her in the shower or in her room."

"She needs to get out of there."

"She won't leave Braden."

"And he'll do whatever it takes to keep his eye candy."

"I told her she could start hanging out and taking showers here."

"You did what?"

"Ben, we're right down the street, and she needs to go somewhere."

"What happened to 'stay ten feet away from her at all times?'"

"I'm pretty sure it was a hundred feet."

"Well, after all that's happened, I tend to agree with you. It's one thing to be in praise band together. We'll never be alone. But her showering here? That can't happen, Meghan. I've done enough to jeopardize my ministry. I don't need you hopping on that train."

"What if we arranged times? Maybe we could set something up so you are at the church or locked in your office and another woman was here as a witness."

"She needs to get out of there."

"I doubt she will."

"Her coming here is not the solution."

"Well, I just thought we should do … something."

He paused. "The fact that you considered it means you're willing to trust me, and that's a big step."

"It is, isn't it?"

He nodded. "It's huge, Meg."

Chapter Seven

TURNING THE CORNER

"I called the insurance company," I announced to Ben from the door of his office.

He was working on his laptop. "And?"

"Since you aren't on the birth certificate, you need to take a paternity test."

A cannon going off in the next room couldn't have caused his head to shoot up and swivel toward me any faster.

"What?"

"They'll send a nurse over to take a swab from you and Caleb; she'll send it in, and then they'll call us and tell us the premium."

"I don't like this."

"What's not to like?"

"What if they find something?"

"Like?"

"A disease. They could drop my insurance."

"If you have a disease, it would be best to know."

"I might not have it now. You can be predisposed to cancer or diabetes or—"

"I don't think they can drop your insurance over that, can they?"

"They could probably raise the premiums."

I considered. "I think they just want to make sure you're Caleb's dad, so they aren't insuring someone they shouldn't be."

Ben rubbed his face. I had seen him as the image of strength and vigor at the beginning of the summer, but now I watched his shoulders slump over his desk and his hands cradle his head. The word *pathetic* passed through my head, but I rebuked it.

He's not pathetic. He's worn, weathered, seasoned, even.

I stood straighter, realizing my own slouch. "Lexie said there's a job opening at the *Post Bulletin* for a graphic designer. Before you say no, it's a freelance position, and I could do it from home. There would probably be meetings, either in person or over the phone to discuss the particulars of a job, but it wouldn't be much."

"You wouldn't quit being my secretary, would you?" Ben asked.

I contemplated.

"Meghan?"

"As long as you match my wage, you have nothing to worry about."

He smiled. "I think it's a great idea."

"You do?"

"Sure. If you were to get pregnant, it wouldn't be a big deal. It's not like it's full-time."

"I won't be getting pregnant anytime soon."

"Oh, why not?"

"For starters, you'd have to touch me. And then there's the business of bringing another life into this mess, and we'd both have to *want* a child."

"Well, I'm not going to touch you until I'm sure you trust me. That seems to be going in the right direction. Neither of us called Pastor Gibbons this week, which may indicate the mess is resolving. I didn't want a child while I was in school and before you knew about Caleb. I'm no longer in school, and rumor has it you found out about Caleb."

"Don't get my hopes up, Ben."

"I think it might be nice to have a sibling for Caleb sooner rather than later. They would be five years apart as it is."

"It's about Caleb then?"

"It's about our family."

"What happens when Becky is done with nursing school? What if she meets someone online and moves to another state or gets a job in the Cities? What if you take a call to Alaska?"

"I think it's fair to say Caleb's going to be in our life in some capacity. He knows I'm his dad. There's no going back."

"I've given up on having a baby anytime soon."

"It wouldn't be that hard to talk yourself back into it, would it? For the last three years, you've mentioned it every opportunity you could."

Pastor Gibbons's voice rang in my head. *Say only what's necessary. Resolve to hold back from jabbing each other with words or taking cheap shots. When conflicted, choose silence.*

I raised my eyebrows and shrugged. How could I explain it wasn't a matter of flipping a switch or that as engrained as it was in me to want a child, the pain of his actions were greater, or that even as I was forgiving him for what he had done, his wanting a child for the sake of Caleb and not me was hardly a motivator?

"Oh, by the way, the pastor's wife in Zumbrota called the other day. She invited me to their women's Bible study on Sunday night. I think I'll go."

"Great."

Great? Why is everything great all the sudden?

Oronoco was halfway between Rochester and Zumbrota. Fifteen minutes south brought you to the hub of health care and business technology, while twenty minutes north brought you to small-town America. Except for the teens dying to be anywhere else, people who lived in Zumbrota wanted to be there. They were willing to drive the extra miles to work in Rochester but live in a place where there were more stars than streetlights, where everyone knew everyone else's business and that was a good thing. Zumbrota, it seemed, was a place to plant a family right along with a garden and establish roots. The teens left, but no one worried, because eventually, almost everyone came back, or at least that's what Pastor Shaw's wife led me to believe when she introduced herself to me over the phone.

A couple months ago, it might have mattered. Now I didn't care if she was inviting me to a Bible study at Disney, because I was there for an hour or two to escape Oronoco and be around strangers who knew nothing of the mess Ben and I were in.

The study was held in the church basement. I parked by the other cars, went in the closest door, and followed the sound of laughter. Liz introduced herself to me as soon as I walked off the bottom step.

"I'm glad you came!" she said, pulling me in for a hug.

"I'm glad to be here," I said.

"Find a seat. We're about to get started."

Four tables were arranged in a square, each of them covered in flowery gold-and-maroon tablecloths. A row of maroon tea candles lined the center of each table. Obviously, this was an effort to make us forget we were in a basement with beige vinyl floor tiles and dark walls. Surprisingly, it worked.

I sat at the end of a table. The older woman I had talked to in the bathroom the day of Ben's installation approached and asked if she might sit beside me. I remembered her because I was all but hyperventilating at the time she emerged from the stall to offer her empathy about how hard a new move and new church must be for a young couple.

"Yes, please," I encouraged.

"I'm Mildred," she said, propping her cane against the table.

"That's my mother-in-law's name," I said, feeling a tinge of regret. "Everyone calls her Millie."

"Same with me!" she said.

"I'm Meghan. I remember you from my husband's installation. Nice to meet you again. Are you from Zumbrota?"

She nodded. "Where are you from originally?"

"Monona, Wisconsin, just outside of Madison."

"It's so good of you to join us," she said.

Was it possible she hadn't heard?

"Okay, ladies, let's get started," Liz announced. She waited while everyone took a seat. "I picked up twenty copies of the book we're studying this year, and by the looks of it, we'll have just enough."

"Do you want us to pay for them?" a woman opposite me asked as she reached to the center of the table for a copy.

"I put a basket by the dessert able. If you want to throw in a couple dollars to defray the cost, go for it. But don't let it be a stumbling block. If, after tonight, you don't think you'll be back, just leave the book. If you don't feel like paying for the book, don't pay for the book. If you don't have money for the book, don't worry about it. If you don't want to write in the book and don't plan on keeping the book, but just want to use it each time you come, that's fine too. The important thing is being here in the Word together."

"How much do the books cost?" another woman asked.

"Thirteen dollars," Liz answered.

Several of the women nodded.

"Most of us know each other, but let's start with introductions, just to be sure."

Liz introduced each person and said a little something about her. When she came to me, she introduced me as her new friend Meghan. She made no mention of me being from Oronoco or being Ben's wife.

The study for the night focused on Moses's sister Miriam, the first woman of leadership mentioned in the Bible. Several statements from the devotion struck me.

"How often don't we throw our hands in
the air when we deal with the people in our

life? Moses was leading two million people who had a rebellious nature. When God decided to destroy them, Moses interceded on their behalf."[1]

I had not gone to the Lord on Ben's behalf since finding out about Caleb. Always, my prayers were for my benefit. We read on.

"Miriam's experiences teach us some important lessons. First, in all situations we ought to give thanks and praise to God for all He has done in our lives, whether or not it is where we want to be. We can always find something that doesn't fit our expectations. It's better to be grateful for the blessings in our lives instead of being disgruntled over the irritants."

I had not given thanks for much the last month, nor was I thankful to be in this situation. I could think of several situations more appealing—like running from a bull or having the mumps or being stranded in the ocean.

"Second, if we are willing to be content with our lot in life, we will not only be at peace in our own regard, but the Lord will be pleased with us as well."

Contentment was not in the top ten adjectives I'd use to describe my attitude about life.

---

[1] From *"Ladies of Legacy"* by Amber Albee Swenson

"And last, we should be mindful of all the people the Lord has put over us: parents, a spouse, pastors, our government officials and the Lord Himself. We ought to give everyone the respect they deserve and the submission of being under their authority, understanding God is the one who put them above us."

I was not mindful of my husband's position; in fact, Ben had fallen from his place of respect in my eyes, and I was slow to give him that respect back.

As we finished the study, Liz asked for prayer requests.

"My friend is struggling with depression," a woman about my mother's age offered.

"Thank you, Betty. What's your friend's name?" Liz asked.

"Rhonda."

"I'd like you to pray for Dora."

I studied the woman who made the request.

"What's going on?" Liz asked.

"She's not living in a good place. I'm worried about her."

Could this be the mother of the Dora I knew? She had a medium-length pixie, with hair just covering her ears and longer hair on the top of her head giving an air of sophistication. Aside from the tiniest wrinkles around her eyes, her skin was flawless. She carried herself in such a way that you knew she could mingle with the elite but would be equally happy to help at your garage sale.

"Is she open to moving?"

She shook her head. "I just don't know. I know she's there for Braden, but I worry about her."

Same Dora.

"Okay," Liz said. "We'll pray for the Lord's protection. Anyone else?"

"Pray for Mira."

"Oh, yes," Liz said. "As you all know, she broke her hip and had to have surgery. So far so good, but let's pray the Lord heals her completely so she can join us next time."

"She isn't that old, is she?" a woman who didn't appear a whole lot older than I asked.

"Maybe sixty?" another offered.

"If that," another woman responded.

"It was a fluke that she fell off her stool and landed that way."

"After hearing about her, I swore off cleaning the top of my cupboards," one woman said.

Everyone laughed.

"Could we pray for the pastor in Oronoco and his wife?" another younger woman asked.

I felt my face warm.

"I feel so bad for them," she continued. "I mean, I know he made a mistake, but he's trying to do the right thing. And she ... we just need to pray that she has the strength she needs to get through it."

Several heads nodded.

"I hope the church is helping them out," an older woman proclaimed. "There's a shortage of pastors as it is."

"Good idea," Liz said. "Let's pray."

Liz went down the list she had been making, praying for each person. When she came to our name, she prayed God would surround us with Christians to hold us up and guide us, that he would provide everything we needed, that he would strengthen our marriage and our will to walk with him, and use this to make Ben's ministry powerful. When she said "Amen," she told everyone to help themselves to the desserts.

I went to Liz and gave her a hug. "Thanks for the beautiful evening. It was just what I needed."

"I hope you'll come back."

I showed her the book I was clutching. "I wouldn't miss it," I said.

"Drive safely," she said.

I threw a twenty-dollar bill in the basket and was almost to the steps when the younger woman who asked to pray for us stopped me.

"I'm Jenny."

"Nice to meet you. I'm Meghan."

"Did you just move here?"

"We moved to the area the end of June. My husband is the new pastor in Oronoco."

Her hand flew to her face. "I didn't know."

"Why would you? Anyway, it was considerate of you to ask to pray for us."

"I feel like such a fool."

"Don't. I could have been elusive and let you figure it out later. It's okay. This year hasn't been what I thought it would be, but God's with us, and he'll get us through. I'm glad I decided to come tonight. You seem like a great group of ladies. I look forward to getting to know you."

"Thanks."

"I'll see you next month."

"See you then!"

A few days later, a card arrived in the mail. The ladies from the Bible study wrote to say they'd be praying for me, were glad I joined them, and were looking forward to what God had in store for me.

I placed the card as a bookmark in my Bible so I would see it every night to pray for the women on the other side of the signatures.

"Everywhere I look, I see babies."

"Tell me about it," Lexie sneered. "It's like an alien invasion."

"You see them too?"

"They were always there. We just didn't notice."

"You think?"

She nodded. "It's our generation's turn to reproduce. I feel the ticking of my internal clock, but with no one to aid me in the process, there's no hope for children for me in the near future. Even if I were to meet a man tomorrow who fell under the spell of my purple bangs, realistically, it would be at least a month or two before I could drug him, drag him to your husband's desk to coerce him into marriage, and then—"

"You'd have to wake him up to perform."

"Right. That would require some explanation, which may or may not go favorably."

"I'm going to start praying you find a husband."

"Grammatically, you should pray I find a man who might become my husband. I know lots of husbands, and honestly, finding them does nothing for me."

"Touché." I took a drink of my tea. "Turns out, Ben is thinking it's a good time to start a family."

"I've been praying he would!"

"I'm glad you're excited."

"You aren't?"

"He only wants a baby because he thinks it would be good for Caleb to have a sibling."

"What's wrong with that?"

"I've wanted a baby for three of the four years we've been married."

"And now he wants a baby, too, not long, I might add, after your newfound best friend began praying Ben would want a baby."

"It's all about Caleb."

"But you'd still be having a baby, so to me, it's win-win."

"Am I the only one who thinks there is at least a remote chance that Caleb won't be part of our family forever?"

"Are you hoping?"

"What do we know of Becky?"

"Well—"

"That was meant to be rhetorical."

Lexie raised her hands ever so slightly. "Sorry. Continue."

"She lied to Ben, not once, but twice about being pregnant. She quit nursing school, started cosmetology school, quit cosmetology school, started nursing school, and dropped her son off to live with strangers."

Lexie lifted a single pointer finger and cleared her throat. "If I may: she had the terrifying experience of going through a pregnancy alone. She listened to the poor advice of parents she trusted, which led not only to her giving up her hopes of being a nurse and finishing the schooling that she had three-fourths finished, but also losing her boyfriend and the father of her child. Then, by no fault of her own, but by an act of God, the ex-boyfriend, who she quite possibly still loves—and his wife, whom he loves—move back into her life, where she gets to see them and their perfect life, free of commitment and debt and insecurities, while they see her life for the mess it is. At this point, she decided maybe the child would be better off with them, thereby twice making the harder choice to save her baby."

"From her perspective, she's given up everything and gotten a mess, whereas Ben's had no paternal responsibility and has gotten to build his life," I interjected.

"Correct. And, nursing seems to be a fairly stable occupation. Why would she go anywhere else when there's a world-class medical center here begging for nurses and offering a good income and benefits?"

"So I'm being irrational?"

Lexie shrugged. "One-sided?"

I rubbed my face.

"If it's any consolation, I think what you're going through is normal, but it's sort of like an older child being jealous when the younger sibling comes along. As predictable as it is, it's still hard to watch and not be annoyed."

"Really?"

"You're competing with a four-year-old, Meghan."

"Have I sunk that low?"

"Unfortunately, yes, you have, but I'm here to raise you from the gutter and get you back to the heights where you belong."

"I'm worried that if Ben wants a baby to be a sibling for Caleb and Becky suddenly comes back into the picture and takes Caleb away, then Ben might wish we hadn't had a baby."

Lexie shook her head. "Even if Caleb did leave for whatever reason, a baby would fill that absence, and you would love that child and the part of the family he or she had become."

"The baby idea is a good one?"

"Yes, but only after you quit smoking."

I sighed. "You can't imagine what good friends those cigarettes become."

She rolled her eyes. "I told you to stop after the second pack, but you had to go all 'Puff the Magic Dragon.'"

"I'm serious. The deepest thoughts come when you're outside all alone—"

"Neglecting your stepson as you attempt slow suicide."

"Just because you've never been in an earth-shattering, life-changing—"

"I'm getting bored."

"Devastating situation that drove you to smoke, doesn't mean you can't sympathize with me."

"It does. I choose different poison. I eat. But I can still judge you because it was a stupid, shortsighted choice."

"Hm."

"What else? You better have something better for number two."

"We're going to have to have sex."

"I'm out," Lexie said, grabbing her purse and her coffee cup. "I have to take communion from that man. No," she said, standing, "you are on your own."

I followed her to the trash can. "Maybe you can pray about it?"

She shook her head and started for the door. At the door, she stopped to whisper, "Not gonna happen, Meghan. When it comes to your sex life, you are on your own. For the sake of my soul, you need to leave me out of it."

"Okay, but again, it's complicated. After something like this happens, you don't just do it," I whispered.

"Some people," she mumbled under her breath as we went outside, "have no idea when they have a good thing."

The mail woman sat alone at one of the two round bistro tables huddling either side of the door on the makeshift patio on the front of the building.

"Hello," I offered.

"Hello."

"It's beautiful out, isn't it?"

She finished chewing a bite of a homemade wrap and swallowed before answering. "September and May are the gems in the Southern Minnesota crown. June and October can be fickle and July and August are hot, but May and September come as close as we ever will to perfect."

"Is that from a book?"

She sighed and shook her head. "Just from the brain of a woman who's been sitting alone far too long. I'm Nora, as in Jones, but without the *h*," she said, holding out her left hand as she held her wrap in her right.

I gave it an awkward shake. "I'm sorry. What?"

"You haven't heard of Norah Jones?"

"Should I have?"

"Only if you like female singers with husky voices and lyrics full of you-know-what and vinegar."

"I'm afraid not."

"What's your genre?"

"Contemporary Christian. I'm Meghan Martins, by the way."

"Nice to meet you, Meghan. Are you the new pastor's wife?"

I nodded.

"He's a brand-new pastor, right?"

I nodded again.

"What a town to come to right off the bat. Small town, full of secrets no one talks about. Don't worry; it won't take long and you'll know them too."

I wasn't sure how to respond, so I smiled and looked down the street. From this spot on the porch, the post office was in full view.

"Would it be possible for the church mail to be delivered to our home?" I asked, remembering that was one of the things on my to-do list.

"Anything's possible. Is that what you want? I'll just need you to fill out a form," she said.

"Sure," I said. "I'll come by sometime and do that. I can't imagine why the church mail wasn't delivered to the parsonage before."

"Pastor Larimer had afternoon coffee at The Strange Brew every day. It was on the way."

Every day? Hm.

"Well, it was nice to meet you Nora, as in Jones."

She smiled. "You, too, Meghan Martins. Welcome to Oronoco."

Ben slid to the bedroom door on his butt. I was on the bed, reading my Bible.

"Is he asleep?" I asked.

"I'm not sure," Ben whispered. "I haven't heard him move in a while."

Ben was on day three of sitting in the hallway just outside Caleb's door at bedtime. Day one Caleb asked every few minutes if Ben was still there. When Caleb went to bed on day two, Ben told Caleb he couldn't talk, but Ben would be there if Caleb needed him. It was twenty minutes into bedtime on day three.

"I never noticed how squeaky this floor was until I tried to stand last night."

I smiled. "Thought you'd slide tonight?"

He crossed the threshold, stood, and stretched before taking a gentle step toward the bed. He stopped and waited before taking another.

"Is it possible he fell asleep without you?"

"I had no idea something as simple as bedtime could be such a challenge."

"I'm not sure we appreciate how difficult it's been for Becky," I mustered, remembering Lexie's speech.

"She was living with her parents. That must have been a big help."

"Yes, but still. She carried quite a burden. She had her parents, but it's not the same as having a spouse."

"What made you start thinking of her all the sudden?"

"Lexie."

Ben raised his eyebrows. "I wouldn't have seen you guys becoming friends."

"Really?"

"Well, the purple hair, fake nails."

"She's real, in a dyed hair, fake nails sort of way."

"Mm hm."

"I wonder what she sees in me."

Ben shrugged. "You're mature and reliable."

Would it be too much for someone to say it's my wit or that aura of coolness or the crazy, unique vibe I give off? "I'm not sure."

"You're right. Tiny town. You're probably one of the only choices for a friend under the age of sixty."

"That makes me feel better."

He smiled. "What are you reading?"

"Portions of 2 Kings and 2 Chronicles. I enjoy hearing about the kings—who was good, who sucked."

"Ahab and Jezebel sucked."

"Jehoshaphat did not suck."

"Joash didn't suck until after Jehoida died, and then he really sucked."

"Don't ruin it. I'm not there yet. This Chronological Bible puts the book of Joel in the middle of Joash's life."

"Sorry."

I closed my Bible. "I've been thinking about starting a family, and I think you're right. I think this would be a good time."

"Oh?"

"Well, Caleb is learning to go to bed on his own, and you're back in our bed, so, you know, we must be qualified."

Ben smiled. "Do you want to try now?"

"As in right now?"

He raised his eyebrows and pointed from me to himself. "We're good, right?"

"Are you keeping anything from me?"

"No. Why?"

"Then we're good."

As he exhaled, I realized a million prayers were being answered at that very moment.

"It's 6:45," Ben whispered.

"That was a short night," I grumbled.

I turned toward his side of the bed. He was dressed in jeans and a long-sleeve jersey shirt, showered but not shaved, cuddling his morning cup of mud.

"I told you as soon as we were in Oronoco it would be all about having a baby, and it got put on the very back burner. I'm sorry about that."

"Really?"

"I've been up praying for the last couple hours. I'm asking God to give us a baby."

"Thank you."

"You're welcome. I'll get Caleb ready for preschool. I just wanted you to know."

As I rolled over and stretched, a bag in the bottom of the closet caught my eye.

I can't believe I forgot about those.

Once Ben and Caleb left, I pulled the bag out of the closet and took it to the basement to look through the assortment of boxes from the move. Most of them were way too big, but there were a few we'd used to pack breakable bowls and candlesticks. I took one, folded Jeff's shorts and T-shirt, and placed them in the box. Upstairs, I retrieved the packing tape and my address book from my desk and debated just a minute about whether or not I should include a note. I decided no, taped and addressed the box, and put it on my desk.

Nora was sitting behind the counter eating a breakfast sandwich when I entered the post office a little after eight.

"Do you want me to come back?" I asked.

She laughed. "Yes. Go out the door and walk around the parking lot two times while I finish these last two bites." She put her sandwich down on a napkin and brushed her hands together. "What do you have?"

"Just this package."

She placed the box on the scale.

"Chicago, Illinois. I have a sister there."

"Do you?"

She nodded. "I'm going for Thanksgiving."

"I went to Northwestern for one year."

"Really? What was your major?"

Screwing up my life, mostly.

"I went through their graphic design program."

"Are you working in graphic design now?"

"I'm freelancing a little. Very part-time."

"Anything fragile, breakable, perishable?"

"No. It's clothes."

"Do you need to insure it?"

"No."

"It's $3.86. It will be there in three days."

I handed her a five. "Great. Thanks."

She handed me the change.

"I didn't say anything before, but I've felt so bad for you with everything that's gone on."

And that's how a perfect morning comes to a screeching halt. My first day without a morning cigarette and it's apparent the whole town knows, whispers, watches. Maybe I should dye my hair pink.

I smiled and lied. "I appreciate that, Nora." Okay, half lied. I appreciated that she felt bad for me, hated that she knew. "Hopefully, the worst is behind us."

She nodded. "Would you want to have coffee sometime?"

Genuinely interested or trying to fill up her gossip tank? Father, forgive me. Here comes another half lie. "Sure."

I gave her my cell number and headed home. Maybe she wouldn't call.

By the time Nora and I worked out a day to meet, September was bowing and October was ready to take the stage. We decided to meet at The Strange Brew for lunch.

"Should we sit outside?" Nora asked as she entered The Strange Brew.

"Why not?" I said, taking my tea.

I put my tea on the table closest to the post office and sunk into a black sling steel chair.

"Surprisingly comfortable," I announced as Nora emerged with a smoothie in one hand and her lunch bag in the other.

"Not surprising if you know Linda."

"Who?"

"The owner," she said, nodding her head toward the door and the woman at the counter. "She doesn't do cheap."

Nora unpacked a wrap.

"I noticed you were eating a wrap before. It smells delicious. What is it?"

"Chicken Caesar. Want some?"

I shook my head, but she tore a bite-size piece off and handed it to me anyway.

"Caesar dressing, grated parmesan, chicken, crushed croutons, and spinach. Not the best for you, but tasty."

I put it in my mouth. "Thanks to the pastor's wife in Zumbrota, I've been taking a stab at vegan recipes. Finding a recipe that is both delicious and nutritious is like finding gold."

"Cooking for one isn't as fun as you might think. As much as husbands can drive you crazy, when they're gone, it's almost unbearable. My husband ran a nursery. When he died, I sold it to the guy who worked with him. The three months after selling the nursery before I started this job were the worst of my life."

"Why?"

I waited while she finished chewing her bite. "I had no reason to live, nothing to get up for. I didn't know what to do with myself."

"I can see how that could happen. It isn't as if the house gets messy."

"You can only clean so much. I'm thankful this job opened and I still have the wherewithal to work."

"You aren't that old, are you?'

"I'm nearing seventy."

"I would have guessed mid fifties."

"Well, you are sweet, but if it weren't for Revlon, I'd be as gray as an elephant."

"Do you have grandchildren?"

"I never had children. I have a stepson in Illinois and a stepdaughter in Owatonna."

"Are you close to them, relationship-wise?"

She shook her head. "Roy and I married in our forties, a few years after he and his wife divorced. The kids lived with their mom. Roy saw his children when they needed him. They've never given me the time of day."

"Was it a messy divorce?"

"She left him. I understand why—not that I agree with the decision. From March to November, the nursery was his life, and you were an afterthought. He expected clean clothes and meals when he was hungry, but you never knew when that would be. He was a hard worker, but he hated bookkeeping. He'd come home and empty his pockets and leave the receipts on the table. I was supposed to figure out his expenses from that. Then, from November to February, he was home most of the time. It was just enough to get used to, and then it was over for another nine months."

"I take it you had a winter wedding."

"We eloped on Valentine's Day."

"Where did you go?"

"Across the border to Iowa. I was managing a flower shop and had been at work since three in the morning trying to keep up with the deliveries and orders. Roy stopped by the shop at four that afternoon and said we had an hour to get to a courthouse if I wanted to go. Off we went."

"Had you ever been married?"

She shook her head.

"Had you been dating long?"

"Just over a month."

"I thought Ben and I were crazy. We weren't even dating when he asked me to marry him."

"That *is* crazy."

"It worked. Kind of."

"You know complicated now, too, don't you? It makes answering simple questions fun."

I told her about the Bible study in Zumbrota. "You should come sometime," I added.

"As much as I hate sitting at home alone, I have a terrible time getting the motivation to go out, especially at night."

"I've got your phone number. I think I could motivate you."

"Incessant calling?"

"I was thinking of a text to remind you. Incessant calling might be more effective."

She laughed. "Till I turn off the phone."

I shrugged. "That might hamper it."

"What do you do for exercise?" she asked.

"I run, but not for exercise. I do it for sanity."

"I need something for both, but I'm not going to run. I do some walking on the route, but a lot of the delivery is done in the truck." She put her container back in her lunch bag. "I'll have to remember if I see you running, you're probably running from something."

"I've heard that a couple times now. Everyone says I don't handle things well. Maybe it's not that I don't handle things, but I avoid them."

"Half the women of this town would join you if they could. There's a lot of mental unrest here. I'd run too if I had the stamina. It's easier for me to sit home by myself and mope."

I took a drink and cradled the cup, swallowing her words. I shivered, despite the afternoon sun. My tea was quickly cooling, and I longed for the warmth to linger. She'd mentioned twice now the secrets and mental unrest. *What is Oronoco hiding?*

"Hey," Lexie said, rounding the corner and climbing the steps.

"Hey, Lexie," I responded. "Do you know Nora?"

Lexie shook her head. "Nice to meet you."

"Nice to meet you too," Nora said.

"Do you want to join us?"

"I can't. I'm just grabbing a coffee before I head back to work."

"I should get back to the post office," Nora remembered.

"I have nowhere to go," I said.

Lexie smiled. "Give me a minute. I'll be back."

"She works at the paper," I said as she went in.

"I don't recall anyone with that name."

"Technically, her address is in Rochester," I clarified. "Just outside the Oronoco boundary."

"That's where the nursery was. I still live over there."

"Maybe you're neighbors," I suggested.

When Lexie returned, I asked where she lived.

"Seventy-Fifth Street. Why?"

"I'm on Seventy-Fifth," Nora announced.

"I'm just off of County Road 112. Where are you?"

"I'm down about a mile farther."

"There you have it," I said. "You live on the same road, frequent the same coffee shop, and, until today, never knew the other existed."

"Small world," Lexie said.

"Sure is," Nora agreed.

"And, as if that wasn't enough, you both dye your hair."

Lexie rolled her eyes and waved as she went down the steps.

Nora stood. "It was good to talk. I enjoy getting to know you."

"I agree."

I walked her to the post office and then went home to figure out what to make for dinner.

Chapter Eight

LIFE OR DEATH

I walked the aisles of Walmart in a state of semiconsciousness, not unlike singing a hymn or saying the Lord's Prayer without cognizance of the words. Most people, I suspected, were home watching their favorite TV show or relaxing after getting the kids to bed or scrolling through Facebook. I amused myself by trying to surmise why those at Walmart were there at that hour. The young man with the case of Mountain Dew obviously had a paper to write that would take most of the night. The woman with the disheveled hair and no makeup getting groceries was a mom to three young children whose husband was finally home. The high school (or were they college girls?) looking at makeup likely had their eyes on boys.

A false sense of security had led me to abandon Target, my usual go-to, when realistically, I probably wouldn't have known any of the people on duty. The regulars I knew were day-shift employees. Walmart was a mile or so closer to home, but navigating unchartered territory hardly seemed worth the effort.

A Band-aid display by the pharmacy caught my attention.

Band-aids make nothing feel better, I reasoned as I perused the designs. *They are cool in the "get to pick the color of your cast" cool. Or "pick out your casket" cool. You're still broken or dead, but at least you have a choice as to what you or someone else stares at.*

I sighed and continued on the trek to find a pregnancy test hidden among birth control and feminine hygiene products. When I finally found them, I grabbed what seemed a reliable brand and slowed my pace to remain inconspicuous.

A barrel-chested, middle-aged cashier monitoring the self-checkout seemed to be reading me. I smiled when passing it to him to make it easier. Married. Happy. Wants a child.

On the way home, I deliberated. *Do I take the test with Ben or on my own? Why bother him if it's negative?*

And yet, Ben's previous experience with a pregnancy test, abstract as it was, was a nightmare. If done right, this experience might rectify that.

"Everything okay?" he asked when I stood in the doorway to his office.

I held up the box.

He glanced at it and then swiveled to face me. "Are you late?"

"Three days."

He smiled. "Really?"

"I'll get it ready. Do you want to see the results?"

"Uh ... yeah."

When he arrived in the bathroom, I handed him the stick. Color was just starting to appear in the window.

"What are we looking for?" he asked.

"A plus sign is positive. A minus sign is negative."

"Makes sense."

I closed my eyes, praying it would be yes. *Silly that such a little stick holds so much power. What if it's negative and I was mentally making myself late?*

I felt his lips on my cheek.

"Congratulations," he said. "You're a mom."

I grabbed his hand, pulling the plus sign closer so I could see for myself.

I couldn't wait to tell Tonya and Lexie. When Tonya and I met for coffee a few days later, she whooped a silent scream and stomped her feet, and before I blinked, we'd talked babies and pregnancy for an hour. She clutched me in a tight embrace before we parted, promising another meeting soon.

I had already known for nine days by the time Lexie's schedule cleared so we could meet. I was positioned in my chair, tea in hand, smile on my face, and news on my tongue. When Lexie arrived five minutes late, she sauntered to the counter and mumbled an order. She didn't wave or acknowledge me, but waited with her back to me and her hands in her pants pockets.

"What's wrong?" I asked as she plopped into her blue chair in the back of The Strange Brew.

Her lips pursed. "Don't you read the paper we work for?"

I shook my head.

"Watch the news?"

I shook my head again.

Disgust dripped from her face like sweat off a toilet on a sweltering day.

"It's been on the front page for two days."

"What?"

"Jane Allen was found murdered outside the Metropolitan Marketplace Apartments."

Should I pretend to know Jane Allen or the Metro apartments?

"Hi, my name is Meghan Martins. I just moved here three and a half months ago."

"Jane Allen," she insisted.

I shook my head, wondering if this was pregnancy related. I'd heard stories of lapses of memory and inability to think coherently. Did it occur this early? Technically, I was six weeks already.

"Police Chief Jane Allen."

"Lexie, I worked in the newsroom of the *Milwaukee Journal* four years and I'm not sure I'd know the name of Milwaukee's police chief. I just do graphics and layout." Unable to shake her from the aloofness regarding my ignorance, I implored again. "Give me a chance. Jane Allen. Police Chief Jane Allen. Super-important person Jane Allen."

"The first female police chief in Rochester, one of the 1 percent of police chiefs that are female nationwide."

"Really?"

"Really."

"Murdered?"

"Brutally. Closed-casket brutality. Hundreds of officers from around the country are here for the funeral tomorrow. They're expecting thousands."

"What happened?"

"She was bludgeoned to death with such brutal force—"

Saliva geysered around my tongue as warmth crept into my face. I brought my hand to my mouth, rebuking the nausea and the mental image that ensued and daydreaming of butterflies while Lexie finished the account.

I took a drink of my tea in a failed attempt to wash away the queasiness.

"Any suspects?" I managed.

"I've been stalking Stacy Lannon, our investigative reporter. She's been to all the news conferences and has friends on the force."

"The 'force be with you' force?"

Lexie's head snapped back, as if my lack of knowledge was now a plague, one she may unwillingly succumb to if she breathed my air. "The police force."

I nodded and mentally warned myself to restrain from further comments that might annoy Lexie and/or corroborate my incompetence.

"Whatever suspects they have are not being disclosed at this time."

She read it like a statement written on her hand, though her skin held no words.

"Any chance she was working undercover?"

"Chiefs don't work undercover. It is a conundrum as to what she was doing at the Metropolitan Apartments," Lexie murmured.

"The possibilities are endless," I began. "Maybe she saw something suspicious or has a friend living there, or a lover, or—"

"She was pregnant."

"What?"

"Three months. It's all in the paper."

"Wow," I muttered. "You never know what the week will hold. One week you're dying inside. The next week, there's new life. Or there's new life and the next week you're dying."

"I'm going to get a scone."

"Wait," I said, grabbing her arm and motioning her to sit back down.

"I'm pregnant."

"Really?"

"Yes. Really."

"That was fast. When are you due?"

"June."

"Congratulations. That's great."

"Thanks. I wanted you to know."

"I appreciate that."

As she went for her scone, I remembered how I felt seeing Ben with Caleb for the first time. My news was a reminder of what she didn't yet have.

I called for Ben, and when he didn't answer, I turned toward the clock. 7:58. He must have taken Caleb to preschool. I struggled to reach the phone on his side of the bed.

He answered on the third ring.

"Where are you?"

"Just down the road," he answered.

"Something's wrong," I managed.

"What?"

"I don't know."

I opened my eyes when I heard him on the steps.

"What's the matter?" he asked.

"I don't know," I told him again, clutching my stomach and willing the pain to stop.

"Should I call 911?"

"I don't think I can walk."

He grabbed the phone. I closed my eyes, trying to think of a place far from Oronoco. Lake Michigan. Sky blue. Calm waves. Sinking beneath the surface.

The Oronoco first responders were the first to arrive. John Higgins, a member of the church, and another man took the sheet off our bed, wrapped it around me, and carried me down the steps so I was ready when the ambulance arrived from Rochester a few minutes later. I was lifted onto a stretcher and into the ambulance. A female paramedic started an IV, while a male paramedic called ahead to the hospital and reported a suspected ectopic pregnancy.

Darkness.

If I trekked through Death Valley in record-setting heat, my mouth could not be more parched and my strength more sapped than when I tried to sit up. Sunspots danced across my field of vision whether my eyes were open or closed.

"Don't try to get up," a woman warned. "You are in the recovery room, just waking up from surgery. I'm going to write down your vitals and get you to your room."

Surgery?

"Ben?"

"I'll take you to him now."

She peeled patches off my shoulders, chest, and lower abdomen and unlocked the cart. I stopped her as she turned the corner to warn her I was about to throw up.

She pulled a cardboard bucket from beneath the cart. Vomiting emitted pressure.

The nurse held the bucket and my head until the rebellion in my stomach died down enough for us to continue. Another turn, a hallway, the elevator, more heaving. Another hall, another corner, and she turned into a room.

Mom, Dad, and Ben were standing against the wall looking as if they'd swallowed some serious tragedy.

"Mom, Dad? Why are you here?" I managed as the cart came to a stop.

The nurse locked the cart into place then dumped my puke bucket in the toilet. Two nurses came in and slid me to the bed.

My nurse moved the cart, tapped my hand, and walked out. Another nurse introduced himself.

"I need to hook you up quick and then I'll get out of your way."

Quickly. You'll hook it up quickly. Thank you, Lexie.

He screwed tubing into my IV, adjusted the drip, and walked out.

Ben came forward. He looked as if his face had been attacked by a swarm of hornets.

"Do you remember this morning?" he asked.

I tried to think. *What day is it?* I shook my head.

"You called me. I was on my way home from taking Caleb to preschool. You said something was wrong. Remember?"

I was in a lot of pain. "Yes."

"Do you remember the ambulance coming?"

"Vaguely."

"You lost a lot of blood."

"I don't remember bleeding."

"I didn't see it until the EMTs moved you. The sheet beneath you was bloody. You passed out on the way to the hospital. They took you right to surgery."

"Surgery for what?"

"The baby."

Ben stopped.

Is he waiting for me to say something?

"It was attached to the opening of your uterus. It never would have survived."

I nodded. The baby was gone.

"Meg."

Ben saying my name was not unlike Jesus saying Mary's name in the garden on Easter Sunday. One word tackled delusions and forced truth. To Mary, Jesus brought life. His voice must have been solid and sure. Ben's voice cracked. He was struggling, unsuccessfully, to hold back tears. They poured down his face like chocolate from a fountain, but not nearly so beautifully, and there were no strawberries, no marshmallows. *What could be so bad?*

"They couldn't stop the bleeding. They had to do a hysterectomy."

The word hit fast and hard. "You let them?"

"They didn't ask my permission. They did what they had to do. You almost died."

I turned away from him. "They should have let me."

Mom came and touched my hair. She had three children. I had nothing to say to her. Then Dad came. He put his hand on my cheek and cried.

What was it Elijah said under the broom tree? *Take me now, Lord. I have had enough.*

God heard. When my nurse came in to do vitals a few minutes later, my blood pressure had dipped low enough to make the staff uncomfortable. Ben and my parents were ushered out of the room. Nurses lowered my head and increased my fluids, checked to see how much I was bleeding. A doctor arrived and ordered more blood.

In the flurry of activity, I wondered how long it would take. I was mostly numb, thanks to the anesthesia, though I was not a fan of having my head lower than my legs.

Please just let me wake up in heaven.

Heaven, it turns out, was not the intended destination, but rather the ICU at Saint Mary's Hospital. Twenty-five-year-olds, with or without a uterus, were not allowed to just drift off into eternity.

There were, I was told, visitors that came to the hospital, but I was spared the pleasure of their presence thanks to nurses who were unyielding. I was in no condition, they said. The only exception was Scott Fredin, Tonya's husband, who Ben brought in when he stopped by very late that night to pray over me. The main lights in the ICU were lowered and everyone walked around in a hush. I saw his head above me, heard him say hello. I think I answered, but maybe I didn't. Talking took effort. Lifting my hand took effort. Listening took effort.

In his own way, God answered my prayer, at least that first night. I was too weak to do anything but sleep, and when asleep, I felt nothing.

Mom put clean sheets on the bed before I arrived home two days later. They were new, I noted, and flowery and bright blue, my favorite color. I wanted to burn them.

I was home on bed rest for a day or two and then "up as I was able, increasing, but not overdoing my activity each day." I had no intention of getting up ever again, other than to use the bathroom. I was still hoping to fall asleep and wake up in heaven.

The doorbell rang often as word spread. Everyone was being sufficiently comforted and meals were brought and no doubt everyone was hopeful they might catch a glimpse of the uterusless woman.

Even I was taken aback when I hobbled to the bathroom, against doctor's orders, by myself. I was Elmer's glue-bottle white. My eyes were sunken, zombiesque. I couldn't stand and look because I was weak and needed to sit down. Once on the toilet, I realized my mistake as the world went black. Again.

Foolish. That's what I was told again and again. I didn't have enough blood in me to have it all pool in one place for the bruise that would cover my left side, a consequence of passing out on the toilet. That and my poor dad had to see me with my underwear around my knees as he and Ben helped me back onto the can. Ben propped me up while I went to the bathroom, and then Ben helped me back to bed and determined to stay nearby at all times.

The smell of food repulsed me, my throat was inflamed—the result of an emergency intubation—and everything from my belly button to my butt threw a fit every time I moved. The nurse had explained that my GI track was likely on standby, thanks to narcotics during and after the surgery, and that contributed to a feeling of being full.

Ironic that I felt full, but utterly empty. It was best to sleep.

Ben came in shortly after I woke. "I snuck away to get you this." He produced a cup from behind his back. "It's a chocolate shake from the gas station. It has absolutely no nutritional value and might even contain chemicals. You need to sit up," he said, propping my head with a pillow.

I reached for the cup.

He handed me a spoon. "No straws till your throat heals."

I frowned.

"How is it?" he asked when I had taken a bite.

I nodded my appreciation.

"I'm thinking we should come up with a name."

"For what?"

"Our baby."

"We don't have a baby."

"We did. Just because it died before it was born doesn't mean it wasn't there."

"We don't know the sex," I reminded him.

I took another bite.

"Do you think losing my uterus was my fault?" I asked.

"It wasn't lunch money. You didn't lose it, Meg."

"I've held a grudge."

"I know."

"How?"

"The smoking, for one."

I nodded. "I get a lot of pleasure from that." I stretched my neck. Too bad about the sucking. I wouldn't be able to do it for a while now.

"I had this mental affair going with Jeff for a while too."

"I know."

"You knew?"

145

He half shrugged.

"These last weeks have been better. I got rid of the clothes."

"I noticed."

"Why didn't you say anything?"

"When I worked on Dad's farm, there never seemed to be a time when everything was done. When the crops were in and the cattle were sold or the chickens were butchered, then you looked at the mess the sheds had become because we never had time to tend them. Some things took priority. When the cows got out, the fence had to be repaired. When the combine broke, it had to get fixed. Morning and night, the cows needed to get fed."

Did they take a portion of my brain along with my uterus? What is he saying?

"We're never going to make each other perfect. We deal with what we need to deal with, and the rest will work itself out. And, no. It's not your fault. If everyone had to be perfect to have a baby, the human race would have died out immediately."

"I could've been a better mom to Caleb. Maybe God saw how I felt about him and decided—"

"Meghan, stop."

Ben's tone conveyed finality, like a gavel slamming judgment.

I handed him the three-fourths-full glass. "I'm done."

The door creaked and Caleb peeked in. "Dad, can I see Mom?"

"I don't know what your mom is doing right now, Caleb."

"I mean this mom."

"Come in," I replied.

"Are you sick?" Caleb asked me.

"I got cut."

"Can I see?"

When he came to my side, I placed the sheets in position to cover the unmentionables and lifted my nightgown just enough to reveal the incision.

"Does it hurt?"

I nodded.

He ran out of the room.

"And that's why God decided we shouldn't have children," I pronounced.

We heard him open the cabinet in the bathroom. He ran back carrying a box of Band-aids.

"Want a Band-aid?" he asked.

"Caleb," Ben started.

"I might need more than one," I interjected.

Caleb unwrapped a Band-aid and pulled the tabs off. I helped him maneuver it so the nonadhesive part was over my incision.

"That *is* better."

He smiled. "Want another one?"

"I think I do."

We decided on three perfectly uniform bandages against an inflamed, protruding gash.

"Caleb," Ben said. "That was nice of you."

He smiled.

"Do you want to come up on the bed for a while?"

He shook his head. "Grandpa's going to take me to the park."

Ben nodded. "Can you shut the door when you leave?"

"Yup."

"Would you mind taking this pillow?" I asked Ben as Caleb left. "I need to lie down."

"You have a bunch of cards downstairs. I'll bring them up and put them next to the bed so you can read them when you're ready."

Which will be never.

"I'm going to get my laptop so I can work next to you. Would it bother you?"

"What about the visitors?"

"Your mom can handle them for a while. Besides, I can hear the doorbell from here."

"What are you telling everyone?"

"That I'm thankful you're alive. If I'd stopped somewhere after dropping Caleb off, I probably would have come home to a corpse."

"Don't be so dramatic."

"Okay. I'll tell the next person you stubbed your toe."

I laughed and then clutched my incision and groaned.

"I'll bring your pain pills too."

He had barely left the stairs when I heard Mom's footsteps. *Why did Ben leave the door open?*

"Knock, knock."

Cute didn't work for my mom. She wasn't the baby-talking, shed-tears-with-you type. She peeked around the door.

"I'm still here," I uttered. "Unfortunately."

When she came in, she was carrying three of Ben's dress shirts on hangers. She walked to the closet and hung them up.

"I washed and ironed them," she explained. "When I put the sheets on the bed, I noticed they were a little wrinkled. I scrubbed the collars too."

"That was nice of you." *Not that he'll notice. I'm sure some of the older women in the congregation will though.*

"The last time you looked like death, I was afraid you had finally done yourself in. This time, death was looming over you, and you squeaked under by the seat of your pants."

"Like Troy making his curfew by twelve seconds."

She smiled. "'I'm not late till it's 12:01, Mom.'"

"I was always on time, if not an hour early."

"You always wanted your sleep."

"My friends all worked. We couldn't be up half the night when we had to get up the next morning."

Ben's steps were deliberate. When he saw Mom by the door, he set his laptop and the pile of cards on the bed and left the room. It wasn't long before the water in the shower was running.

"To many people, it probably looks like you've had the perfect life," Mom declared.

"Doubtful."

Mom shook her head. "You took college credits in high school, got your graphic design certificate from Northwestern. Got married when you were young to Ben, landed jobs right away. Even when you were so skinny, some people would have found that attractive."

"Some people know nothing."

"Meghan, your husband is a pastor. He leads people spiritually."

It must have been the Holy Spirit that kept my mouth from dropping in sarcasm to cry, *What? Since when?*

"You can see God as a hard-hearted jerk who stole your future, or you can trust him and his plan for your life."

"What does this have to do with Ben being a pastor?"

"As the pastor's wife, you have the power to set the tone for this."

"You obviously have never been a pastor's wife. I don't have any power."

"I've been married almost thirty years. A woman has incredible influence over her husband. You have been acting like God owes you something since you found out about Caleb. Maybe you aren't saying it. Maybe you aren't even conscientiously thinking it. But your actions are speaking loud and clear."

"Consciously."

"What?"

"You said I wasn't *conscientiously* thinking it. You meant *consciously*." *That's where I get it from.* "Anyway, what actions?"

"Smoking, for one."

Why would Ben tell them?

"Mom, I doubt you can fathom what my life has been like since we moved here."

"When Ben asked you to marry him, one of the things he said was that he chose you because he thought you would be a good pastor's wife."

"So pastor's wives can't smoke when their life falls apart?"

"You can. You can try retail therapy. You can get drunk. You can slip into despair. But I think when Ben married you, he was hoping you'd choose to lean on the Lord instead."

"Is that what he told you?"

"No, and so you know, it was Dad who asked him how you had been dealing with everything. Ben didn't offer the information."

"Well, he certainly wouldn't make a good spy. You asked, and he caved."

"You almost died, Meghan. I don't think you understand that."

"I wish I would have. I don't think *you* understand that."

"What about Ben and Caleb?"

"What about them?"

"Ben was begging God to spare your life. Doesn't that mean anything to you?"

"Ben could easily get remarried."

"He doesn't want to get remarried."

"Mom, I wanted children. I don't think that was too much to ask of Ben, and I don't think that was too much to ask of God, and they both let me down. Caleb is Ben's child, and I can love him, but it's not the same."

"Be careful, Meghan."

"Careful of what?"

"Caleb has been through so much. He's got a chance to be part of a family."

"He had a family, Mom. It isn't like he was in an orphanage or living on the street."

"Every child wants a father and a mother. He has grandparents and that is wonderful, but it isn't the same. He has a dad now. Yes, Becky is his mom, and she always will be, but Caleb is living in your house. You can teach him what a family should look like."

"When Caleb moved in, I all but disappeared."

"Everyone responds to love," Mom reminded me.

The water in the shower turned off, and Mom took that as her cue to leave. Good thing, because Ben came in wrapped in a towel.

"I'd do anything for a shower," I lamented. *And a cigarette. A cigarette in the shower would be delightful.*

"Not for a few days," he said, going to the drawer.

"Just kill me already."

He turned to stare at me. "Okay."

"You'll kill me?"

"No. I'll take you to the shower."

He towed my legs over the side of the bed and helped me sit up, then steadied me as I got to my feet.

"I hope Mom doesn't come up," I said, noting the towel around Ben's waist wasn't covering much.

"She's probably seen worse."

"I'll let my dad know you said that."

He chuckled.

I worked to get my clothes off while he started the water. When he was content with the temperature, he helped me over the tub and into the shower.

The water wrapped me like a blanket. I let it course through my hair and down my back.

"How's it feel?" Ben asked, stepping in.

I gave him the thumbs up.

He reached behind me for the loofah, squeezed shower gel onto it, and started lathering my neck. He made his way down my torso until he reached my incision.

"I'd like to name it, but I can't name it a girl's name if it was a boy, or vice versa," I said, noting his hesitation where the baby would have been.

"We could pick two names," he offered.

"We could."

"How about Autumn?" he suggested. "She was conceived in the autumn, lived all of her life in the autumn, and died in the autumn."

"Autumn Grace?"

"Beautiful."

"I bet she would have been tall," I decided.

"Dark skin."

"Dark hair?"

"Definitely dark hair," he affirmed.

"Hazel eyes. Your voice."

Ben groaned. "I'm a tenor. I think she'd be in the soprano-alto range."

"Your vocal ability," I corrected.

"Agile. I played soccer."

"I played basketball," I reminded him.

"She'd do both."

"And long fingers to play the piano."

Ben popped up from washing my legs. "Not guitar?"

I shrugged. "Maybe. But she'd probably have my impatience."

Ben smiled. "God help me."

"And your messiness. God help me."

"She'd have to marry someone to keep her in line," Ben noted.

"We'll never get to see that."

"It would have been great."

I nodded. "What would our son be like?"

"A rascal."

I snickered.

"I'd have rallied for the name Pierce," he said.

"Pierce?"

He nodded as if I should understand.

"It's probably good that didn't happen."

"It seems impossible this happened."

The somberness of his words was too much even for the water to comfort. As my face crumpled into sobs, he buried his face in my hair, and we cried until the warmth gave out.

"How are we going to do this tomorrow?" I asked, as Ben lifted my legs on the bed.

"Do what?"

"Church."

"You shouldn't go," he said. "I'll announce it and say a prayer, and then everyone will know."

"I was there when you announced the Caleb ordeal in church. I think I should be there tomorrow."

"You're too weak."

"Dad can drive me, and I'll sit in the back. If I need to leave, Dad can bring me home."

Ben looked at me and nodded.

Mom, Dad, Caleb, and I snuck into the back pew during the last verse of the first song.

After the offering, Ben relayed the events of the past week. The baby implanted in the mouth of the uterus, he said, causing a rupture that required a hysterectomy to stop the bleeding.

"Meghan is understandably weak after losing so much blood and undergoing emergency surgery, but she's alive," he said. "And I am thankful for that."

One by one, the usher excused the congregation after the service, and one by one, people stopped by the last pew to hug and put an arm around me, to shake their head in sympathy and give my arm a squeeze with promises of prayers. Lexie waited impatiently for her turn, and when she came, she wrapped her arms around me.

"Even I'm starting to hate Oronoco."

"I would have bled to death in Milwaukee. I was at the hospital fifteen minutes after Ben called 911 and in surgery minutes later. You can't put a tourniquet on a bleeding uterus. Any longer and I wouldn't be here."

"Oh, man."

"John Higgins carried me out, believe it or not."

"I've always wanted a man to sweep me off my feet, but not like that."

Ben came and put his hand on my shoulder.

"I'm really sorry," Lexie said to him.

"I'm just glad I didn't have to plan a funeral," he said. "Living without Meg would have been a huge loss."

"You'll have to fill me in on the investigation," I said.

"Don't worry about that," Lexie said.

"No, really. I'd like to hear about it. Maybe we could have coffee sometime this week."

"Sure," she said. "If you're up for it, give me a call."

When I stood, I noticed Millie, the older lady from Zumbrota, standing in the church entrance. As Lexie left, Millie ambled forward: cane, step, cane, step.

"Millie, why on earth are you here?" I rebuked as I hobbled toward her.

"I heard what happened," she said. "I felt so bad. I just had to come."

I wrapped my arms around her in a tight hug.

"I lost a baby," she said. "She was four months old and died in her sleep. It was so painful. My heart hurt, and there was nothing anyone could do to make me feel better."

"Oh, I'm sorry," I said.

"I had another baby," she continued, "but it was different. One doesn't replace the other."

There would be no more chances for Ben and me. Millie seemed to remember too.

"I brought you some food," she said. "I can't do much else, but I can still cook and bake."

"That was nice of you," Ben said.

"Others have to hold you up when you can't do it yourself," she said.

Ben helped me to the car and then went to Millie's vehicle to retrieve the food. I wondered how full the freezer was and if the day would ever come that I would be hungry again.

Chapter Nine

UNDERCOVER

"Why are we here?" I asked Lexie as she parked her Malibu in the lot of the People's Food Co-op. I tried to get out of the car gracefully, despite the ache that accompanied standing and sitting.

"We're going to get a coffee."

"Here?"

"The guy who works at the coffee counter in the People's Co-op found Jane. He was 'allegedly' returning home after a night with friends. He lives in the Metro apartments."

She pointed up, apparently at the Metro apartments.

"I don't envy him."

Lexie gave an almost missable shrug.

"No, but seriously. Why are we here?"

"Maybe we'll see something."

"Something the police missed. That's likely."

"You never know," she said, strolling through the sliding doors.

The People's Food Co-op was like any other small grocery. Seven checkout lanes, produce, boxed goods, frozen foods. As we sauntered down the aisles, I started reading the labels of "organic" and "environmentally safe" products.

"What are you doing?" Lexie grilled.

"I'm fitting in. Anyway, I kind of like this stuff. I may want to become a regular."

"Stick to the mission."

"We have a mission?"

"Come on," Lexie muttered.

"You stink at undercover work," I mumbled.

Lexie led me to the deli.

"Did you want a sandwich?" I teased.

She ignored me and continued to the pastry case. Next to the case was the coffee bar, which we soon found offered a very limited selection of drinks.

"Can I help you?" a man with moppish sandy-brown hair asked as he maneuvered his way behind the counter.

"Two chai teas," Lexie ordered.

"I'd like a turtle mocha, actually," I interjected. "If that's okay."

Lexie stared at me in bewilderment. "Whatever."

"One or two shots?" the man inquired.

"Shots?"

"Of espresso."

"Oh, one, please. And skim milk, if you have it."

"I do," he said. "Are you first-timers?"

"It's our virgin voyage," I responded.

"Maiden voyage," Lexie mustered through obvious embarrassment.

"Sorry."

Mophead smirked. "Easy to do."

"The blood loss must have affected my brain activity," I whispered.

"You were always like this," Lexie altered.

"Was I?"

She nodded.

"What happened?" the man asked.

We stared in obvious confusion.

"The blood loss," he said. "What happened?"

Is he thinking of Jane Allen and the blood-stained pavement? I found myself suddenly guarded. *My baby is not his business.* Lexie's displeasure showed. She was all about the undercover mission of her own making. *Play along, Meghan. Play along.*

"My uterus ruptured."

Once I said it, I resented both of them.

Mophead cringed. "How'd that happen?"

I scanned his nametag. Jake. *It should be Pete. Sandy-haired, mophead, surfer dude should be Pete, or Will,* I decided, *as in "Will you please stay out of my personal life?"*

"Ectopic pregnancy."

His glance shifted to my right hand, which was covered with my left. "Are you new to town or just to the store?"

"She's new to town," Lexie announced.

"For school?"

I shook my head. *What's up with the twenty questions?*

"Have you been to The Brew House yet?"

I shook my head again. "I haven't been much of anywhere."

"My friends and I hang out there on the weekends. You should check it out."

I looked at Lexie and shrugged. "Maybe."

He handed us our drinks. "Pay at the registers, ladies."

"Thanks."

Lexie paid for our drinks and we sauntered to the car.

"What was that about?" I asked.

"Act natural. He could still be watching us."

She unlocked the car and we got in.

"Smile and act like we're having a conversation," she said with a grin.

"You got it," I sang, buckling my belt as she started the car.

I took a sip of my turtle mocha. "Surprisingly good."

I sipped again. "'Come back again' good."

"I've been regretful of many things," Lexie said, stopping at the light. "Don't make bringing you here today top the list."

"'This might be my new favorite store' good."

The light turned green. After one block, she turned onto Broadway.

"Do you know with certainty he was the guy who found Jane?" I asked.

"No."

"We went down there investigating, and you don't know if Jake's our man?"

"That name sounds right."

"None of it matters if he isn't the right guy."

"What did we find out anyway? He's single—"

"Or in a relationship that doesn't matter to him. He all but asked us to the bar."

"Asked *you* to the bar," Lexie corrected.

"He seemed more interested in me once he knew I couldn't have children."

"So?"

I shrugged. "Why would he be interested in a woman who couldn't have kids?"

"Because he's too young to care about kids, like most guys under thirty. They are about a good time and no strings attached. He was probably turned on knowing you had been sexually active."

"But he 'found' a body two weeks ago that was as mangled and gory as it gets. Doesn't that do something to you?"

"Yes, unless you're happy she's gone."

"I don't know, Lexie."

"I've got to talk to Shirley and find out the detective's name in charge of the case. Maybe an off-duty police officer could hang out at The Brew House on Saturday night."

"Lexie, you don't just tell the police to send an off-duty officer to a bar because a guy asked some girls to hang out at a bar." I took a drink. "I hope he didn't have anything to do with it. The world needs more people who can mix a drink like Jake."

"Forget today happened. I'll take you home. You can rest, and we can both go on with our lives."

"What lives?" I mumbled.

"I think I should tell Ben."

"That we went to the Food Co-op and a guy asked us to the bar? Not worth his time."

"We are never going down there again. Thank you very much, but I love The Strange Brew."

"So, you're all done investigating murders?"

"Totally."

I let it go, but I knew she was lying.

Who is young enough to go to The Brew House with me Saturday night? Tonya was both young and pretty, but she was pregnant. Lexie wasn't an option. I called Dora.

"Any chance you can get away for a bit Saturday night?"

"It depends on Chris's plans."

"Check into it and get back to me."

"What time?"

"What time does Braden go to bed?"

"Between 7:30 and 8:00."

"How about right after that? Oh, and would you mind driving? I'm not supposed to for a while."

"I'll let you know."

"Perfect."

"Mind clueing me in?" Ben asked. I couldn't tell if it was exasperation or worry in his tone.

"What do you mean?"

"You're going out on a Saturday night. Is this a midlife crisis or PTSD?"

"Are we that old already? Don't most twenty-five-year-olds go out once in a while?"

"Most, yes. You and I, no. Are you going to drink?"

"I wasn't planning on it."

"But you're going to The Brew House?"

"Only because there's a guy that's going to be there and I want to observe him."

"Perfect. You're going to watch a guy."

"I have no interest in him, but I want to see if he's a sleazeball or just an immature dopehead."

"Sounds reasonable."

"No, it probably doesn't. He's the guy who found the police chief dead a week before we lost the baby. Or, at least, Lexie thinks he is. He works at the People's Food Co-op. Lexie and I went there the other day for coffee, remember?"

He nodded.

"He mentioned he hangs out down there. No. He deliberately threw it out, and I want to find out why."

"Why would you want to be involved?"

"I'm not sure. I've just got a gut feeling."

"What time will you be home?"

"Ten. No later."

"For sure?"

"Positive. If I'm running late or decide to stay longer, I'll call."

"Okay, but I'm putting this in my 'you're not the easiest person to be married to' file.'"

"And I'm putting this in my 'why I love being married to you' file.'"

"I'll remember that."

The Brew House was a quaint bar on the top floor of a beloved and overpriced Rochester restaurant. In the twenty seconds it took to get to the steps, I observed diners with fancy clothes taking tiny bites off fancy plates as violin music applauded their affluence.

Once we opened the door to the second floor, though, the lights were low, neon beer signs glimmered, and the music was just loud enough to make a quiet conversation a challenge, but low enough to hear the slightly intoxicated guy next to you repeat the escapades of the night before.

We snatched a table in the corner next to a window overlooking the street. I angled my chair farther into the corner so I could observe the entire room.

"Welcome, ladies. What can I start you off with tonight?"

Mandy wore her nametag on a lanyard around her neck. She was a brunette with hints of caramel in her messily styled ponytail. She smiled lazily while shrewd eyes deciphered how much time she'd give us.

"Iced tea for me," I said.

"I'll have a raspberry tea," Dora said.

The waitress left, and Dora ventured into the "How are you managing?" territory.

"Physically, I'm tired and still a bit sore, but that's to be expected."

"And mentally?"

"Everything reminds me of babies. I see the waitress and think, 'She can have kids. I wonder if she has kids.' She asks about drinks and for a second I think, 'I shouldn't drink,' and then I realize the baby isn't there and never will be."

"It's only been a couple weeks."

"But I don't want my daughter to think I wasted my life. When I meet her in heaven someday, I want her to be proud of me."

"It was a girl?"

"Ben liked the name Pierce for a boy and I wasn't thrilled with it, so I'm hoping it was a girl."

"I don't know. Pierce seems fitting to me. He pierced your heart."

"When you put it that way ..."

"Did you have a girl's name?"

164

"Autumn Grace."

"That's beautiful."

"Thanks."

Mandy brought our drinks, and I glanced around the room. No sign of Jake yet.

I wanted to keep talking about the baby, but I was sensing, even with Ben, I had to measure my words. People expected me to move on even when I didn't want and couldn't fathom moving on.

"What about you? How are you managing?"

"Nothing's changed."

"What are you going to do? In less than a year, you're getting married. What's going to happen to Braden then?"

"I don't know."

"Ben thinks you should get out."

"So do my parents, but I don't want to leave Braden, and don't have the money to live anywhere else."

"What about your parents' house?"

"It's a half hour to Rochester. That's fine when you're working a twelve-hour shift. It doesn't make a lot of sense when you have a one- or two-hour class."

"Does the college have campus apartments?"

"Not for a hundred dollars a month. I'm trying to get through as many classes as possible before getting married, and that means not having a lot of time to work."

"I hate the idea of your safety being a factor."

"Chris isn't one to force himself on someone. He screams, and he'll go home with any willing party, but I don't think he'd ever rape me or beat me up. Spy on me? Yes. Go through my drawers? Maybe."

"That's creepy."

"Could be worse."

"Could be better. One of the things I'm learning is that doing something you know your spouse, or fiancé, wouldn't like is a form of rebellion. I could have told Ben how sexual the environment was at the Milwaukee paper, but I figured he'd want me to get another job, and I didn't trust that I'd find one where I could make as much money. That may or may not have been the case. Maybe he wouldn't have made me quit. Maybe he'd have been there to support me and advise me how to handle it. Maybe I would have gotten a better job, or gotten pregnant or been around more so he would have told me about Caleb. I don't know what your fiancé would say, but I'm pretty sure he wouldn't be too excited about another guy going through your underwear drawer."

She sighed. "I know."

I peered around the room. Was that Lexie sitting at the bar? Her button-down white blouse was unbuttoned and/ or missing a couple buttons near her throat. A man leaned against the bar next to her, his form-fitting jeaned legs crossed beneath him. His pale-gray sweater had brown patches on the elbows, I noticed as he raised his beer bottle to take a swig. She twirled her straw and took a drink.

Mandy came back, and we ordered meals. Lexie's "date" motioned the bartender, who flipped the top off another bottle of beer and placed it in front of him. A moment later, a small glass was placed in front of Lexie.

I groaned.

"What?"

"Do you know Lexie Felps?"

"The name sounds familiar."

"She goes to our church. Purple bangs."

"Oh, yes. Standing in front for praise band, you see pretty much everyone."

"She's here, and someone's trying to get her drunk."

Dora swung around and looked toward the bar. "From the back, he's kind of hot."

"He's a good dresser," I affirmed.

"How do you know he's trying to get her drunk?"

"She isn't halfway through with her first drink and she's got another in front of her."

"She's going to hate us if we rescue her."

"And we're going to hate ourselves if we don't."

"Do we get to eat first?" Dora asked.

"Might as well. I can watch her from here. If they start to leave, we'll intercept."

When Mandy came with our order, we asked for the bill so we'd be able to leave as soon as we finished eating. She was happy to oblige.

The guy next to Lexie was on a barstool now and swiveled to face her. The first drink was gone, and she was on her second.

Dora noticed my anxiety.

"Maybe she's going to call it a night after this. Maybe they aren't even here together. Should we consider the chance that she is here to drink alone and he's keeping her company?"

"Or, he's just about to sweep in and catch his prey," I said, motioning their way. "You can keep eating. I'll see what I can do."

As I neared, the man stood and I recognized him, distinct though incognito initially because his hair was not the frizzy, disheveled mop it was the first time I met him. Instead, his hair was slicked behind his ears. I briefly imagined him in a smoking jacket and mustache but shook the image away.

"Hello again," he offered happily as I approached.

"Meghan, you remember Jake?" Lexie stated flatly.

"I do. Nice to see you."

"And you," he said.

"I'm going to use the restroom before we leave," Lexie told him.

"I'll come with you," I said.

"So?" I asked when we got to the bathroom. She went to the stall.

"I am not a drinker," Lexie admitted when she emerged. She leaned against the counter and looked in the mirror. "Those drinks are going straight to my head."

"Where are you guys going now?"

"He didn't say."

"I don't think you should leave with him, especially if you don't know where he's taking you."

"You're probably right."

"Great. Wash your hands and we'll get out of here."

She obeyed, and we walked back to the bar.

"I think I'm going to call it a night," she told Jake.

He smiled. "A bit of a lightweight, are you?"

"No one has ever called me that before," Lexie muttered.

"Are you sure you don't want to sit down and have a drink?" he asked me.

"It's been a long week," I said.

"Okay, then. I'll see you around."

"Good night," I said.

He turned back to the bar, and I nodded for Dora to come.

"Where's your car?" I asked Lexie once we were outside.

She pointed down the street.

"We'll go to your car and then drive Dora to hers. Technically, I'm not supposed to drive yet, but—"

"I haven't been drunk in a long time," Lexie moaned.

"Probably a good thing."

She was slowing down, and I looped my arm in hers in an attempt to make her go my pace. I aimed the keys and started clicking the unlock button. The headlights lit up. I looked at Dora and pretended to wipe my brow. *What did people do before automatic unlocking devices?*

Lexie got in the front, and Dora slid into the back. I took a deep breath before crunching my abdomen into a sitting position. I exhaled as I repositioned the seat, and then I started the car. It had only been eleven days since I'd been behind the wheel, but it felt foreign, like the feeling of trying to find your legs after getting off a really good roller coaster. We dropped Dora at her car and waited until she was buckled and ready to follow.

"I have a general idea where your house is," I told Lexie, "but I'm going to need your help."

She grunted.

"I thought you were going to forget about Jake. We don't even know him, you know?"

Lexie did not know. She had her head against the window and appeared asleep.

Broadway I knew, but many of the other streets were still a mystery. When I saw Second Street, I turned, knowing it would take me to Highway 52, and Highway 52 would take me to the Seventy-Fifth Street exit. Less than a mile onto Seventy-Fifth Street, I saw a nursery and made a quick stop and hard turn to get into the empty lot. Dora pulled up beside me. I scrolled through the contacts in my phone until I got to Nora.

"I'm across the street. Come to my house," Nora offered as I explained my predicament.

She turned on the outside light so we'd know we were in the right drive.

"I'm in my pajamas," she apologized, wrapping a robe around her.

"Not a problem," I said.

Dora met us in front of my car.

"Lexie is out cold," I said.

"That's a little strange, isn't it? How much did she drink?" Nora asked.

"One drink and a few sips of another," I told her.

"In how much time?" Nora prodded.

"An hour?" Dora guessed.

Nora shook her head. "That's not enough to do it. She's not a small girl."

"Do you think she was drugged?" I asked.

"One drink shouldn't knock her out," Nora held.

"I'm calling Ben."

I told Ben of Lexie's condition.

"Call the police," he said.

"The police?"

"How else will you find if she's been drugged?"

"That seems drastic."

"Call the police, Meghan."

I obeyed.

"911. What is your emergency?"

"I think my friend has been drugged."

Chapter Ten

THE KISS OF BETRAYAL

"I can't do a breathalyzer on her when she's unconscious, and I'm not convinced we need to test for anything else," an older officer with thick, curly gray hair and a lisp told us.

"How many drinks does it typically take to knock someone out?" I asked.

"Several."

"She had one in an hour."

"It must have been a doozy."

"Is it possible the bartender deliberately spiked it?" Dora asked.

"It's possible," the officer murmured. "He might have seen a guy out to get a girl drunk and decided to help him out. But honestly, if she's not a drinker and she had a strong drink, well—"

"Don't you think we should find out?" I pushed.

"Sure. You can take her to the hospital."

"Getting her to the hospital is not a problem. Getting her out of the car may be," I said.

"I don't know how they'll handle that," the officer grunted. He had already arrived at the not-my-problem phase. "Take her in. They'll let us know if they find something."

He went to his patrol car.

"Do you want to go home?" I asked Dora when he left.

"I have no reason to rush back to Chris's house."

"Do you mind if we leave Dora's car here for a while?" I asked Nora.

She shook her head. "Keep it here as long as you need."

"Do you know how to get to the ER?" I asked Dora.

She nodded.

"Great. You drive."

I went into the ER while Dora waited in the illegally parked car outside the emergency room doors. I explained the situation, and after much discussion, both in front of me and elsewhere while I waited, a security guard and phlebotomy technician went to the curbside to draw Lexie's blood. Lexie stirred a bit as the needle poked her arm but didn't rouse.

"The nurse behind the desk asked if I felt comfortable taking her home or if I wanted to bring her in to have her checked out. If she has been drugged, we need to make sure she doesn't quit breathing," I reported to Dora as we drove away.

"That's scary."

"That's what I thought. It's already been an hour and a half. Let's hope she's as far gone as she's going to be."

"Probably depends on what she was given and how big of a dose."

"It's too cold to leave her in the car. There's no way we'll be able to carry her in."

"Why not?" Dora countered. "There are three of us. One can take her legs and one can take each arm. We should be able to get her to a couch, or at least inside the house."

"I can't lift anything. I wasn't even supposed to drive."

"Maybe Nora and I can manage."

"Then what?"

"I can stay with her. I have no reason to get home."

"I hope Nora's okay with that plan."

Lexie had not given me a choice. She needed me at The Strange Brew, in my normal chair, in twenty minutes.

"Thanks for meeting me," she started, humbly.

"I don't have long," I confessed. "Ben has a couple coming for counseling in an hour and I promised I'd watch Caleb. I wanted to let you know Vespa Adams is happy to do sewing repairs if your blouse from the other night is missing some buttons."

She wrapped her forehead in her hand. "Dora already sang 'Desperado,' so I think we can let it drop. And speaking of your husband, I don't think I'll be able to face him again knowing he helped carry me into Nora's house."

I waved my hand to dismiss the idea. "He was coming to pick me up anyway."

"Still, him seeing me with missing buttons and all—"

"Except for the protruding bosom, you looked nice, by the way."

"Oh, good. Now I feel better."

"I talked to Dora after church. She said you were out a little over three hours. Did you find out what it was?"

"Rohyphol."

"Which is?"

"Illegal here but readily available south of the border."

"Nice."

"I ran into Shirley at work on Monday."

"Investigative reporter Shirley," I clarified. After the super-important Jane Allen fail, I couldn't take any chances.

"The same."

"And by 'ran into' you mean 'purposely made your way' to her office?"

"Of course."

"And?"

"She ran my incident by her detective friend, and he wants me to go back to The Brew House to see if Jake will do it a second time."

"They want to use you as a guinea pig?"

"I've got the body for it."

"No," I said decisively. "Absolutely not."

"Look at you, getting all protective," Lexie said, cradling her cup of Strange Brew coffee.

"What's the point?"

"Evidence."

"Evidence of what?"

"If Jane Allen received reports of Food Co-op guy drugging and raping girls, wouldn't that be motive for murder?"

"I didn't think mophead had it in him."

"He wasn't moppish on Saturday."

"I noticed."

"Sort of makes you wonder how much hotter you could be with the right hairstyle, doesn't it?"

"Not until this moment," I answered. "Anyway, don't they have the evidence they need? Your blood test proves you were drugged."

"The test proves I had it in my system, not how it got there."

"No one would drug herself!"

Lexie raised her eyebrows. "Correction. You and I wouldn't drug ourselves. There are plenty of others who would—and do."

"They need to see him put the drug in your drink? How's that going to happen?"

"They can do a blood test prior to my meeting him and one afterward, and that should be the evidence they need. Besides, there will be undercover police at the bar, so they'll be watching from different angles."

"How will they keep you safe? Where's he going to take you when you're passed out?"

She lowered her voice to an almost inaudible whisper. "Did I mention there will be lots of undercover police officers? Some will be inside The Brew House, some outside it. Some will be waiting by his apartment."

"He's not going to his apartment. You were passed out shortly after you got to the car. There's no way he could get you from the parking garage to his apartment without being seen."

"Maybe that's what Jane Allen saw."

"Him transporting an unconscious body?"

Lexie shrugged. "She was by the parking garage."

"I watched you for most of an hour and I had no idea that was him with you. Are we sure his name is even Jake? What did he tell you about himself?"

Lexie's face colored. "He mostly asked about me."

"And you told him?"

"Pretty much everything; where I work—"

"Where you live?"

She nodded.

"You didn't tell him your parents are down south and you're alone in the house, did you?"

"I might have."

I sat back in my cozy blue chair. The faux fire danced in a ridiculous attempt to bring warmth to the situation.

"Don't you see why it's important I do this? I'm the perfect candidate. He knows I'm alone and vulnerable."

The Strange Brew was strangely empty, even for a Tuesday morning.

"I'm going to meet with the detective tomorrow," Lexie asserted.

"Won't Jake be suspicious?" I countered.

"For all he knows, you dropped me off at home, and I went to bed and slept it off."

"What if he has a police scanner?"

"A police scanner?"

"What if he heard dispatch send a unit to Nora's house for a possible drugging?"

She shrugged. "What if I do nothing and he keeps doing it?"

"When's this going to happen?"

"I'll let you know when I know. In the meantime, you and I never had this conversation. No one can know. I don't want to blow my cover."

"From now on, I'll refer to you by your undercover alias only. Hm. What should that be?" I took a drink. "How about Mop Hoar?"

Flavored coffee shot out of Lexie's mouth. I used my napkin to wipe my sleeve.

"Excuse me?" she shrieked.

"As in pig," I explained. "Guinea pig and all."

"Boar," Lexie clarified.

I shrugged. "Hoar. Boar. It's all the same thing, isn't it?"

"Well, it's never a bore meeting you, I'll give you that. You and your inadequate usage ... grammar ... vocabulary."

"Stop, really. My self-esteem has reached its limit."

She smiled. "Next time you see me, I'll be a seasoned—"

"Guinea pig. Seasoned and ready for the spit."

"I was going to say informant."

I leaned forward. "Send me encrypted code to let me know when and where we can meet again."

It was only two blocks home, but the chill from the October air left me shivering. At least, I hoped it was the air.

I grabbed the mail from our box at the end of the drive before heading into the house. Ben came down the stairs when he heard me come in.

"Everything okay with Lexie?"

"Fine. How'd it go here?"

"Uneventful. We've been playing Frank and Bob."

I smiled. "Are all the cars working now, Frank?"

He raised his eyebrows and gave a nod. "I'm Bob."

I smiled and scanned the mail. "Oh, look. This is from VEBA. It must be the results of the paternity test. Want to open it and see if you're predisposed?"

He took it with a scowl. "You won't think it's funny if the rates go up."

"The rates *will* go up. Caleb's going to be on the plan."

Ben sat down on the couch and opened the envelope. I opened the fridge and tried to decide what I'd make for supper. Out of the corner of my eye, I saw Ben disappear into his office.

"Ben?"

The letter was still on the couch. I sat down and skimmed and then stopped and re-read.

"We are unable to insure Caleb Benjamin Ellingson under your insurance policy, as the paternity test showed you are not Caleb's father."

I could hear Ben from the office. I went to the doorway.

"I don't care what you have going on. Cancel it."

When I heard Ben's tone, I knew two things with certainty: one, I needed to remove Caleb from the house; and two, unless I wanted to unleash a fury I had never known, I would not say a word.

I went upstairs and called Dora.

"Are you home?" I asked her.

"For another hour."

"Any chance you and Braden could hang out with Caleb at the church for a bit? We've got a situation."

"I'll be right there."

I packed a snack for the boys and had Caleb put some toys in a backpack. Dora arrived looking pale. I had never seen her without makeup, and her hair was in a sloppy ponytail.

"Everything okay?" I asked when Braden and Caleb were in the Sunday school room unpacking the contents of Caleb's bag.

"I'm leaving tomorrow," she whispered.

"To go?"

"Didn't I tell you that Nora said I could move in with her?"

"No, you didn't."

"She'll let me live there for free."

"Do we even know Nora?"

"I sat up most of the night with her on Saturday."

"And you're sure it's safe?"

"Safer than where I am."

Have all my friends lost their minds, or is it me? Did my brush with death leave me hugging a wall? "Does Chris know?"

She shook her head. "I'm going to bring Braden with me and leave a note for Chris telling him he can pick him up when he's done with work."

"I'll pray it works out. I better get back home. I'll get Caleb as soon as I can. The church door is locked, so no one can get in without a key."

"We'll be fine."

When Becky arrived, Ben opened the door and shoved the letter at her.

"Caleb isn't my son, Becky. Do you have any idea what I have gone through in the last five years? Do you know and understand the pain you've caused? If there was any doubt, why didn't you have a paternity test done before you told me I had a son? And who's Caleb's father?" Ben demanded.

Becky looked at Ben and shook her head. "I talked to him while I waited for you to get home from class."

"It was one of my suitemates?"

"One day, he kissed me. I started to push him away and … then I didn't."

"He raped you?" Ben asked, with sudden urgency.

She shook her head. "I don't know why we didn't stop, but I guess we both got caught up. We knew it was wrong. It was the only time."

"Which one, Becky? Who is Caleb's father?" Ben demanded.

"Matt."

I felt the breath leave my body. I had been standing by the steps but turned and sat on the couch.

"Was that before or after you and I had sex?"

She looked down.

"Answer me!"

"Before."

Ben went to his office and slammed the door.

Becky looked so pathetic it was hard not to be compassionate. I wasn't sure what to do. I didn't know if Ben would come back out or if she should go. The couple he was supposed to counsel would be here momentarily, but surely he was in no mood to—

Ben charged out of the office. "I'm going to Madison."

"Alone?"

"You can come if you want, but I'm leaving now."

"What about Caleb?"

"I can watch him," Becky offered. "But I can't take him to the apartment."

"You can stay here," Ben said.

Desperate situations do *call for drastic measures.*

"Are we staying overnight?" I asked.

"No."

"Can you get Caleb from the church while I get a few things together? Did you cancel your appointment?"

"It's taken care of," he said, walking past Becky and out the door.

"So, for supper tonight," I started, heading to the fridge.

Two months ago, I had been the one speeding along this road. How many times would we take this path before the past wasn't hitting us over the head?

For nearly an hour south of Rochester, the fields dipped and winded along the contours of the land. Combines sent clouds of dust and dirt across the landscape. The sun offered brightness unreciprocated in the temperatures. In March, forty degrees was balmy, but in October, it came as a shock to the body.

As we neared the Mississippi River, the fields became dense with trees in full autumn hues. Because I didn't have to watch the narrow, curving road, I was able to take it all in: the cliffs, the meandering river still teeming with fishermen, the eagles gliding and returning to their perches.

I brought a book, but after reading and rereading a few pages, I knew it was a lost cause.

"Can I offer a suggestion?"

"What?" Ben grunted.

"Think about where you're going to meet Matt. Don't bring this into their home. If you want to meet him alone, fine. If you want Amanda there, then they need to find a babysitter, and that may take a bit of time."

"Why would I want Amanda there?"

It occurred to me that Ben wasn't thinking one second beyond seeing Matt and taking a swing. "She needs to know. We've just been through this in our marriage. Now

Matt has a son, and she needs to be part of the decision as to what to do."

"You better call her, then."

"What do you want me to tell her?"

"Tell her we're coming into town about four and we'd like to meet her and Matt somewhere alone for a bit."

I called Amanda and delivered the message. She said she'd work on getting a sitter and get back to me. I was not used to being elusive, squelching her excitement at our unexpected arrival, and then lying to her to assure her all was fine.

I put my phone in my purse. "Ben, this is going to turn their world upside down."

"Maybe they already know."

"How could they?"

"Don't you think Matt thought about it back when she thought she was pregnant the first time? There's no way it didn't go through his mind. I told him about Caleb this summer just before we moved to Oronoco. It had to go through his head again then."

He figured out how to tell Matt, and not me?

"I don't think Amanda knows. And I don't know what she's going to do."

"All I want to know is what they want done with Caleb. Technically, he isn't our responsibility anymore."

"As much as he's gotten on my nerves at times, I think this better be handled right. He's only had a dad in his life for a few months. I'm not sure how he'll react if you tell him you aren't his dad."

"I just got used to being his dad."

"I'd just gotten used to being okay with Becky."

Ben stiffened. "She's a scheming—"

"But—" I interrupted.

"I know," Ben finished. "I fell for it. Stupid."

We arrived at the Schumacher Farm Park a half hour before Matt and Amanda planned to meet us. It would have been nice to have stopped to pick something up to eat, but food was not on Ben's radar.

He turned the car off and stretched. I brought my seat up from the reclining position and prayed Ben's mood would soften before Matt and Amanda arrived.

"I'm going to take a run," he said.

I quickly surmised my options were to hang out in a car at an unfamiliar park or go along.

"I'll come," I decided.

"Are you sure that's a good idea?" he asked.

It had been two and a half weeks since the surgery.

"Do you know how far this goes?" I asked.

"Not more than a mile or two," he said.

"I'll do what I can."

I stretched as he locked the car and walked to the trail.

"Ready?"

"I guess."

Running would not be the word to describe what I was doing. Speed walking or slow jogging, maybe, but compared to normal, I was mostly dragging. Ben stayed with me, but he reminded me of a dog on a leash, obviously not happy about the pace but unable to change it.

Woods enveloped either side of the path. Squirrels scurried and birds flitted away as we approached. Not all of the leaves had turned, and only a few had fallen.

The path twisted and brought us to a stone fence where several Canadian geese were resting. As we neared, they scattered, all except one, who ran a few feet and stopped.

I pulled Ben's sleeve to stop him. "His wing is broken."

"What do you want me to do about it?" he snarled.

"Let's just go around him so he doesn't have to move."

"We can turn here and go back to the parking lot. It's just as well."

I had been struggling to keep up with Ben's pace. Now I slowed to walking and let him run. Even if I lost sight of him, I'd be okay if I was headed in the right direction.

When I reached the car, he was bent over, catching his breath.

"It seems to me Caleb has the most to lose here," I reminded him.

"Or gain," Ben said. "Matt and Amanda have other children. A brother and sister wouldn't be a bad thing."

"You don't think Matt and Amanda would have him live with them?"

"Why not?"

"Becky's in Rochester. She's letting him live with us because she's ten minutes away. Three hours is a whole different ball game."

"It's not our problem to figure out, Meghan."

Ben's curtness was frustrating. "I'm not sure we should have come today, Ben. You aren't in any mood to deal with this tactfully."

Matt's truck turned into the parking lot.

"Nothing's going to change," he said. "I'll feel the same way tomorrow and the day after that and the next day."

Amanda hopped out of the truck and came to the car.

"What's going on? You didn't drive to Waunakee on a weekday to meet us in a park for nothing."

Matt got out of the truck and came over.

"How could you?" Ben demanded.

Matt looked Ben in the eye and shook his head.

"What are you talking about?" Amanda asked.

"I would never do that to you," Ben affirmed.

"You didn't have to. Girls were always looking at you. You could have been with anyone you wanted to be with. The only reason she noticed me is because she was waiting for you."

"And you put on the Matty charm."

"I never thought I had a chance with her."

"You shouldn't have been looking for a chance with her! If you were attracted to her and she was with me, you should have walked away."

"I should have, but I was twenty years old."

Amanda looked at me. "Are we talking about Becky?"

I looked at Ben.

"Stop talking around me! Stop ignoring me! You wanted me here. I'm here. What is going on?" Amanda cried.

Ben looked at Amanda. "I took a paternity test. Caleb isn't my son. Becky said the only other person she was with was Matt."

Amanda's head flew to face Matt. "You slept with Ben's girlfriend?"

"Once!" Matt shouted. "One time! We were talking and then we were kissing and then we were having sex."

"So Caleb is yours?" she said. "And the lies I've been hating Ben for were your lies?"

Amanda looked at Matt, then at Ben, then at me and walked away. I went with her, once again finding myself struggling to keep up.

"You think you know a guy," she mumbled as I caught up to her. "What else is he keeping from me?"

"I thought the same thing when I found out about Caleb."

She spun around. "And was there more, or has Ben convinced you that was all?"

"As far as I know, everything he was hiding from me was related to Caleb: the tutoring jobs he took to pay child support, the checking account to pay child support."

She shook her head. "You know how many times I've thanked God I wasn't in your shoes?"

"I didn't want to be there either, Amanda. When I found out, I thought Ben and I were done. I couldn't imagine staying with someone who kept something so big from me. It wasn't until I talked to Jeff—"

"Don't talk to me about Jeff! He slept with your best friend one week after you broke up. What is wrong with you?"

"There's always been something about him."

"You're sick!"

"You're right. That's why Jeff and I agreed we couldn't talk anymore. It's too dangerous. I'm grateful Jeff didn't kiss me the night I found out about Caleb, because at the time, I didn't care about hurting Ben."

"I can't relate to that, Meghan."

"If you had asked me any day prior to that if I was capable of cheating on Ben, I would have said no. It never crossed my mind."

"So what are you saying? I'm just supposed to excuse this? It happened on the wrong day? It was a momentary lapse of judgment? I don't buy the 'we were just talking, then kissing, then having sex.'"

"Like Ben said, Matt was putting himself in a position for it to happen. He was courting her while she was waiting in the suite for Ben. I didn't put myself in a good position going to the beach with Jeff when I was hurt. It was wrong. But it happened."

"All this time, he let Ben pay child support. He let Ben take the fall."

"I don't know how often Ben and Becky had sex, but I would imagine if Matt and Becky only had sex once, he didn't think it could be his."

"We only had sex once when we got pregnant with Abby, Meghan."

"Oh."

"We're barely living together as it is. I don't want to have sex with him when he's drinking, so I sleep in my own room with the door locked."

"You're kidding."

"Do I look like I'm joking?"

"Why didn't you say something?"

"It's not something you broadcast."

"But you made a big deal about Ben sleeping with me."

"Ben *should* sleep with you. Matt *should* be sleeping with me. It's just not the way it's going."

"You need to get help."

"Matt doesn't want help."

"This is what happened to Earl and Margaret."

"Earl and Margaret?"

"Remember my old landlord from Evanston?"

"Good grief, Meghan. Matt's not about to start strangling women."

"I didn't say he was. It just reminded me of what she said. He was drinking, she was working, and pretty soon, they were living separate lives. He was staying at the apartment complex while she was at the house."

"I'm not taking Caleb. That's not an option."

"What is the option?" I asked.

She turned and headed toward the guys. Ben was leaning against the hood of the car.

"Where's Matt?" she demanded.

Ben shrugged. "Restroom?"

"I'm not taking Caleb," she told Ben.

"So what do you want to do with him?" Ben asked her.

"I don't care. I don't even know if he's Matt's. How do we know there wasn't someone else?"

"He'll have to take a paternity test."

"Fine."

"I have a child living under my roof that I have no legal right to," Ben reminded her. "I have no insurance on him. If he falls and breaks a leg, I've got nothing."

"If he falls and breaks a leg, you call Becky and she takes him to the ER. She has a legal right to him, and surely, she's insured him."

"I'm not so sure," Ben said. "She's cut her ties to her parents; she's working at a restaurant part-time and going to school."

"She's probably on the state," Amanda decided. "And if she's not, she should be."

Matt reemerged from behind the barn.

"You're going to have to take a paternity test," Amanda told him.

He nodded.

"And you owe Ben five years' worth of child support."

"I'm not asking for that," Ben said.

"Money isn't a problem, Ben. Matt's parents are loaded. You know that." She turned back to Matt. "I can't stay married to you."

"Hold on, Amanda. Calm down," Ben said.

Matt held up his arm. "Don't worry about it, Ben. Our marriage has been over for a while."

"You have a family," I reminded them.

"It's a charade. Perfect family. Boy and girl. Amanda always wanted everything perfect. Remember the wedding? That was a joke. I wanted something small and quick, but she insisted on the gloves and the flowers and the ice sculpture."

"The idea was to get married once!" Amanda cried.

"We'd been sleeping together ever since she moved into my parents' house. We couldn't have a quick wedding beforehand. We had to have the best of everything. It's always been that way. The kids have to look good. I have to look good."

"What's wrong with wanting to look good?" Amanda demanded.

"We look good while our marriage falls apart."

Ben stood between the two of them. "You're saying a lot of things you don't mean."

"I've meant everything I've said," Matt said.

Ben held his hand up. "Stop, Matt. This is not the time to determine the strength of your marriage. We went through the same thing. No decisions should be made tonight. A lot has happened, and everyone's feelings are hurt."

"I haven't done anything wrong," Amanda shrieked.

"You haven't kept anything from Matt?" I asked.

"Nothing."

"I thought the same thing, until Jeff pointed out that I hadn't told Ben about the perverts who harassed me at work all the time."

"I still don't understand why you stayed there," Ben chided.

"To pay your bills."

Ben put his hands on his hips. I turned to Amanda.

"You don't do anything that he doesn't know about?"

"Meghan, I don't have secrets."

"You hire babysitters and go shopping," Matt announced.

"That's not a big deal."

"The amount of money you spend is."

"Since when?"

"My parents have been asking me to talk to you for a while. In less than four years, you've been putting the business and their future in jeopardy."

"That's an exaggeration."

"It's not. It's house projects, the furniture, the patio, the kids' stuff, your clothes, the hundred dollar trips to the salon and the nails and—"

"In God's eyes, it's all the same," Ben said.

"Not true!" she screamed. "Matt slept with your girlfriend!"

"You slept with someone out of wedlock too," Matt reminded her. "You've betrayed my family. They were willing to be generous with you, and you've taken advantage of them."

"This isn't about me!" she yelled.

"Amanda, it's about all of us. It's what I told you before. I was so hurt that Ben didn't tell me about Caleb that I committed adultery in my heart. I was mad that Ben was keeping secrets from me all the while I was keeping a secret from him. Matt slept with his best friend's girlfriend, and you slept with him. He's lied. You've lied. We're all in the same boat," I said.

"You've got a lot to work on. We've got a lot we're working on," Ben added.

"What if I don't want to work on it?" she touted.

"You made a promise," I reminded her.

"I didn't think it would be like this," she said.

"I didn't either. Trust me. I couldn't have imagined the last few months," I assured her.

"I wish you'd stop comparing our lives. You and Ben have been the golden couple until now. We've had four terrible years."

"Our first four years weren't all bliss," I countered.

"Oh, really? What have you had to endure?"

I looked at Ben and sighed. "When Ben started the seminary, I was working. He had such a busy life and was always around people, but he didn't put any time into us. He did the usual routine of not taking care of his clothes or the dishes or me, and it made for some hard feelings."

"Meghan's way of dealing with it was predictable," Ben huffed.

"Hold on. I dropped plenty of hints."

"If you did, I didn't get them, so by the time we'd been married six or seven months, she was miserable."

"I didn't notice at our wedding," Amanda rebutted.

"Trust me, Amanda, we could make it look good for a weekend," Ben assured her.

"I enjoyed your wedding because Ben and I spent time together," I added. "Most of the time, I was coming home to a dark apartment and a cold bed more often than not, and when he finally got home, he was excited after being with the guys all day, and I was ticked off."

"Once spring came, she started running. Every day. We went home one weekend and Mom asked if Meghan was pregnant. She said she looked thin and sickly."

"So Ben asked if I was pregnant—as if he wouldn't know. I was furious. His solution was to demand I see a shrink."

"A Christian counselor," Ben corrected.

"You never told me that," Amanda noted.

"I went to one appointment."

"*We* went to one appointment," Ben corrected. "And Meghan refused to go back."

"And Ben gave me an ultimatum. He told me I had two weeks to get myself back on track or he wasn't going to give me a choice about the matter."

"What did you do?"

"I told him he had two weeks to change his rude, domineering tone that not only made me want to run, but also lose my appetite or I'd be scheduling an appointment with the pastor I worked for."

"You didn't!" Amanda hissed.

"She did," Ben acknowledged.

"He treated me like a child he needed to correct."

"So what did you do?" Amanda asked Ben.

"Ben had my parents come for an intervention."

"Hold on," Ben said. "Before you think I was out of line, Meghan was scrawny thin, she was getting headaches all the time, and she wouldn't talk to me."

"Because you were never there to talk to."

"That's not true."

"When I came home to a dark apartment at 11:45, I was already angry, so when you came strolling in at 12:15, I was in no mood to talk."

"What did your parents do?" Amanda asked.

"My mom told me to quit running, but it didn't mean a thing. What changed everything is what my dad said to Ben."

We all looked Ben's way.

"He said if Meghan was miserable, it was my job to fix it."

"How'd you do that?" Matt asked.

"Her parents were no more than out the door and Meghan got her running shoes on. I was thinking how nothing was ever going to change, and stewing, and then I thought about what her dad said and got my running shoes on and found her. I picked her up and carried her home. She told me to put her down and let her go, but I held on to her and told her she was my wife and that was not an option."

"You carried her the whole way home?" Matt asked.

"It was only a few blocks. I'm a faster runner. Anyway, I had to. I knew if I put her down, she'd run away."

"I would have too. I had had enough."

"I'm surprised no one called the cops," Matt said.

Ben looked at me and shook his head. "When we got home, I plopped her on the couch and asked what it was going to take to make our marriage work."

"And I said I wanted to see you and spend time with you and feel like I mattered to you."

"And my heart broke. I was so into myself and my school and doing what I wanted that I didn't notice what I was doing to her."

"You did the same thing when Caleb moved in," Amanda pointed out.

"I know. I've always assumed Meghan would be there, and because of it, I push her to the back burner when I feel overwhelmed."

"She's tried to tell you she's not happy, and you don't listen to her," Amanda accused.

"I'm guilty of that," Matt admitted. "Amanda tends to be vocal, and after awhile, I tune her out."

"The drinking is the ultimate zone-out," Amanda pointed out.

"I know."

"We haven't made any decisions about Caleb," Ben reminded everyone.

"I'm with Amanda, Ben. Maybe that makes us bad people. We've got a ten-month-old and a three-year-old. As far as I'm concerned, you can be his dad. I can pay you back—"

"It's not about the money," Ben insisted. "First, we need to make sure you're Caleb's dad."

Matt nodded.

"In the meantime, I don't want anyone else to know," Ben demanded. "Caleb doesn't need to be in the middle of another rumor, and until we decide what to do with him, it's best he hears nothing."

"You don't have to worry," Matt said.

"Amanda?" Ben prodded.

"What about my mom?"

"Your mom is fine," I said. "You need to be able to talk to someone about this. Just ask her to keep it to herself, at least until we know if Matt is the father."

"Okay, then," Ben said.

I gave Amanda a hug. "This isn't the end."

"That's what I'm afraid of," she retorted.

I gave Matt a hug. "We'll be praying."

Ben held Amanda in a hug for a long time and whispered something in her ear. When he let her go, she wiped a tear from her cheek.

Matt approached Ben. "I can't tell you how bad I've felt."

Ben sighed. "Just get your life together."

"Easier said than done," Matt said.

"You've got to start somewhere."

For the first time in a long time, they parted without shaking hands.

Once we were buckled and in line to follow Matt out of the parking lot, I asked Ben what he said to Amanda.

"I told her I've never wanted to kill a man before today and she could call me if she wanted to rehearse murder scenes together."

I didn't respond. Someday, Amanda would tell me what he really said.

$$\overset{+}{\underset{+}{}}$$

Chapter Eleven

NO DAWN ON
THE HORIZON

I had not understood Exodus 10:21. Darkness I had seen, but the plague of darkness that God told Moses was coming was one that could be felt, one that paralyzed the Egyptians for three days.

Ben's side of the bed was empty when I woke up at 3:17. I wrapped my robe around me and headed downstairs, feeling an ache with each step, the result of trying to keep up with Ben and Amanda at the park.

The light was on in Ben's office. It occurred to me I may want to brace for the worst, only to realize I didn't know the worst Ben was capable of. *If I don't know what my husband would do in his deepest despair, do I know my husband?*

He was in the leather swivel desk chair his parents gave him when he graduated from the seminary taking full advantage of the reclining feature. His stocking feet rested on papers haphazardly strewn across his desk. His hand was raised, holding a pencil. Only God knew the depths of his thoughts, I decided when he turned to face me. The sheen in his eyes made me wonder if he had been joking when he talked of killing Matt.

I sat in the chair opposite him, knowing he was unreachable, the way I had been so many times in the last months.

"Would you like a cigarette?" I asked at last.

"I thought you quit."

"I did. A couple times already. I keep a pack in the crockpot just in case."

I retrieved my contraband and grabbed a blanket from the couch. When I opened his office door, he followed me onto the porch. I lit a cigarette and handed him the pack and lighter, only to realize this was not his first cigarette.

"Matt taught me to smoke the fall after everything happened with Becky," he explained.

Matt smokes? That's what he was doing behind the barn. I wonder if Amanda knows?

"We smoked half a pack in a half hour, one right after the other. I could barely talk when I got up the next morning."

"That's one way to get a sexy singing voice."

"Leave it to Matt to use cigarettes to console me after he'd ruined my life."

"Is that what you think? Your life is ruined?"

"Have you read the story of the woman who lost the borrowed necklace and worked ten years to replace it, only to find it was a fake and she'd given up everything for nothing?"

"I don't think so."

He exhaled condemnation, an obvious violation of an assumed smoker's nonjudgment code.

"It hasn't been ten years," I pointed out.

"Right," he said. "I worked my butt off to pay child support, ruined my reputation, and damaged my marriage for the sake of a boy I was deceived into thinking was mine."

"Or—" I hesitated, remembering the feeling of being in the wagon at the top of the hill in my backyard as a child, wondering if I should pick my foot up or keep it down. Once it started, the wagon would be full speed ahead until the hill leveled or I fell out. "You might consider how even though Caleb isn't yours, he just as easily could have been."

Ben ground his cigarette into the decking beneath us. "Not helping."

The door shut behind him, leaving me to a moonless night. Looking out over an ill-named street where no oaks grew and no leaves gathered on the side of the road in a last parade before winter, I couldn't see, but I knew there was nothing ahead of me but darkness. I crushed what was left of my cigarette and hurried into Ben's now-vacant office, locking the door before going up the stairs to bed.

It had been nearly a week since I'd talked to Lexie. The texts I sent went unanswered. She hadn't been in church. One last text, I decided, and then Caleb and I would head into the paper office to make sure she was okay.

She responded with: Strange Brew?

My response: Twenty minutes?

Hers: Got it.

Caleb was working his way through a peanut butter and jelly sandwich. I tapped on Ben's office door before opening it a crack.

"I'm meeting Lexie at The Strange Brew for a bit. Would you like a sandwich before I go?"

He had not spoken to me since our cigarette on the porch four days ago, and he'd offered little more than grunts to Caleb. Caleb was, by all appearances, unphased.

I had been to the crockpot twice already in one week and noted I was not the only one depleting the supply. Two recourses had come of my sanity smokes. Pastor Gibbons told me to call sooner rather than later, and if that didn't work, there was always the option of calling Ben's parents. I doubted that would shake him out of it, though, since the intervention Ben called with my parents had done little to help me. I kept thinking Ben would come out of it on his own, hoping the next day would be better.

When Ben didn't answer my question about the sandwich, I shut the door and headed upstairs to get ready.

We arrived early to claim a table. "Do you want a smoothie?" I asked Caleb after we'd shed our coats. "There's strawberry banana or mixed berry. Which sounds good?"

He shrugged.

"Let's get mixed berry, and if you don't like it, I'll drink it."

I looked at Linda. "Small, please."

She nodded. "I can put a bit in a cup and let him try it."

"That would be great."

Caleb's face showed neither pleasure nor displeasure when he took a sip.

"Do you like it?" I prodded.

"It's okay."

I turned back to Linda.

"Chai tea?" she asked.

"How about a turtle mocha with skim milk and one shot of espresso."

"Switching things up?"

"I overheard someone else order one. It sounded good."

I refrained from telling her I'd already tried it and knew they were both delicious and effective.

"They *are* good. Do you want whipped cream?"

"No, thanks."

"White or dark chocolate?"

"Dark, please."

"Got it."

I was carrying the drinks to the table when Lexie arrived.

"What did you get?" she asked, slipping off a pink cable-sweater jacket and wrapping it around a chair.

I repeated my order.

She nodded and went to the counter. "Large turtle mocha with dark chocolate and two shots of espresso, please."

"Whipped cream?"

"Lots."

Linda smiled.

"Meghan's going to live longer," Lexie explained. "But I will have more fun."

"Conjecture," I interjected.

"Uh oh. She pulled out a big word."

"Rough week?" Linda asked, handing Lexie the drink.

Lexie and I answered, "Yes," simultaneously.

Lexie glanced my way and raised her eyebrows. I smiled and turned to Caleb.

"How's the smoothie?"

"Okay."

"You can play with the toys in your bag."

He opened the bag and took out an orange, a yellow, and a blue car.

"How are you, Caleb?" Lexie asked when she sat down.

"Do you recognize Lexie?" I asked when he didn't answer.

He shook his head.

"She goes to our church."

I looked at Lexie and shrugged.

"Pastor gone today?" she asked.

I shook my head. "Just in a mood. I didn't think it fair to leave him."

She nodded her understanding.

"I sent you several texts."

"I was under orders. It was for your protection."

"How is the undercover world?"

"Horrific, but I paid my debt to society, and I'm moving on."

"You finished the mission?"

"I did."

"How'd it go?"

"Long or short version?"

Caleb moved the cars around the table. "See how far we get."

"The plan was to go into the People's Food Co-op, find Jake, apologize that our time got cut short, and see if he wanted to set up another date."

"How did Jake act when he saw you?"

"A bit surprised."

"I bet! And how did he respond to your offer?"

"He was thrilled. It was nearly five, and he was about to get off work."

"Convenient."

"That's the way we planned it."

"Why?"

"Since your arrival foiled his first plan, we figured he'd want to be spontaneous if he had sinister intent. That way you or someone else wouldn't accidentally hone in on us. But honestly, my heart sank a little when he said he got off work in a couple minutes and asked if I wanted to catch a drink."

"Because then it seemed apparent he was up to no good?"

"More so when he got back from his apartment and insisted I go in his car."

"Were you nervous?"

"Yes and no. There were undercover police outside the Food Co-op and at The Brew House, but I didn't know if he'd take me there or go somewhere else. I wasn't sure if the bartender was responsible or if it was Jake acting alone."

"Was his hair moppish?

"When I first arrived at the Co-op, yes, but he went to his apartment and put his designer jeans and a baseball cap on."

"Did he take you to The Brew House?"

"He did."

"So the bartender was in on it?"

"Very much so. And this time, they decided not to take any chances."

"Meaning?"

"They gave me the knockout-cold dose."

I leaned in to whisper to Lexie. "I don't get it. What is fun about having sex with a girl who is out cold?"

"They didn't do it to have sex with me," she whispered back, her hand covering the side of her mouth nearest Caleb.

"Then what was the point?"

"Well ..." she started, as if to say, *There is much more to this story.* I glanced over at Caleb and reminded him his smoothie was there.

"It didn't take long and I started feeling woozy, so Jake suggested we leave. I made it to his car, but soon after, the world went black. Unbeknownst to me, Jake did not go to his apartment, but instead drove to Highway 52 and headed north."

"I bet your undercover police team was enjoying this."

"They weren't too worried yet. Detective Halbert put an app on my phone to track me, but they didn't know if Jake was smart enough to get rid of the phone or not. Initially, he wasn't."

"Can I go to the bathroom?" Caleb asked.

"Yes," I said. "It's right over there. Make sure to wash your hands when you're done."

He darted off.

"Where did he take you?"

"Saint Paul."

"What!"

Lexie nodded. "Eventually, the state patrol, Saint Paul and Minneapolis police were all involved."

"The undercover police followed the whole way?"

She shook her head. "The team that left The Brew House followed us to Oronoco, at which point the group that had been at the apartment caught up to us."

"How did they get there that fast?"

"His apartment isn't far from 52. Once they were on the highway, they sped to catch up. The other team got back on at Pine Island. They kept in contact via text."

I gasped.

"There were two people in each car," she assured. "One man, one woman to make it look like an ordinary couple. The woman's job was to text location while the man drove."

Caleb emerged from the bathroom.

"Can we go home?" he asked.

"In a little bit. Do you want to sit in the big chair by the fire? Take your books with you," I said, pulling his *Racing through the Alphabet* and tractor books out of the bag.

He hoisted himself onto the comfy chair and opened his book. I turned my chair so I could see him.

"Okay. What happened when Jake got to Saint Paul?"

"He dumped my purse in the garbage at a gas station."

"That's obvious, isn't it?"

"He stuck it in a paper bag and then wrapped it in a plastic bag filled with fast food wrappers. Thankfully, it was a prop given to me by the police department. I didn't bring any credit cards. I had twenty dollars and an ID."

"But that's how they were tracking you, right?"

"According to Detective Halbert, they had eyes on the car at all times. That was just the point that it became critical they didn't lose sight of me, all the while not tipping off Jake, who was getting increasingly paranoid."

I wiped my hands on my jeans.

Caleb peered around the chair. "Can we go?"

"Soon. You're being a good boy. Just give me a couple more minutes."

"I'll walk you home if you want," Lexie offered. "Caleb can go inside and play, and we could talk on the porch."

"That will work," I acquiesced. "Pack up your stuff, Caleb."

We loaded his toys and books into the bag, grabbed our cups, and headed into the crisp October air.

"Hold my hand while we cross the street, please," I reminded him. When we reached the church parking lot, I let go. He skipped ahead of us. Lexie took this as her cue to continue.

"The Saint Paul police were on call, waiting for a location. When Jake finally stopped the car, the undercover Rochester police called for backup. Little did they know, Jake wasn't staying there. Just about the time they were rallying to rescue, Jake got back in the car, and off we went. In hindsight, this was a blessing, because the undercover Saint Paul officers were there and picked up the tail."

"And they know the area."

Lexie affirmed. "This time, Jake pulled into a driveway away from the road, and two guys came out of the house and carried me in. Within ten minutes, police were raiding the house."

"Look before you cross, Caleb!" I called. Caleb skipped across the road to the parsonage.

"Ten minutes is a long time for you to be alone in a house with three men."

"They didn't touch me. They carried me to the basement and put me in a dog kennel."

"A dog kennel?"

She nodded. "One of those chain link things you put outside."

"No!"

"There were eight down there total, all with blankets, pillows, and a bucket."

"Bucket?"

"That would be the toilet."

"No!"

She nodded again. "There were more than twenty women living there—in some cases, three to a kennel."

"For what?"

"Sex trafficking."

"No way!"

"They weren't all there at the time. Some were working."

"They were going to turn you into a prostitute?"

"Probably not. Likely, they would have raped me in front of the other girls."

"What is that all about?"

"Fear. Intimidation. Most of the girls down there were fourteen to eighteen years old. They videotape the rape and tell them they'll show it to all their friends and their family and everyone will think they are promiscuous."

"No."

"Oh, yes," she said.

"In truth, they'd never show anyone because it's evidence of a rape," I declared.

"Most likely, they use the tape to relive the experience."

I cringed. "So disgusting."

Lexie nodded. "I was probably chosen to be a caretaker, looking after the girls, making food, cleaning them up before appointments, emptying the buckets, etc."

I unlocked the door and let Caleb in. "Come in," I urged Lexie. "It's chilly. We can sit..."

Ben was making himself a sandwich in the kitchen. His hair appeared to be confused as to which way it should go. It was greasy and flat in some places, sticking up in others. His unshaven face grizzled turmoil. There was a good chance he'd been sleeping in his clothes for at least a couple days, though he hadn't come to our room, so I couldn't account for his sleeping—or absence of.

"Hello, Pastor Martins," Lexie offered.

He gave the slightest nod before cutting his sandwich, taking his plate, and retreating to his office.

"What was that?" Lexie whispered.

I shrugged. "I don't think you have to be embarrassed about him seeing you in a compromising position anymore."

Caleb went to his room. I sat on the couch and motioned for Lexie to do the same.

"What happened when the police arrived?"

"They arrested the guys and, upon searching for me, came across the other young ladies. After what they found at that house—the women and the sex tapes—they were able to get a warrant for the first house and found more of the same there."

"How can this happen?"

"I have had several days to think about that, Meghan, and the question I have come to ask is not, 'How can this happen?' That's an easy answer. It happens because men pay for sex and images of porn on the web. It's a lucrative business. By the way, did you know that the majority of those who pay for sex are married white men, over half of whom have children at home?"

I shook my head.

"The questions we should ask are, 'Why don't we know this is happening?' and once we do, 'What are we going to do about it?'"

"Where did the girls go once the police found them?"

"First stop was the hospital. From there, social services works to get them back home—if there's a home to go to—and if there isn't, they place them with organizations that help women get out of the world of prostitution."

"Did you see anything, or were you out the whole time?"

"I woke up in the emergency room with Greg leaning over me, calling my name."

"Greg?"

"Detective Halbert," she explained. "Believe me, it was one of the best images I've ever woken up to."

"I hope you didn't tell him that."

"I did."

"What did he say?"

"He asked me out."

"What?"

"Not just that second. He debriefed me and told me how courageous I was and how my actions will lead to the undoing of one sex trafficking ring and the release of thirty-seven women. When I answered it was the least I could do, he assured me that was not true, because I could have done nothing. And then when I said, 'You're going to make me blush' he said, 'I'd rather take you to supper.' At that point, I said, 'I'm done dating strangers.' He pulled out his badge and said, 'I've had a background check, and there are ten officers in the emergency room who will vouch for me.' I told him to send them in."

"Are you going to go out with him?"

"I don't know. He's called to check on me a few times. I'd like to, but I'm scared."

"Beneath the purple hair and the nails, you are just a softie; in fact, I think you use those things to hide the fact that you feel vulnerable."

"Let's not go all Dr. Phil on me. I *am* going back to my normal hair color."

"Oh?"

"I can't explain it except to say this experience has changed me."

"You don't need to explain. I completely understand. You know what you need?"

She shook her head.

"You need to find someone to go on a double date. I'd offer, but—"

"Bear Grylls has taken your husband captive," Lexie finished.

I wrinkled my face.

"*Man vs. Wild,*" Lexie prodded.

I shook my head. "Never seen it. At least you're safe and it's over."

"Your drama will come to an end too."

I shrugged. *One can hope.*

Amanda answered on the third ring.

"How are things on your end?" I asked.

"If you think the devastation after World War II was paradise, then we're in paradise."

"Same here. Ben's not talking."

"That'll make for an interesting sermon."

"He did the service, but once he came home, nothing."

"You mean total silence?"

"Total silence. I feel like he's on a raft drifting farther and farther away."

"What can you do to pull him in?"

"I thought of calling his parents."

"Sort of sounds like what he did to you at the seminary."

"I know. I never understood that."

"Funny how that works."

"Isn't it? How are you coping?"

"We're not coping, Meghan. I isolate myself. He drinks. We pretend it's all good while I loathe him and he escapes the guilt and shame."

"Could that be why he started drinking?"

"To mask the guilt, you mean? I don't know. It could be, I suppose."

"Are you going to get help?"

"That's a great idea, but I don't know where to go. Who do you tell the worst to?"

"Amanda, I knew nothing of your struggles before last week, but now that I know, I don't think any less of you. You didn't know all Ben and I went through while he was in school. Does it make you think less of us, knowing Ben took me to a shrink and I ran as a means of gaining control?"

"No. It makes you more human."

"Exactly. We're all struggling with something. It seems to me the only way to get through it is to let others in."

"You always make it sound so easy, Meghan."

"If you think what I've gone through in the last two months has been easy, you haven't heard my thousands of prayers asking God to just take me home."

"If it weren't for Max and Abby, I'd be right there with you. To be honest, I'm not sure we're going to make it through this."

"You will. This is what we promised on our wedding day. When the worst comes, we said we'd stay."

She sighed.

"Oh," I said, remembering. "What did Ben say to you just before we left the other day?"

"He said if I wanted to go through murder plots, he'd be happy to."

"No!"

"He did. Then he said that if we were willing to kill Matt, we'd better be ready to die for all the crap we'd done too. He told me to hang on. My marriage was worth fighting for."

I had not talked to Ben's mom since the day I confronted her in the garden.

"Millie, it's Meghan."

"Oh, Meghan!"

She caught herself, I imagined because she felt like a contestant on *Deal or No Deal* looking at the row of briefcases. The right words would mean repairing the relationship; the wrong could mean things staying as they had been. "I'm so sorry about the baby. How are you?"

Well played.

"Physically, I'm fine."

I stopped, not sure I wanted to share my raw and honest emotions, a thought that never would have occurred to me three months ago. *Take a chance.*

"Sometimes I forget about it for a while, and other times, it is hard to get out of bed. Usually, it's hardest at night, for some reason. Sometimes I get mad at Ben."

"Oh?"

Another well-played response, I noted.

"All these years I asked if we could have a baby, and he dismissed my feelings. He had a son, and he didn't want a baby."

"But now he doesn't have a son and he doesn't have a baby."

She knew? "When did he tell you?"

"I guess it was Thursday."

We met Matt and Amanda on Wednesday, had the cigarette early Thursday morning.

"Meghan?"

"He hasn't spoken all week, not to Caleb or me. He made all of us: Matt, Amanda, and I, promise we wouldn't tell anyone, but calls you. I don't get it."

"I think he called for perspective. When you're in the battle, all you see are bullets flying. When you back up a bit, you see the situation for what it is."

It was hard for me to reign in the sarcasm. "What did you tell him you see?"

"A boy without a dad, a woman who has endured almost more than a person can, and a man who has the power to make it better for both of them, but who is too self-consumed to want to."

A unicorn flying across the sky with a leprechaun on its back couldn't have shocked me more.

"Meghan," Millie said. "Ed and I are here for you."

Chapter Twelve

PEOPLE ARE NOT WHO THEY SEEM

Two days later, Ben broke his silence a little after eleven a.m. with the declaration that he'd like to take Caleb and me for a ride, and if we could get ready, he'd like to leave soon. He had showered and shaved and was wearing a pair of nice jeans and a sweater I gave him two Christmases ago.

"Where are we going?" Caleb asked.

"It's a surprise," Ben said.

In the span of the next five minutes, I mentally broke multiple commandments.

After bundling Caleb and myself, I dropped into the passenger's seat, buckled up and assumed the best "I hate you" position I was capable of, complete with crossed arms, irritated scowl, and an utter fascination with the nothingness outside the passenger window.

The first stop was the post office. Ben left the car running. A few minutes later, he deposited a package into the trunk. From there, he drove across the street to The Strange Brew.

"What do you want?" he asked.

"Linda knows," I said. "Tell her I want it Lexie style today."

He returned and handed a cup gingerly to me. "I asked for a medium, but as you can see, she decided you needed a large."

"I love Linda."

I meant it as a jab. On our first trip to The Strange Brew, just a week after we'd arrived in town and before I knew about Caleb, Linda had asked Ben if he was the new pastor in town. When he responded that he was, Linda offered him luck, saying, "I belonged to that church for a while. Too many hypocrites," to which Ben responded, "Probably some gossips and murderers too."

She replied, "You've got that right."

Ben claimed the coffee was mediocre and overpriced, but I knew Linda was the reason he hadn't been back before today. I took a sip and decided Linda was one of my favorite people on earth for her ability to mingle sweetness and acerbity so deliciously.

Ben turned away from Highway 52. We passed Lexie's and Nora's houses on the way. Dora's car was in Nora's drive, a reminder to call and see how the new living arrangement was going.

Children at play scurried across Resurrection's soccer fields, I noted as Ben slowed to turn.

A different day, I would have asked Ben where we were. It was a church; that much was obvious. He circled to the back of the building to a hill where three crosses stood.

Four and a half years ago, on a hill with three crosses six and a half hours away, Ben and I came to the end of seven days of fasting and praying about our future, seven days without speaking to one another, and committed our lives to each other.

Ben retrieved the package from the trunk and handed me the box.

"Open it."

I worked to tear the tape. Pushing aside the cardboard flaps brought me to Styrofoam peanuts and, as I pushed them aside, a glass heart. It was rustic red and orange, not unlike the maple leaves I used to find in my parents' backyard each fall, on a street that had more than pines. A white C-shaped swirl started on one side of the heart and ended on the other. On the base, a plaque said "Baby Martins."

"When you lose a baby before twenty weeks, you have the option of getting some ashes," Ben explained. "They aren't just our baby's ashes. They cremate several babies together, and from what I've read, the ashes are mostly made of what is left of the wooden box they put the remains in. Our baby was tiny—not much more than a speck. Typically, they'd just dispose of it when a miscarriage occurs that early, but the nurse in the OR kept what they took out of you and put it in the cremation bin. I got a call several days later telling me that I could pick up our portion of the ashes."

He leaned over and traced the swirl in the heart. "Those are the ashes. I was going to put a date on it, but the more I thought about it, the more I decided it wasn't just the ashes of this baby, but of any baby we might have had, so I decided against a date."

"That was thoughtful. And sweet," I managed.

Ben turned to the backseat. "Meghan and I can't have any babies, Caleb. It's a good thing we have you."

I looked back to see Caleb smile and nod.

"Are you glad to be with us?" Ben asked.

"Mostly," he answered.

The slightest smile made an impromptu appearance on my face.

Ben kissed my forehead.

"Should we go for Chinese food?" Ben asked.

Caleb disapproved.

Ben turned back to face him again. "You don't like Chinese?"

"No."

"That will change today."

Ben drove like he knew where he was going.

"Is there something you want to tell me?"

"We're meeting Scott and Tonya."

"Ben, I know Tonya's called several times, but she's still pregnant. I just can't. Don't you understand?"

"He took a call, Meghan. They're moving to Arkansas. They leave in a week and a half."

Another time, a different place, we might have been good friends.

"All the area pastors and their wives were invited."

"That would have been nice to know. I would have dressed different, taken a shower, gotten a gift, even, or at least a card."

He stopped at a red light and looked at me. "We both know you wouldn't have come."

"Why do you want me there?"

"You're my wife."

"You haven't talked to me in a week."

"I decided not to talk until I wasn't angry anymore."

"Were you mad at me?"

"No."

"Then why couldn't you talk to me?"

"I needed time to think."

"And today you woke up and you weren't angry? Or you wanted to go to this farewell so you suddenly got over it?"

"This is why I didn't talk for a week."

"Because the last time we talked, I suggested you weren't entirely blameless in the situation?"

"Do you want me to take you home?"

"I want to go home," Caleb offered.

"That," I whispered, "is why I don't lock myself in my room and refuse to talk for a week."

"And that's exactly why I did," Ben rebutted.

When Ben pulled into the parking space, he turned off the car and faced Caleb.

"I have a friend who is moving a long ways away. I'd like to say good-bye to him. Could we have lunch at this Chinese restaurant and not fight or complain?"

"Sure, Dad."

Ben looked at me.

I lowered the visor. In the few minutes I'd had to get ready, I'd put minimal makeup on and thrown my hair in a ponytail.

"Any chance you have a hat in here?" I asked Ben.

"Caleb, is there a hat on the floor somewhere?"

Caleb unbuckled his seat belt.

"Right here," he said, handing Ben a black-and-white hat from a farm store Ben's dad frequented.

I adjusted the band at the back, wove my ponytail through the loop, and lowered the visor.

"You look better without it," Ben said.

"I think I have some bobby pins in my purse."

"We'll go in and find a seat. Come in when you're ready."

That will be never. I slid the ponytail out and twisted my hair into a French roll. I only had four pins, but at least the twist was secured. Thank God I'd put on makeup and a pair of jeans and a sweater. I closed the visor and prayed for the courage to go in.

Most of these women don't know me, so all I have to do is sit by Ben and smile. One hour. You can do this. Don't talk about the baby. Don't talk about Ben. Ask a lot of questions about them, and pray they don't bring up kids.

I took a deep breath and slowly got out of the car. It was getting easier to move. Part of me mourned that. The ache reminded me of the baby, and I didn't want that reminder to go away.

The Chinese restaurant was in a strip mall. Neon lights outlined the window. Inside the door was a set of double doors. An Asian man dressed in a short-sleeve T-shirt and a smile that could melt snow and seemed to say, "You're safe here with me" welcomed me.

"I'm with a group," I said, looking around and seeing no one familiar.

"They're in the room over here," he stated, leading me to a small room on the other side of the cash register, where my husband and several men were sitting along one table and Tonya and several women were sitting at another. Tonya jumped up when she saw me and wrapped her arms around me in a tight hug. It took me a few seconds to react.

When she backed away, Ben's face spoke of pity. Or was it empathy? Or "Please don't kill me?"

"We're not moving," Tonya blurted.

I turned to Scott. "You're not?"

Tonya shook her head and started to cry.

"It was my ploy," a tall, lean man with speckled gray hair said, standing up. "I'm Dave Larimer, the former pastor at Grace."

I felt my face getting warm as everyone stared my way. Maybe the kind-looking Asian man could come back. Perhaps his smile had the power not only to melt snow, but also the floor beneath me so I could sink into oblivion. Or possibly Christ could choose this minute to return. Either option would be welcome.

"We've all felt terrible about all that has happened in the last few months and decided it was time to show our support."

This is how you show support?

"We told Ben Scott had a call and asked him to bring you and Caleb because we didn't think the two of you would come if we told you we wanted a chance to talk to you and encourage you."

"Where *is* Caleb?" I asked, realizing his absence.

"My mom took him and Eli to our house to play for a while and eat macaroni and cheese," Tonya said.

They walked out the door of this restaurant and to a car without my notice while I was in the parking lot doing my hair? That should earn me the stepmom of the year award.

"He'll appreciate the macaroni and cheese," I managed.

Ben still looked sheepish but nodded his agreement.

"Come sit down," Tonya ordered, pointing to a chair in the middle of the women's table, across from her. "I'll introduce everyone. I'm sure you met most of us at Ben's installation, but that was so long ago."

She introduced each woman and told me the church her husband pastored. When the introductions were finished, Tonya said, "Really. How are you, Meg?"

In an effort to keep going and not be pitiful, I had deliberately tucked all my unmet dreams and emotions into a cavity deep within the chambers of my being. Unbeknownst to me, the key to unlocking that chamber, which I thought was well fortified and inaccessible, was simple sincerity followed by the endearing term of Meg.

The older woman next to me put a box of tissues on the table. On cue, Pastor Larimer directed the men out of the room, leaving us alone.

"I feel like a shell of a person," I admitted when they left. "I've got a vacuum that I don't know how to fill."

It was not me, but others who reached for the tissues, as they nodded.

"For most women, mothering is a big part of their identity," one offered.

"Even more so for pastors' wives," another said.

"Our husbands run the church, and we have a bunch of kids and hang out at home."

"My only ambition in life was to be a mom," I stated. "All the work I did the last four years was about working toward that."

"It's hard when we have different plans than God," the lady sitting next to Tonya said. "Our seven-year-old was killed in a car accident fifteen years ago, and I couldn't see how God could want that for us. I can relate to the vacuum."

"My dad died two weeks after Carl and I moved here," the woman sitting across from her said. "My mom was all alone four states away. It seemed impossible at the time, but we moved her here. She had thirty years of friends and memories there and wasn't keen on leaving.

"But it's been such a blessing. She was a helping hand as we raised our children. We didn't know back then of the health problems she'd have these last years. The clinic has offered much better care than she would have gotten there. God provided her a great friend who was recently widowed, too, and they comforted each other.

"But I'm telling you this in hindsight. Believe me, at the time, I felt like my world was falling apart, while Carl was excited about starting his ministry."

"I don't have any problems," a middle-aged woman with red hair sitting in the corner declared.

Everyone laughed.

"Two years ago, I fell and crushed my hip. I've had two surgeries, but I still walk with a cane," she admitted.

"She used to run marathons," Tonya told me.

"Not anymore," the redhead said.

"Two of our sons have walked away from God," the woman across from her admitted. "I have never been so burdened."

"If it weren't for these women," Tonya offered, "I'm not sure Scott and I would still be married. I was immature and selfish when we first came. They've been opening their hearts and lives to me and giving me small bits of advice and praying for me, whether I knew it or not."

"I thought you said the area pastors' wives rarely get together," I reminded her.

"We don't," the woman sitting next to me said. "We get together like this when it's important that we do so, but we keep in touch via e-mail and text, and you can expect a card in the mail from Wanda Larimer."

The women at the table all nodded.

"We all bear a cross," she continued, "and it would be so much harder if we didn't have others to help us bear them."

They all nodded again.

"How is Ben dealing with it?" Tonya asked.

I looked around. "Where *are* the men?" I asked.

"At the buffet," someone offered.

"Shouldn't they be back?" I asked.

"I'm sure they found a table out there. That way we don't see all the horrid food they're eating."

"Or how much," another woman offered. "Fred is supposed to be on a diet."

"Carl needs to watch his salt."

"Good luck with that here."

"I know."

We laughed. I looked at Tonya, who winked at me. I had avoided Tonya these last painful weeks, and yet here she was, crying over me and laughing with me. *Who would have guessed?*

It was nearly December by the time the paternity results proved Matt was Caleb's father. When Amanda called to give us the results, I asked how things were going.

"The same," she said.

"Is Matt still drinking as much?"

"He tried to slow down, but he got cranky, so—"

"Don't give up on him."

"I don't know, Meghan."

"We're praying."

"How are you guys doing?" she asked.

"Peaks and valleys. Good days and bad. Sometimes Ben drowns himself in his work. I haven't decided if it's because he's so committed or if he's trying to get away from me."

"What do you do when he's all consumed?"

"I talked to the pastor's wife in Zumbrota. She told me years ago, she made an appointment with her husband via the church secretary. He wasn't very thrilled to find out she was his one o'clock appointment, but now they schedule time every week. I've started putting an X on one night a week, and that's our night. We spend it with Caleb until he goes to bed at 7:30, and then the rest of the night is ours."

"Caleb goes to bed early now?"

"Ever since he started preschool. It's such a blessing."

"That's progress."

"We were waiting for the results, but now that we're sure, we're going to set up a day to meet with Becky and decide what to officially do with Caleb. Does Matt still want to revoke his parental rights?"

"Oh, yes."

"Well, I don't know what Becky will want. She has a boyfriend now."

"I didn't know that."

"I don't know if they're moving toward marriage or not, but they are both in school for nursing, and they'll graduate in the spring. She's expecting again."

"You're kidding!"

"No. She's actually pretty far along. She was due before me, sometime in May, I guess. I'm thinking they might settle down and get married. Maybe they'll want to raise Caleb with their baby."

"How would you feel about that?"

"Hopefully they'll make their home nearby so we'll be able to stay involved in his life, but I keep reminding myself that Becky's the only one that has any right to him, and she's the one who ultimately gets to make the decisions."

"It would be hard to go back to an empty house."

"I know there's a plan. And there are days Caleb still drives me batty."

"Any child will do that. I just can't get over that she left him with you in the first place. I can't imagine dropping Max off and just not coming back to get him."

"You're in a different place though. She was never able to finish school. She felt held back. Then she got into the fight with her parents and moved to an apartment where she couldn't have Caleb, and then she got pregnant and was sick and tired and going to school. She was probably thrilled to know he was somewhere where he'd be taken care of."

"Being pregnant and watching a toddler was not fun. Caleb's older, but I don't blame her for that. Those were long days."

"Well, I don't know really what to expect. I keep praying for God to prepare us for what's ahead."

"Have you met the boyfriend? Is it serious?"

"We asked them over for Thanksgiving."

"Were your families there too?"

"Just Ben's folks."

"How did that go?"

"I was probably the only comfortable one in the room. Ben's parents had never met Becky, since they dated while they were at Wheaton."

"Did they stay overnight?"

"We told them they could, but they drove up that morning, went to church, came over for lunch, and drove home."

"Did they say anything to you?"

"Millie said I was doing a wonderful job taking care of Caleb, despite the circumstances."

"That was nice."

"Yeah, it was. Unfortunately, the relationship just isn't what it was. I still hesitate to open up to her. I don't know why. I just feel betrayed."

"I know the feeling. Ever since Matt told me how his parents felt about me spending money, there's been a great divide between us too."

"Really?"

"I've quit shopping altogether. It's not like we need anything anyway. The house is finished. We have furniture and more than enough of everything. I even dyed my hair so I don't have to keep putting in highlights. Matt asked me the other day if I wanted to go get my nails done, and I told him to go you-know-where."

"It should make his parents happy that you aren't shopping."

"I don't care, really. I hate that it all happened behind my back. If Matt had ever said anything to me about spending money, it would be one thing." She sighed. "Anyway, enough of that. What's Becky's boyfriend like?"

"Well, he's not as cute as Ben."

"Pff." Her silence made me wonder if she was still there. "I just gagged on some water."

"He's cute in a homely sort of way. He's in the nursing program and seems devoted to Becky, so that's a good thing."

"How is he with Caleb?"

"Michael didn't spend much time with Caleb. Mostly, I think he was just trying to get through an awkward day, like the rest of us."

"Michael, huh?"

"Yep."

"Not Mike?"

"Nope."

"Sounds stuffy."

I chuckled. "I guess he likes to dance."

"I sure hope he has other qualities," she teased.

"It's like dating someone because they have nice teeth."

"Or ears."

"Yeah. That'll come in handy," I quipped.

She laughed. "It's good to talk to you, but I should run. The kids will be up from their naps soon. If I don't talk to you before then, have a merry Christmas."

"You too!"

Becky and Michael came over the first Sunday in December. They had supper and we played a game of Yahtzee with Caleb before Ben took him upstairs to brush his teeth and say prayers.

"Are you coffee drinkers?" I asked while I put away the game.

"Only in the morning," Michael answered.

"I usually make myself a glass of tea at night. Can I make you one?"

"I'm fine," Becky answered.

"Soda? Ben has Pepsi and Mountain Dew, and it looks like there's a Diet Coke left from Thanksgiving."

"I'll take that," Michael said.

When Ben came down, he joined us at the table. Michael and Becky sat together on one side, and after I started the dishwasher, I sat opposite Ben.

"Michael and I have decided to get married," Becky said, looking at Michael.

"Congratulations!" Ben exclaimed. "That's wonderful."

I nodded my agreement.

"We'll probably do that sooner rather than later, since in a few months, I won't look so great in a dress. It's not going to be anything fancy or big, just the two of us and a few friends."

"There's nothing wrong with that," Ben assured them.

"We're thinking about traveling some when we get done with nursing school," Becky started.

"There are organizations that hire you as a traveling nurse, and you spend three months at one assignment and then go to the next," Michael explained. "You may be in Boston for three months, then in New Orleans, Vermont, or Chicago. It seems like now might be the best time to do that. Neither of us have a house. We don't have furniture or much for belongings, so it would be easy to pick up and go."

"With a baby?" I asked.

Becky shifted in her seat. "We're thinking eventually we'll settle back down here, maybe in a year or two. The Mayo Clinic will always need nurses, and hopefully, at some point, I'll have a better relationship with my parents. Michael's parents are in Kasson, so the long-term goal is to come back."

"And the short-term goal?" Ben asked.

Becky looked at Ben and lowered her voice. "Caleb thinks you are his father, and I don't see any reason to lead him to believe anything else. He's happy here."

She looked at me. "You've taken great care of him. You feed him good meals, get him to bed, read books to him. I don't know how you found it in your heart to love him, but ..."

A knot crept into my stomach. *But*—there's always a *but*.

She took a deep breath. "We were wondering if you'd consider adopting Caleb," Becky said. "I'd like it to be an open adoption, so I could be involved. I'd like to be part of birthday parties, and Christmas, and other holidays as much as I'm able. I'll have to work some holidays, of course, as an RN, and may be gone for a while traveling."

I looked at Ben as I tried to decide if she was extremely generous or extremely selfish.

"And," she continued. "We were wondering if you'd consider adopting this baby too."

This, I was not prepared for.

"You mean 'adopt the baby until you get back' sort of thing?" I asked.

She shook her head. "We'll be putting this child up for adoption either way. I know what it takes to raise a child, and for now, I'd like to start my career and have time with Michael."

"We just thought maybe you'd consider, since we know you would give the baby a good home."

Since we know you can't have a baby of your own.

"The ultrasound is Friday. If it's something you're interested in, you could come and see the baby yourself."

"Meghan and I will need to talk it over," Ben said.

Thank you, Pastor Gibbons.

"We'd expect that," Michael noted.

When they left, I went to the closet for my shoes.

"Where are you going?" Ben asked.

"For a run."

"It's dark."

"I won't be long," I said, hurrying out the door.

Every year since I could remember, the weather at Christmas was less than magical. It was either snowy, making traveling difficult, or cold, making shopping and errands unpleasant, or there was no snow, and in the upper Midwest, we looked forward to our white Christmas. This year, the weather had been perfect. Temperatures hovered around thirty, which meant the precipitation came as snow, falling in dustings that required no shoveling. The streets weren't sloppy, the lawns were white, and the temps meant you could linger.

I ran almost a block before the lights became streaks and the sobs took over. I stopped and bent over, letting the tears fall.

"Rough night?"

I straightened. Chris was at the end of his driveway, smoking. Normally, on a twenty-degree night I'd be wearing a winter coat, but I hadn't taken the time to put one on. Chris wasn't wearing a jacket either.

"I didn't see you," I explained as I wiped my face and wondered if he could run. He had at least six inches and a hundred-pound advantage on me.

"You're Dora's friend, aren't you?"

I took a step back. *How does he know me? Had he watched us talking from the window the day I saw her after praise band?*

"My husband is the pastor at her church," I said.

He took a drag off his cigarette and blew it away from me, nodding.

His calm produced the opposite effect in me. I thought of Lexie. *How awful to be so close to home and have no one know where you are.*

He said something that I hadn't heard. "Excuse me?"

"The tears. Eventually, you get numb," he replied.

"I'm hoping to avoid that—and temporary fixes," I mustered.

"Did you quit smoking, then?"

Goosebumps emerged across my neck and arms. "A couple times already."

"Yeah, me too."

"Meghan?" Ben called.

I exhaled my relief. "That's my husband."

"See you around," Chris said.

I turned and hurried to Ben.

"Everything okay?" he asked.

"I just want to get home."

As we neared the porch, I told Ben about Chris.

"He knew I smoked. I never smoke anywhere but next to the house. He's watched me. I can't remember the last time I was so terrified."

"Did he threaten you?"

"I don't think so. He was just there."

"That's probably how it happens," Ben suggested. "Some situation at home has a girl running straight into the arms of someone ready to take advantage of her."

Ben opened his office door. I slid my shoes off and slumped into an armchair. My heart was still racing and my limbs felt weak.

"We don't have to adopt Caleb," Ben assured me, leaning against the door, which he'd just locked.

"Of course we do. He thinks you're his dad. If we don't adopt him, who will?"

"Becky's parents might."

"That would be great. He can go back to falling asleep on the couch and sucking on a pacifier."

"Well, we don't have to adopt the baby."

"It may be our only chance to have a baby. You prayed for a baby, and God is providing—through Becky, of all people."

Ben crossed his arms. "Can we trust her?"

"Will she want the baby back in three years or four or eight? Or, what if they decide last minute not to go through with it and we're left with a nursery and broken hearts?"

"She knows what she's getting into," Ben said. "And Michael doesn't seem overly fond of children."

"He is a bit … sterile, isn't he?"

"He'll make a good surgical nurse."

"What if the baby has a birth defect or a predisposition to a disease? We don't know anything about his family."

"It's too much to think about."

I nodded my agreement.

"Let's go to bed," Ben decided.

I followed him upstairs.

Once in bed, I realized sleep would be a long ways off. I was hyperalert, hearing the creak of the furnace and the motor of the fridge, the ice as it dropped into the bucket.

When I finally drifted into sleep, I was being chased and held down. I woke in a sweat, realizing Becky was not the worst thing to happen to a person.

The ultrasound was at nine on Friday morning. The 7:30 alarm was a brutal and unpleasant intruder. There had been too many weeks of too little sleep and too much emotional drain. I stumbled to the shower while Ben and Caleb headed down for breakfast.

I took my time, hoping the hot water would somehow seep into my skin and praying God would give me strength for whatever the day would bring. Finally, I shook myself into action, remembering Ben still needed to shower and our twenty-gallon hot water heater was more miserly than generous. I was just stepping out of the shower when Ben opened the bathroom door.

"I know. I know. I've got to move. Can you shut the door? I'm freezing!"

"There's been an accident," Ben said, stepping in and shutting the door.

"What?"

"Scott called. Do you remember the Bentleys?"

"Of course. They led the battle march to get Pastor Larimer back after you admitted you had Caleb and, when he refused, promptly joined Resurrection."

"Their son Gabe was in a car accident last night. Scott went to the hospital to be with the family from three to five a.m."

"Is he going to make it?"

"He's got a pretty good head injury. I'm thinking we should drive two cars. I'd like to go to the hospital."

"Do you think that's a good idea?"

"They still live in Oronoco. I'll just let them know I'm praying."

"Why don't we both go? I can wait in the waiting room. If he's in serious condition, you probably can't stay long, anyway. Is Scott still okay with us bringing Caleb to their house while we go to the ultrasound?"

"Tonya's fine. She stayed home and slept."

I waited in the car while Ben delivered Caleb to Tonya.

"I told her we'd call before going to see Gabe," Ben reported, getting back in the car. "If it's not working with Caleb, you can drop me off at the hospital, get Caleb, and then come pick me up."

"I wonder what's going through the Bentleys' minds right now."

"Please God, don't let him die or have a permanent brain injury," Ben surmised.

"It puts a little different spin on the ultrasound."

Ben nodded. "As in, if the baby's healthy, just shut up?"

"And if it isn't, then that baby needs a family and love too."

He nodded.

I'm not sure who felt more uncomfortable about Becky's belly being bare, but there was enough discomfort to go around—and to make it hard to imagine Ben and I being present for the birth, even if we did adopt this child.

The tech pointed out the four chambers of the heart, the kidneys, ten toes, ten fingers, the three strands of the umbilical cord. When he had all the pictures he needed, he asked if we wanted to know the sex.

Becky affirmed that she did.

He moved his probe until he was content with its position and then froze the picture and announced, "It's a girl."

"You're sure?" Becky asked.

"Yes—99.9 percent," he said.

After thanking Becky for letting us be there, we left her to her doctor's appointment. Tonya assured us all was well, so we made our way to the visitor's parking ramp at the hospital several blocks away. At the information desk, they directed us to the seventh floor; the same ICU I had been in two months prior.

As we passed the waiting area, we saw Rebecca Bentley, Gabe's mom, surrounded by a crowd of what I assumed was family and close friends. When she saw us, she left her friends and came to us, wrapping her arms around me in a tight hug.

"Thank you for coming," she said.

Ben nodded.

"Rob is with Gabe," she said. "I'll take you to the room."

"Did you want me to stay here?" I asked.

"No. You can come."

She pressed the button and we went through first one set of double doors, then another.

Walking into the intensive care unit brought a surge of sadness. My dreams died the day I was here.

The unit was a semicircle of rooms huddling around a nurse's station abuzz with doctors and nurses and lab techs and a pharmacist, all hovering like paper wasps around a nest.

The nurse that dismissed me was one of the wasps. She recognized me at the same time I recognized her. I waved, and she came over as Rebecca ushered Ben into Gabe's room.

"How are you?" she asked, putting an arm around me.

I shrugged.

"I know, right? Changed forever."

"Yes. That's a perfect description."

"We see a lot of it up here."

"Surprising you keep coming back to work with all the sadness."

"The sadness will happen whether I'm here or not. I'd like to think I'm helping to relieve some of the hurt, even if just for the little bit that's in front of me."

"You guys were awesome."

"Do you know Gabe Bentley?"

"They went to our church."

She nodded. "I helped settle him when he came in."

"How's he doing?"

"He'll have a long road ahead of him, but most of our patients do."

That was good news. "A long road" was much different than "lucky if he makes it." I said my good-bye and made my way into Gabe's room.

Gabe was connected to a ventilator and had IVs coming out of both arms. His head was in a neck brace and swollen, at least two, maybe three times bigger than normal. His face was purplish gray.

Rob Bentley was sitting in a chair, holding Gabe's hand. He and Ben were already midconversation. Rebecca was on the other side of the bed, near the vent.

"You never want it to be you," Rob stated. "You never want to get the call or to sit here."

Ben nodded. "I told him you had been just around the corner," Ben said to me. He turned back to Rob. "Do you know what happened?"

"We know they rolled and they hit a tree. And we're pretty sure alcohol was involved. Other than that, there's a whole lot of who knows?" Rob said.

"What happened to the passenger?"

"He's a couple doors down. Gabe took the brunt of the impact with his head, and the other guy, Mark, got it in the legs. He's pretty smashed up. They're not sure what the likelihood is of him walking again."

Ben grimaced.

"They're taking Gabe to surgery within the hour to relieve pressure. They'll put in a drain and put him in a halo to keep his head in one position," Rebecca explained.

"We'll be praying," Ben said.

"We're so sorry about what happened to you," Rebecca said, looking at me. "John Higgins is one of our best friends."

John Higgins was the first responder who carried me out of the house. I still had a hard time looking him in the eye.

"We weren't there for you," Rebecca continued. "You lost your child."

Rob's eyes met Rebecca's, and tears fell down both their faces.

"I didn't see the people who were there," I managed. "Ben liaisoned. I was pretty much out of commission."

"We were too big for our britches," Rob said. "In some ways, I guess we thought you had it coming." His gaze was directed at Ben now.

"None of us could stand under God's judgment," Ben said. "In fact, I was hoping I could have a devotion with Gabe."

"We'd welcome that," Rob said.

Ben approached the bed and placed his hand on Gabe's shoulder.

"Gabe," Ben said, leaning over him. "It's Pastor Ben Martins. I met you a couple times. I took over for Pastor Larimer when he retired. I want to read to you from Mark Chapter 2."

He pulled out his tablet and read about the paralytic, brought by his friends and lowered through the roof to be put in front of Jesus. Jesus first forgave the man's sin and then healed him.

Ben put his tablet back in his pocket. "I read this to you today, Gabe, because I want you to know your sins are forgiven. We all make mistakes, but God meets us with his grace. I'm praying for God to heal you. That's important. But even more important is knowing you have peace with God."

A tear rolled down Gabe's face.

Rob pressed his hands around Gabe's while Rebecca quickly wiped Gabe's tears, only to soak his face with her own.

"I'm not sure you're doing a lot of good there," Rob said.

"I know," she cried, wiping her tears to keep them from falling on Gabe.

"We'll let you two be with him," Ben said. "We just wanted to stop by."

"Thank you," they both said.

"Come again," Rob added.

Ben shook his hand. "I will."

Once we were in the car, I called Tonya to let her know we were on the way.

"Do you want to just have lunch with us?" she asked. "It's nearly eleven anyway."

"We've put you out as it is."

"Nonsense," she said. "Caleb was great. He kept Elijah happy all morning. I've got meatloaf in the oven and potatoes on the stove, which is more than you've got ready."

"I can't argue with that."

"Good. It's settled. See you in a bit."

Caleb barely acknowledged us when we arrived. He and Elijah had built tracks and were weaving cars around the buildings they made with blocks. Elijah was fascinated with Caleb, and Caleb was in all his glory.

"I've never really seen him play with another child," I confessed, taking off my coat and joining Tonya in the kitchen. "Preschool must be working. When our friends brought their son for the weekend the end of August, Caleb didn't want anything to do with Max. He stayed by Ben the whole time."

"Well, I was pleasantly surprised," she said. "How was the ultrasound?"

"The baby's healthy, or so it appears. It's a girl."

"Really?"

I nodded.

"And?"

"It was amazing to be able to see everything."

She read my face. "Bittersweet."

I nodded again. "It would have been different if it was Ben and I having an ultrasound and seeing our baby. As it was, it was Becky, which was awkward. And we haven't given her a definite yes. We said we were interested enough to want to go to the ultrasound, but I think we're afraid to say yes because of all the 'what ifs.' Even if I was holding the baby and carrying it out of the hospital, I'd be afraid to call it mine."

"None of these children are really ours. We just get to take care of them."

"I know. I'm just slow to accept this as God's plan. My plan looked so different."

She carried the potatoes from the stove and dumped them in a colander in the sink. "It's hard not to get in the way of God's plans."

She gave the colander a shake before transferring the potatoes to a mixing bowl. Steam followed her. She plopped some butter and milk in before turning on the mixer.

"Do you want to round up the men? I'll get everything on the table."

Scott was using a downstairs bedroom for his office. I assumed the men were there.

From the hallway, I could hear Ben's voice.

"It took me off guard. I hadn't been attracted to her before."

"That's always the danger. Anytime you're around another woman, you have to be on your guard."

I stopped.

"And yet," Scott added, "it isn't as if we won't be around them."

I took a few steps back toward the steps, called for the men to come eat, and then went back up to help Tonya with the boys.

Chapter Thirteen

OUR DEPRAVITY MEETS HIS DIVINITY[2]

"You're quiet," Ben said on the way home. "Everything okay?"

I decided against answering with Caleb in the car.

Ben's habit was to check the answering machine immediately upon arriving home. Caleb's newest habit was to go to his room to play with the train set Becky and Michael gave him for an early Christmas present.

I had yet to develop a habit upon returning home. Other than hanging up coats and putting away shoes, I had nothing awaiting my attention. More often than not, the dishes were done; the laundry was put away. Usually, I was lucky to get an e-mail or two a day, and those were from businesses reminding me they still wanted my money. I made a point of waiting until Caleb was asleep to turn Netflix on, and though it was fun to daydream

---

[2] "When our depravity meets his divinity it is a beautiful collision."— David Crowder

that Dr. Spencer Reid, the young but brilliant FBI agent from *Criminal Minds*, anticipated my return each evening, the truth was less optimistic.

My lack of a habit was metaphorical of my life, I decided as I trudged the stairs to sit at my desk. *Lost. That's what I am. Untitled. Not Dr. Meghan Martins or FBI Agent Meghan Martins or super-important, though dead, Police Chief Jane Allen. Not even stay-at-home mom. Just Pastor Ben Martin's wife, stepmom, freelancer. Freelancer* sounded painfully similar to *freeloader.*

Ben's desk screamed of a body that couldn't keep up with the creative portals of a mind. The only sign of occupation on my desk was the wedding picture of Ben and I framed in sterling silver roses. That and the stack of cards people brought to us after my surgery.

"What are you doing?" Ben asked, no doubt sufficiently filled with messages of people wanting to keep him in the know or needing advice. He stood in the doorway, his arm raised to the trim opposite of where he was standing, as if he was holding it all together.

"Reading these," I said, holding one up. It was the first one, and the envelope was still sealed.

"Is something wrong?" he asked.

"What makes you think that?"

"I may be ruggedly attractive—"

"Slightly arrogant."

"Musically inclined—"

"Obsessed."

"A decent preacher—"

"So-so."

"But if there's one thing I've always stunk at, it was reading minds. Thanks to intense therapy and friends who point out the obvious, I have come to note that you ignore me and/or lash out when you are ticked off. That and the fact that unless you have X-ray vision, it would be impossible for you to be reading those cards, leads me to the conclusion that something is, in fact, wrong."

"When I came downstairs to tell you lunch was ready, I heard you saying that you were attracted to someone."

"Ah."

"Were you talking about Becky?"

"No."

"Then who?"

"It isn't a sin to be attracted to someone. Some women put a lot of time into making themselves attractive to men. To notice that is not a problem. What you do with that determines if there is a problem."

"So it's not a problem?"

"Not a problem, especially when I'm admitting it to Scott."

"It's just that you didn't say, 'She's attractive.' You said, 'I'm attracted to her.' There's a difference. You can be attracted to someone who isn't all that attractive if your personalities match. Sometimes, that's a harder bond to break."

"Scott's my mentor and accountability partner. The idea is to be open about these things and to realize it and pray about it, to be held accountable."

"What is it that you find attractive? Her hair? Her chest?"

"I am not a fan of a big chest."

"Said no guy ever."

"Have you seen an older woman with big boobs that weren't halfway to her belly button?" He grimaced. "I'm happily thinking that won't be an issue with you."

"That's comforting."

"Dad, can I watch a movie?"

Ben turned to Caleb and released his grip on the doorframe. "Go for it, bud."

Caleb skipped down the stairs.

"Forget it, Meghan. I knew for months you were struggling with an attraction to Jeff, and I didn't make it into a big deal. I prayed for us. Give me the same benefit."

"Is it someone in our church?"

"Meghan, let it go."

I sighed.

"What did you think of the ultrasound?"

"I don't know. It was beautiful and awkward."

Ben nodded. "On the one hand, God's all but handing us what appears to be a perfect baby girl."

"And on the other hand, it's Becky's baby girl."

He agreed.

"Everyone complains about pregnancy. Maybe I'm the lucky one getting a child without all the side effects."

"I wonder how many people think we're the lucky ones?"

"According to my mom, quite a few. You have a job you feel called to do and a wife who has stood by you to take care of you and everything around the house so that you don't have to concern yourself with when the bills are due or if you have enough money in the bank, or with what is for supper."

"And you have a husband who lets you run off to investigate murders and meet people for tea whenever you want and rescues you from crazy men in the street in the middle of the night."

"I'm thankful for that."

"It's not all bad, Meg."

"No. It isn't."

So why does it feel like it's not all good either?

"Lexie's been waiting to go on a double date," I reminded him as I remembered.

Ben crumpled his face like he had just asked for a cookie and I gave him a piece of blue cheese. "Why does that not seem appealing?"

"Greg might end up being your best friend. He's the detective who helped rescue Lexie from the sex traffickers."

"At least he's had a background check."

"That's what he said."

Ben smirked. "Okay. You read these cards and I'll go on your double date."

It was my turn to take the stinky cheese. "Ben—"

"We could go through them together."

"Or we could poke an eye out or stab ourselves with forks or, I don't know, go swimming in the icy Zumbro River."

"Are you afraid to feel the emotions these might bring to the surface?" Ben asked.

"I've never hurt like in the days after my surgery," I confessed.

"If you keep burying it, Meghan, it's going to keep resurfacing, but when it does, it will get uglier. The lashing out, avoiding people with kids, it never makes you feel better. Somehow, we have to start dealing with it and accepting it."

"If I really let myself feel, then I may not be able to pick myself off the floor."

"I'm okay with you not being able to function if it means dealing with it. I've cried in my office. One night, I punched the couch."

"Why the couch?"

"I didn't want to break my hand or wreck anything, but I needed to punch something. I walked out of my office and there it was. Easy target. The point is that I am going through the stages of grief, but I think you're stuck in denial. You block out people like Tonya and talk about anything but what happened."

"What's there to talk about? Nothing we say changes anything."

"Can't we admit it hurts?"

"Maybe I don't need to go through the stages. And is it so hard to imagine me having a hard time seeing Tonya? She's showing. It's a constant reminder that she has what I don't."

"By not letting her in, you aren't being a very good friend to her. She wants to help."

"She has lots of friends. And what if I am stuck? Are you somehow better for sailing through the stages of grief? Congratulations! You're an overachiever, and I am ... nothing."

Ben's tone softened. "What were you before you got pregnant?"

"I was the person who couldn't wait to get pregnant, Ben."

"That was the basis of all your future happiness? What if I would have been sterile and we only found out after three or four years of unsuccessful trying? Would I be nothing because I was unable to reproduce?"

"Ben, you don't understand."

"No, Meghan, I do. Before the surgery, you didn't feel like you were less of a woman because you didn't have children. There's no reason you should think you're less of one now. You were important and valuable then, and nothing has changed. The sooner you figure that out, the sooner we can get on with life."

Ben's words reminded me of what my dad used to call "point of reference." When I complained about something, he'd tell me that was *my* point of reference, *my* perspective. Many times, he was able to show me where the other person involved was coming from. Maybe Mom wasn't so out of line asking me to do something, or maybe a friend had said this because of this, or maybe my boss was looking for one thing, which is why he was less than pleased when I did something else.

For the past four months, my point of reference was that I had been wronged by Ben, by life, by God. For the most part, I was unconcerned with the weight Ben carried, because he didn't burden me with the weight. When he was in the pit of despair, I was quick to show him how his sins could have contributed, but ruminating on my iniquities and how they may have added to the mess I was in was not helping me. I was fed up with Ben when he took a week to come to grips with the deception and ramifications of being wronged, even when his silence spared me the complaints and bemoanings of his tortured soul. Now I was angry with him for moving on, but bitter because of my own paralysis.

I didn't want to sink back to where it hurt to breathe and open my eyes, but I loathed every happy thought, because to be happy meant I was not mourning, and I wanted, needed to mourn, not just a baby, but my future. My point of reference was that I needed to mourn alone. Well-wishers could say they understood or could try to understand, but my pain was my pain, and they couldn't feel my pain. They didn't know my ache. Maybe it was just a baby to them, but to me, it was everything, and if they didn't understand that, then they couldn't understand anything.

That is why I hadn't opened the cards. What could anyone say to comfort me? I imagined nothing but shallow words and empty promises, or worse, the mostly benign-sounding but deep-cutting words of Job's friends. Didn't we all want to let Job scrape his wounds in the dust by himself?

Ben's ultimatum was for me to read the cards and he'd go on the date.

Oh, Lexie, if you knew the lengths I've gone to for you.

There were seventy-six cards. I divided them into seven piles of ten and one pile of six—stacks I deemed tolerable. After a deep breath, I grabbed the first card off the first pile. It was a reminder that Jesus was with us even now. Signed prayers and hugs. Not horrid. The second card was "thinking of you with prayers for peace in this difficult time." Signed: "I've cried so much since I heard the news. So very sorry for your loss. From Will and Diane Lapper."

Will was the president of the congregation. He let Ben and me into the house when we first arrived into town. Our first and only time at The Strange Brew, Will had come in to get a coffee on his way into town to buy more patio pavers. His wife had bought a patio set that was too big for the patio, so Will was going to add three feet to each side. "Sort of like buying a couch and deciding to add on to the living room," he added. "These are the crazy things retired people do."

The third card was from Dora, and the card itself was blank, but her writing filled both sides of the inside of the card, telling of how I'd been such a good friend to her in the few months we'd known each other and how my concern for her had made a difference in her life. She hoped she'd be able to be so caring to others. She ended her card with: "You and Pastor Martins are such beautiful people. I know God must have something really amazing planned to work this out for your good."

Three cards. Each felt like a hug, not a jab, from the sender. Three cards that made me eager to open more.

"So?" Ben asked when he came back upstairs.

I had moved to the bed and surrounded myself with the cards.

"You should read these," I said. "They're amazing, all of them."

Ben raised his eyebrows. "You didn't know so many people cared so much, did you?"

"Did you?"

"I see and hear from people every day."

"Then why didn't you say something?"

He frowned. "I guess it kept slipping my mind."

"You know, Ben, I think we're just different. When something huge happens to you, you shut down and deal with it until you come to terms with it. That was my plan when I got home from the hospital, but my mom put the kibosh on it."

"The difference being that you wanted to die."

"Well, yeah."

"I don't mind how you handle it as long as you aren't getting bitter and hurting other people in the process. God decided to give Tonya a biological child. That's not her fault."

"I've always thought Old Testament Rachel, Jacob's wife, could have stepped up and been the bigger person. Instead of fighting and moaning and being jealous and having her husband sleep with other people, I've thought she should look at all the good; you know, like being beautiful and being loved."

"You're beautiful and you're loved."

"But now I know the other: the pain and the hurt. It's not so easy to just love and look at the bright side."

"It's impossible, Meg, if you do it alone. If you let us in, we'll help you."

January announced its arrival with viciously cold temperatures and notable snowfalls, which left homeowners aware of the dimensions of their drives and the muscles in their back.

Ben shoveled once, but the snowflakes were relentless when we left to pick Lexie up at her house and drop Caleb and a fresh batch of vegetarian chili off with Nora and Dora. Greg met us inside the double doors of La Casa Fiesta. He offered a hand to Ben.

"I'm guessing you're Pastor Martins. Nice to meet you."

"Call me Ben."

He shook my hand next and gave a nod and smile to Lexie. The hostess took us to a table.

Greg helped Lexie out of her coat before taking off his black waist-length matted wool jacket. His slender frame reminded me of Professor Ambrose, though his handshake had been more firm and Greg was clean shaven. He wore a gray turtleneck and a darker gray zip-up sweater. Nothing about him seemed detective-like to me, and I mentally wondered what I needed from him. *Glasses? A stern look? Maybe a pipe. Yes, that would help.*

Lexie, too, seemed out of character. Not only were her fingernails au naturel, but her clothing and makeup were more muted too.

I grabbed her hand to examine her nails. "Were they booked solid, with the holidays?"

She shook her head. "I set my nails free. They haven't seen the sun in a few years. It's time."

"Free at last?"

"Something like that. I finally know there's more to life."

"So they're gone forever God of love?"

"It's Thine Forever God of Love," Ben corrected without looking up from his menu.

"Are you Lutheran, Greg?" I asked. "Or is that reference lost on you?"

"I was baptized Catholic, went to a Missouri synod grade school, and, in recent years, have attended a Baptist church. And no, the reference wasn't lost or even misplaced."

As far as I was concerned, Lexie could set a wedding date.

"Where did you grow up?" Ben asked. "Rochester has plenty of Catholic schools."

"My parents had a falling out with the Catholic Church."

"A lot of people left because of the scandals. Tradition is such a part of the church, especially for Catholics," Ben noted. "When they get the feeling their tradition was betrayed or hypocritical, they become disheartened."

Greg nodded. "I always got the feeling—"

Knowing they would be occupied, I took the opportunity to talk to Lexie.

"This whole thing has thrown you for a loop, hasn't it?"

"I understand you better. Changed forever. Did you decide what you are going to do about the baby? Are you going to adopt?"

"We've decided to do it. It's not the time I would have chosen, because our baby would have been born just a month after she's due, but there's nothing I can do about that."

"I think when you look back, you'll find it was the perfect time. I suspect the baby will bring a lot of healing."

I shrugged. "I hope."

"Are you going to decorate the nursery?"

"I still have a hard time believing Becky will go through with it. If she changes her mind, it would feel like going through the hysterectomy all over again."

"That won't happen. She knows what she's doing."

"She's married now though. It's not like with Caleb."

"When did she get married?"

"They had a New Year's Eve wedding. Won't he want to raise the baby when he sees it?"

"He knows you guys will do a good job, and you'll still be in their life. If they want to see her, they'll come see her."

"What if they want to take her to the Mall of America and they don't watch her the way I do?"

"You ask to go along to help. You're overthinking this."

"Am I?"

"I subscribe to the 'don't worry till there's something to worry about' camp."

"I'm more of the 'don't tell them what they have to worry about, and pray they don't find out till after it's done' camp," Greg volunteered.

"I noticed," Lexie said with a smirk.

"Hey, guys, I'm Dave, and I'll be your server. Is it a special occasion tonight?"

"First date," Greg answered.

Dave pointed to Greg and then Ben.

Greg shook his head again and pointed to Lexie.

"My bad," Dave said.

"There's a first time for everything," Ben announced when Dave walked away.

"I get it all the time," Greg announced.

"You do?" I asked.

"I'm not one to hang out at the bars, and I'm not egotistical, so assumptions are made."

"I've gotten that too," Lexie added. "One of the many blessings of prolonged singleness."

"I've been meaning to ask about Jane," I remembered.

"Jane?" Greg asked.

"Super-important Police Chief Jane Austen," I reminded him.

"Allen," Lexie corrected.

"Hm?"

"Jane Austen is the novelist. Jane Allen was the police chief."

"I'm not sure I understand how she tied into the whole Jake thing."

"The People's Food Co-op is fairly new to that location, and with a baby on the way, Jane became interested in organic and health food. All Jake knew is her presence put his way of life in jeopardy."

"How did he know what she did?" I asked.

"Jane wasn't one to slip in and out of a place without being noticed. She liked to talk, and she loved her coffee."

"Kind of like you," Lexie pointed out. "I can go in and out of The Strange Brew without saying anything but my order. You stop to talk to the post lady and in five minutes know where she lives, that she dyes her hair, and what she eats for lunch."

"Unlike me, she worked during the day," I pointed out. "I have time to jabber."

"The Government Center is a couple blocks from The People's Food Co-op and was her choice for coffee. It's where she went every day and sometimes even twice a day," Greg explained.

"He did make good coffee. In fact, I went back for a mocha after he drugged you the first time."

"You did?" Lexie squealed.

"What!" Ben screeched.

"The guy made good drinks."

"Thank God you didn't blow the case," Greg murmured.

"What did you say to him?" Lexie asked.

"I ordered and told him I was new to the world of whole foods and non-GMOs, and we talked about the evils of eating poor food."

"You talked groceries with the guy who drugged me and would later take me to be sold to traffickers?" Lexie accused.

"Lexie," Greg offered, "it put him at ease. It's why he tried again. It's why he's in jail now and those women are free."

"I'm with Lexie, Meg. Why would you go back knowing what he'd done?" Ben accused.

"Because it was the best drink she'd ever had," Lexie said. "Some women are bought with wine. Meghan, she's after the right combination of chocolate and espresso."

"It was the first thing—the only thing, really—that tasted good after losing the baby," I reported.

Lexie softened. "I'm sorry."

"I still don't understand," I said, slipping away from the baby conversation. "How did Jake kill Jane? It was night. The Food Co-op wasn't open."

"Jane had met friends at Twigs the night she died."

"Twigs?" Ben asked.

"It's a restaurant two blocks from the co-op. She parked in the co-op parking lot, a decent place to park on a Friday night. She probably never saw the blow coming."

I shook my head. "Jake really did it, huh?"

"He moved here six months ago from Austin, Minnesota. While he was there, four women disappeared. Two of them were found in the Saint Paul rescue."

"Where are the other two?" Lexie asked.

"Typically, sex traffickers move their victims to keep from being detected. The other two could be in Miami or New Orleans, Seattle," Greg offered.

"What a shame for the families," I said.

"Two families have restoration," Ben offered.

"That's the way you have to look at it," Greg admitted. "It's too depressing to focus on the failures."

"In life in general," I added. "I think they should have Jake serve as a full-time coffee maker for community service."

"It might be hard making coffee with handcuffs on," Greg pointed out.

"It's too bad. Mophead really could have had a future in coffee."

Amanda called twice during our meal. Both times, I rejected the call. When she called Ben, he excused himself to answer.

"Everything okay?" I asked when he returned, knowing, of course, that it wasn't.

Ben nodded. "They're fine."

Ben stopped at Nora's for Caleb, and then we dropped Lexie off and headed home. Once Caleb was tucked in, Ben followed me to the bedroom and shut the door.

"Do I need to sit down?" I asked.

"Matt started feeling off while they were eating supper. Amanda had to call an ambulance."

"Is he okay?"

"She's pretty convinced he's using drugs. She said she is leaving him."

"She's been saying that for a while."

"I think she meant it this time."

"They'd be the first of our friends to get a divorce."

"Let's pray it doesn't come to that."

Ben shoveled while I called Amanda. She was unyielding. If the incident was related in any way to drugs, she was filing for divorce.

I listened, remembering the time not that long ago when I, too, was ready to sign the papers and give in, when I wanted nothing to do with being Ben's wife.

Ben sat on the bed and took a drink of his coffee. Was it the jostling of the bed or the acidic aroma that roused me to consciousness?

"What time is it?" I asked, not yet ready to open my eyes.

"Almost eight."

In fifth grade, I made it to the spelling bee finals. Standing in front of the whole school, I heard my word (*rough*), hesitated, then spelled "*R-U-F-F.*" A very kind classmate announced my mistake by barking one high-pitched, "Ruff."

The first waking moment of every day brought the same expectancy, hesitation, and disappointment. Nothing had changed. I was still childless and incapable of producing, carrying, or bringing a child into the world.

"I texted Amanda. There weren't any drugs in his system," Ben began.

"Then what happened?"

"He was going through withdrawal."

"He was trying to quit?"

Ben nodded. "His body can't function without alcohol. He needs to taper down slowly. He's been transferred to inpatient treatment."

"That's good, right?"

"Very."

"I'll have to call her."

"Maybe you should go see her."

"How's the weather?"

"It quit snowing by midnight."

"I suppose I could take Caleb. He might get used to Max. I could probably stay with my parents for a couple days."

Ben nodded.

"Are you trying to get rid of me?"

"No, but I think if Matt and Amanda are going to make it, they're going to need help. I can't leave today, with church tomorrow. Matt's going to be in treatment for a while, and he can't have visitors the first week, so there's not much use in me going now. You, on the other hand, could be a huge help to Amanda."

"I'll start packing."

"I'll make you breakfast. Want eggs?"

"Not so much. Now, a cup of Linda's turtle mocha ..."

"The car needs gas anyway."

Chapter Fourteen

WHERE THE HEALING BEGINS

I knocked on the door, remembering how much I hated the knocks that came in the hours and days after I returned home from the hospital.

Amanda answered wearing pajama bottoms, a T-shirt, and a red bandana.

"Goodness. Looks like I arrived just in time."

"Are you going to go Mary Poppins on me?"

"Likely, yes," I said, handing her a skinny vanilla mocha. Thanks to all that memorizing at a Christian day school as a child, I remembered things like what Amanda asked for in September when I ran into the Caribou to get our drinks before heading to the park.

I prayed Caleb would fraternize with Max or Abby— or both—so Amanda and I would have time to ourselves. As I stepped in and waved Caleb to follow, I realized I was stepping into much more than I anticipated.

The entry was strewn with shoes and boots— haphazardly misled from across the room shoes. The coats, Amanda's and the kids, were dropped where they'd been shed.

"Where would you like our coats?" I asked.

She opened the closet and pointed to the hangers. I hung the coats, refusing to gawk at the packages, tightly packed shopping bags, and boxes with shipping tags, all unopened and stacked methodically from the floor to where the shelf ran across three-fourths of the way up.

She led us to the living room and invited us to sit. I moved a bowl with soggy cereal and milk onto a stack of books on the coffee table, brushed a pile of magazines to the side, and took a seat. Caleb stood silently surveying the room. My silent prayers were answered as he maneuvered around the piles of toys to the corner where Max lay on the floor running cars up and down a track.

My sympathy shifted from Amanda to Matt. I'm not sure I ever craved an alcoholic beverage, but sitting in the tumult of a therapy shopper's hoarding den mingled with the disorder of a woman who had long given up housekeeping, my turtle mocha with one shot of espresso didn't seem adequate.

"What can I do?" I asked.

My voice caused Abby to emerge from behind a recliner. Upon realizing a stranger had entered the room, she made a dash to Amanda. Amanda scooped her into her lap and rested against the back of the chair.

"It's overwhelming," Amanda admitted. "I've had most of the night and morning to think about how we got here and where we need to go. I don't know how to get out."

"Matt's where he needs to be, isn't he?"

"I suppose."

"How long will he be there?"

"At least thirty days."

Thirty days would be more than enough time to clean a house that was mildly cluttered. Thirty days in this house, assuming the rest of the house resembled the bit that I'd seen, wouldn't be enough for one person, especially when that one person had two other people to care for.

"He's gotten so he goes to work, comes home, eats supper, and goes downstairs till it's time for bed."

"Maybe he doesn't know how to deal with everything, Amanda."

"I don't know how to deal with it, Meghan."

"I will help you. We can start by returning the unopened packages. Then we can make piles to sell at consignment or on Craigslist."

She smiled, but her face conveyed something else, something I couldn't interpret. "I better get dressed."

She held Abby and carefully made her way down the hall. I heard first one door and then another close. I sipped my mocha and wondered how long I should stay. Caleb's preschool started again next week, but if he missed a week, it wouldn't be the end of the world. There was no way I could take him home and return on my own, even if it would be easier without him. Ben alone in the house would be enough of an ordeal to deal with. Ben and Caleb alone in the house for any amount of time and I may come back to a house looking much the same as Amanda's. I shuddered at the thought.

Abby's cries roused me to reality. She banged on a door. Amanda must have taken her into the room with her and she was looking for a quick escape. After Abby's cries turned frantic, I went to find out.

Abby's voice led me to a door, which, when opened, revealed a room with pink walls, a crib, a changing table, and more books and clothes than three children could use. *Why would Amanda shut Abby in her room?*

Max's room was across the hall, door open. The door at the end of the hall was closed.

When I tried to pick Abby up, she screamed, so I left her to an open door, content she could find her way to Max.

I knocked on the door to the room at the end of the hall. "Amanda?"

No answer.

Then I understood the smile. It was my smile when Mom came in the bedroom hours after I'd collapsed in the bathroom. It was the smile of a person thinking, *Say whatever you want, because hopefully, I won't be here long.*

The doorknob was the same as my parents'. The circular hole in the middle of the knob was the key to getting in. I raced to my purse and grabbed a pen, disassembled it and, taking the ink cartridge, made my way back to the door, passing Abby in the hall.

Amanda was on the bed with her hands folded across her lap. The pill bottle on the nightstand was open and empty, and she had earplugs in. The room was cluttered with piles of papers and clothes and books and boxes.

I picked up the pill bottle. "How many did you take?"

"All of them."

I scanned the label. Fifty tablets were refilled the day before.

Five minutes was not long enough to die, but I didn't know how long I had. I raced to my phone.

"911. What is your emergency?"

"My friend just overdosed."

"Do you know what she took?"

"The pill bottle says *A-m-i-t-r-i-p-t-y-l-i-n-e*."

"I'm sending an ambulance."

Abby was standing next to the couch. I cleared a circle from beneath her, so if she fell, she wouldn't get hurt. Max and Caleb were still playing cars.

I ran back to the room.

"Amanda, I know how you feel."

"I've been in your house, Meghan. It's neat as a pin."

"Because I have nothing else to do! I'm barely working, Amanda. The apartment in Milwaukee was rarely clean."

"Everyone would be better off if I was gone."

"Your kids wouldn't."

"You can raise my kids. You'd do a good job."

"Matt wouldn't want that."

"He'd be fine seeing them a couple days a month."

"He was drinking before, Amanda."

"Even if I were to start cleaning today, it would take a year to get through it all."

"I'm in your house, Amanda. Do you honestly think I'm going to sit by while you go to sleep?"

"I was hoping."

I ran back to check on the kids, who were still safely playing in the living room.

"Max, where does your mom keep her purse?" I asked, trying to stay calm.

"In the kitchen," he said, "by the garage door."

I found her phone and scrolled through the contacts. There was only one Tammy, thank the Lord.

"Hello," she said.

"Is this Matt's mom?"

"Yes."

"Amanda overdosed. I called an ambulance."

"Who is this?"

"Meghan Martins. Ben's wife."

"Dear God," she exclaimed. "We'll be right there."

Matt's parents arrived shortly after the ambulance. I had moved the children to the basement and put a movie on to shield them from what was happening.

"I'll have to stay with the kids," Tammy said. "Abby won't go to anyone."

"I noticed. Max held her hand and helped her down the stairs. She cries if I come in her general direction." I sighed. "I'll take Caleb to my parents. Then I can go to the hospital."

"We should let her mom know," Matt's dad suggested.

"Her phone is on the kitchen counter. I'm sure she's in the contacts."

Matt's dad nodded. "We got the call last night."

"I'm sorry," I said.

He shrugged. "What do you do?"

The nurse at the admissions desk in the ER told me to have a seat and she'd get me when I was able to see Amanda. I went past the row of chairs to the hallway and dialed Ben.

"How's it going?" he asked.

"The good news is Amanda waited till I was in the house to try to commit suicide. The bad news is that it's much worse than I could have imagined."

"What?"

"I wish I was making this up."

I relayed, as tactfully as I could, the scenario I'd walked into.

"What can I do?"

"Nothing. You're needed there. Just pray."

When a volunteer finally led me to the room, Amanda had a tube coming out of her nose. It looked to be filled with large granules of black pepper. She was sitting up on a cart.

"I'm having charcoal. I'd offer you some, but—"

"Is that what that is?"

She grimaced.

"Can you taste it?"

She shook her head.

"You didn't have to do this, Amanda. I came to help. I was in your house."

"Meghan, you can't begin to scratch the surface of where Matt and I are."

"Don't you think I know? I've run away from home. I've wanted to die. I've put on all the masks, pretending I'm okay and doing well and even happy. I've avoided my pregnant friend."

"When they told Matt he was going to inpatient, I was jealous."

"You don't have to do it alone. We've had counseling, remember? Poor Pastor Gibbons heard a lot. I've had more than a few coffee dates, too, with friends who listen to what I'm going though and offer their advice."

"I don't have friends."

"I guarantee there are women at the church who would be great encouragers. You just have to step out of your comfort zone and get to know them."

"You're probably right."

"Why does everyone always say I'm 'probably right,' but when it comes to Ben, he's right?"

"Don't delete Pastor Gibbon's number."

I laughed. "For a week, I called him three to four times a day. He was probably tempted to turn his phone off."

"I think Matt does that to me."

"Another reason you need women friends. We love to talk."

"If I got the house cleaned, I could have another mom over, someone who has children the same age as Max and Abby."

"It doesn't need to be perfect. There are people who can overlook a mess. True friends can see the worst in us and like us anyway."

"Sometimes it's hard not to hate you when you're so positive."

"I'm not always positive, Amanda. Some days I can barely put one foot in front of the other. Hate me or not, you just need to take one step at a time."

Linda made the turtle mochas to our individual specifications and we moseyed to the cushy blue chairs.

"Can you imagine if Linda closed the coffee shop?" I whispered.

"She wouldn't do that," Lexie replied casually, unconcerned.

"How do you know? There are never many people in here."

"You're lucky if you can get in the door on a Saturday morning. Anyway, this is how small towns operate. When Linda opened the place, she knew she had a small pool of people to serve, but they're committed, and until something changes, so is she."

"Now that Mophead is gone, I really don't have anything to fall back on."

"There's always Caribou."

I shrugged. It just wasn't the same. Linda and Mophead ruined me. How could I bet five dollars on someone who may or may not be able to make a decent cup of tea or turtle mocha?

"You're an addict. You realize that, right?" Lexie pointed out.

"Me, an addict? Please."

"It's true," Lexie said, gingerly taking a sip of the scalding mocha. "Once you're expending energy working on a backup, it's taken hold of you. For years, I was like that with food."

"You've lost weight," I noticed.

"Greg is not one to sit and watch a movie. He'd prefer to hike or go ice fishing or—"

"You're ice fishing? Doesn't that entail sitting on an overturned bucket in the cold, dangling a rod for endless hours?"

"These days, people have shacks. Said places keep one sheltered from the cold. Greg's is particularly clean and warm."

"You're ice fishing." I said it to convince myself. "What else does he have you doing?"

"Downhill skiing. I'm struggling with the moguls on the black diamonds, but overall, I'm doing pretty well, considering I've only been doing it a month."

"Has it been a month already?"

She nodded. "Our first date was just after New Year's, remember?"

"Going to Wisconsin on the weekends has got me discombobulated."

"How is your friend?"

"It's coming. Every weekend, we choose a room and sort everything into piles. It's her job to deal with the piles before I return. I don't think she's stashing it in the garage, but I guess I'll find out when we get to the garage."

"It was pretty bad, huh?"

I cuddled my cup. "I'm sure there's worse."

"Is her husband home?"

"Just home. Ben's coming this week to see him. We leave tomorrow and come home Saturday."

"Good. You'll finally be back in church."

"That's what Ben said. People are probably starting to wonder."

"Greg is coming to church on Sunday. Do you and Ben want to come over afterward for brunch? Caleb, too, of course."

"Holy domesticated, Batman. Lexie Felps is having brunch. We wouldn't miss it."

I'm not sure what I expected. To me, "treatment" may or may not include electric shock therapy or other *One Flew Over the Cuckoo's Nest* behavior adjustments.

When Matt greeted us, he was not sedated, drooling, or peering at us with glazed eyes; in fact, he was bright-eyed and, after an initial slightly embarrassed smile, he welcomed us with a warmth I hadn't seen from him in a while.

Amanda hurried to the door just as I finished hugging Matt.

"You are Matt's new favorite person in the world," she told me.

"It's true," Matt said. "If I had known how much you two could get done, I'd have left a long time ago."

"All you had to do is ask."

Ben shook Matt's hand. "You're looking good."

"Feeling good too. I should see a lot of changes over the next months and even year."

"Year?" I contended.

"It will take his body time to heal," Amanda explained.

She ushered us in and motioned for us to sit on the couch. Caleb, Max, and Abby found their way to the toys, now that they were accustomed to each other. Thanks to the living room being the room where Amanda and I had started, we had places to sit.

"One of things I learned in treatment is the importance of making amends," Matt began.

"Isn't that a step?" Ben asked.

"Admitting our wrongs is number five; making amends is step nine. I can't begin to tell you how awful I feel about what I've done to you."

Ben raised his eyebrows. "I have to tell you, Matt. There have been times I could strangle you and not feel bad about it."

"That's why I never told you," Matt said. "Loyalty and integrity are big in your book."

"I've tried to imagine the shoe on the other foot," Ben said. "I can't fathom sleeping with my best friend's girlfriend."

"I'm with you, Ben. I can't relate to Meghan's feelings for Jeff," Amanda noted. "Once he'd slept with my friend, I'd have been done with him."

"Hold on, you two," I interjected. "That may be true, but I can't imagine keeping the secrets Ben's kept the past five years."

"And I know you don't understand the problem I have keeping house," Amanda admitted.

I nodded. "We all have different weaknesses."

"But do you think about sleeping with Meghan?" Ben asked Matt.

I looked at Ben in astonishment.

"What?" Ben replied. "If he slept with Becky—"

"That was before I knew Amanda," Matt explained. "Anyway, Amanda, you're not totally innocent. You've always thought Ben was hot."

Amanda reddened. "It's true."

"And it seems to me Ben's struggled with finding another woman attractive," I added.

Now it was Ben's turn to color.

"Not that I have anything to brag about," I declared. "I turned my affection from Jeff to cigarettes, from one bad choice to another."

Amanda glared at Matt. "That's the next thing that has to go."

"You just worry about the house," Matt retorted.

"I don't envy you," I said to Matt. "Oh, man, was it hard to quit smoking, and I'd only done it for a few months."

"Most people struggle with the physical addiction," Ben explained. "Meghan had to get rid of her friends."

"I had an emotional connection right up until I realized our freaky neighbor a block away could see me when I smoked."

"You never told me that," Amanda chided.

"Didn't I? It was the night Michael and Becky asked us to adopt." I looked at Caleb and lowered my voice. "I was going to go for a run. I made it a block before I was crying too hard to see. Chris was smoking in front of his house. He asked if I'd quit. I never smoked anywhere but between our garage and our house, except for once when I was on the porch with Ben. He must have been able to see me from his driveway."

"It cured her. She hasn't smoked since," Ben noted.

I decided against revealing how Ben knew. Obviously, he'd been to the crockpot.

"That's a blessing in disguise," Amanda said.

"I'm not sure what else would have done it," I confessed.

"If I hadn't felt like I was dying, I wouldn't have gone to treatment. I thought I could do it on my own," Matt offered. "Even though I'd tried and failed several times."

"I'd obviously had the chance to fess up to Meg a million times," Ben admitted.

"God knows what it takes for each of us," Amanda decided. "Thankfully, it's all out, and we can pick up the pieces."

I hoped it was all out. The way the year was going, I was afraid to make that assumption.

Ben decided we would stay at the farm with his parents. I had seen my parents a lot in the last month, as Caleb and I stayed with them each time we came to help Amanda clean.

I wanted the farm to be what it had been to me, but my feelings were much like Ben's toward Matt: oscillating between a willingness to trust again and forgive and the deep-seeded anger, hurt, and resentment Ed and Millie's actions had caused.

The smell of Millie's sweet-and-sour meatballs met us as we ambled through the porch. That and her mashed potatoes and homemade Amish bread had me mentally singing, "Comfort, comfort all my people." Her green beans were not the slightest bit soggy, and they were seasoned perfectly. Caleb cleaned his plate and asked for more.

Millie's food had always been a highlight, but this time, I despised her for it. Then I hated myself for feeling that way. Ben could hate Matt for a couple decades. I could hate Millie. Or we could accept their apologies and get on with life.

Ben and Ed talked about the land, the cattle, the machinery. When Ben heard the loader had been stalling, he insisted he and Ed go out to look at it, so once the plates were cleared, Ben, Caleb, and Ed headed to the shed.

"How are Matt and Amanda doing?" Millie asked when Ben left.

It always surprised me how much Ben shared with his mom.

"I think they're in a good place. They've confronted their problems and seem to be dealing with them, so that's a good thing. It's good Max and Abby are so young. Hopefully, they won't have any recollection of this."

Millie nodded. "Ed quit drinking when Ben was five. I don't think Ben remembers much if anything."

"Ed drank?"

"Heavily. It wasn't until I needed him to take me to the hospital when I was in labor with Katie and he couldn't that he finally figured out he had a problem."

"How did you get to the hospital?"

"Ed's mom dropped me off and then came back and got him up out of his stupor. Don't ask me how, because I tried."

"So he was there when Katie was born?"

"Oh, yes. He wasn't feeling too good, and I wasn't very happy with him, but he was there, and it was the last time he drank like that."

"I've never been around alcohol much. My parents never drank, that I know of."

"If you've ever been in a situation where you had to watch or live with someone who abused it, it isn't too hard to give it up."

"Did Ben tell you he got drunk when we were in Port Washington?"

Surprisingly, she shook her head.

"He met some friends from the seminary. I knew nothing about it until they drove him home."

"I'm glad they did."

"I wouldn't want to deal with that on a regular basis. I hope Matt can stay away from it now too. I think a lot of it was guilt over sleeping with Becky and not being able to cope with Amanda's mess."

"I get the feeling Ben is having a hard time forgiving Matt."

"He's having a hard time forgiving Becky and Matt. And yet he expected me to forgive him. I don't understand that."

"The motives are different," Millie explained. "Becky seduced Ben in full knowledge that she'd slept with Matt. She may have even guessed she was pregnant. Even telling you last fall was malicious, if she knew or even guessed Matt was the father. Matt, too, must have at least wondered if Caleb was his, and yet, he stood by and let Ben carry the burden.

"There's a passage in Proverbs that says 'the Lord searches the heart and weighs the motives behind the thoughts.' Becky was cunning. Matt was dubious. Ben was—"

"Misguided."

It came out before I could stop it.

"Ed and I deeply regret advising Ben to keep it from you."

"You must have thought it would come out at some point."

"We kept looking ahead to Ben finishing school. I think all three of us nearly dropped dead on call day because we'd always said we'd deal with it then. Suddenly, it became clear God was going to deal with what we hadn't."

"If this year taught me anything, it is that I have very little control," I admitted.

"Why we thought we could control it or that it would even be good to control is beyond me. It's been amazing to see what you've done with Caleb. Even if he isn't yours or Ben's, I'm grateful God's allowing you to care for him. You are a wonderful mother."

If only she knew the horrid thoughts I'd had about Caleb when he first came or all the times I hoped Becky would pick him up so Ben and I could get on with the business of having our own family.

Like Millie, I'd tried to be in control. Like Millie, all it got me was stuck.

To say Lexie was having brunch was not completely accurate. Hosting brunch, yes. Greg did the cooking. To Caleb's dismay, the menu included fruit compote and bacon and asparagus quiche. To his relief, Greg had also whipped up blueberry muffins.

"When is the wedding?" I whispered to Lexie after filling my plate with Greg's assortment.

"I don't know, Greg. When should we get married?"

"I've always liked October. November would be okay too," he answered.

"Let's do November. Then we can go to a ski resort for our honeymoon."

"Good idea."

Lexie turned to me. "November."

"Good to know."

"We'd like Ben to marry us and you to stand up for us."

"Is this official?" I asked.

"It is," Greg said, moving his full-length apron aside to produce a ring from his pocket.

Was this sane? They'd dated less than two months. And, why wasn't he proposing on the top of a mountain they'd scaled, or shoving the ring in the mouth of one of the icy fish they caught? Everything about this said anticlimactic.

"I proposed last night, but because I wanted it to be a surprise, I guessed her ring size, and I guessed wrong."

Never mind.

Lexie smiled. "It's okay, Meghan. I've done crazier things—like trying to track down a sex-trafficking murderer."

"Let's leave Mophead out of this," I said, wrapping my arms around her to give her a squeeze.

In an attempt to shield myself from all further cases of astonishment, it was probably best to accept that Greg and Lexie were the type to always live on the edge of crazy.

Matt talking about making amends had me thinking. As we left Lexie's house, I asked if we could make the stop I'd talked to Ben about earlier.

When the car came to a stop, Caleb looked up and ran to the door. If it had been unlocked, he would have gone in. Since it was locked, we told him to ring the doorbell.

The man answering the door was average height, a bit broad through the shoulders but slim through the waist. His gray hair was trimmed, and short sideburns gave him a bit of a Wild West air. His rosy cheeks added to the "wind-chapped" look.

Caleb dove into his arms and yelled, "Grandpa!"

He hardly had time to react when a thin-enough-to-be-frail-looking woman with a pixie cut appeared. The lines in her face told of adventure and sorrow, triumph and despair, of regrets and long nights of worry.

"Caleb!" she screamed, wrapping her arms around him.

Her scream produced another body: a very petite, mousy-looking girl with a pointed face, not unlike Caleb's, dark hair, also like Caleb's, and very bushy eyebrows.

"Hello, Alyssa," Ben announced.

That was Alyssa: *the* Alyssa I wasted hours worrying about; *the* Alyssa I feared had stolen Ben's heart or had his baby; *the* Alyssa I almost gave up my marriage for?

"How do you know Alyssa?" Mrs. Ellingson asked.

"She came to see me a few times after I moved to Oronoco," Ben revealed. "I'm Ben Martins, by the way. This is my wife, Meghan."

"It's nice to finally meet you, Ben," Mr. Ellingson responded. "I'm Peter. This is Barb."

We shook hands and they invited us in, taking our coats and hanging them before leading us to the dining room. The mouse went back into hiding. When Barb quit caressing Caleb's hair, she pulled him onto her lap and wrapped her arms around him.

"We've missed you so much," she said to him.

"I've missed you too," he said.

"He goes to preschool three days a week," I informed her.

"You go to school?" Barb cried. "Do you like it?"

He nodded.

"Mom and Michael gave me a train set for Christmas!" he announced.

"They did!" she cried. "How many cars does it have?"

"Four and an engine," he answered.

"That is a super-neat present. Do you know we have presents for you? They're still wrapped and next to the tree."

"Barb wouldn't let us take the tree down," Peter informed us. "She kept insisting Caleb would come, and when he did, she wanted him to know we had remembered him at Christmas."

"Do you want to open your presents now?" Barb asked.

He nodded and started into the living room. Barb plugged in the lights and sat with him next to a still-decorated Christmas tree. She handed him a box. He tore through the wrapping paper, something I had not allowed him to do, and brought a remote control car to Ben.

"That is so cool," Ben exclaimed.

"I have your Christmas outfit here too," Barb said. She turned to me. "Every year, I bought him an outfit and went to Target for pictures. Remember, Caleb?"

Caleb nodded. She handed him the package, which he dutifully opened to produce khaki pants and a green sweater. We slid the sweater over the dress shirt he was wearing.

"Maybe Grandpa Peter can take your picture. It's not the same as the studio, but for this year, it will do."

After Caleb posed for a few pictures in front of their fireplace, Ben asked if Peter and Barb would like to be in the picture.

"We're not dressed up," Barb replied.

"You look fine," Peter urged.

As they huddled next to him, sliding their arms around him, I realized their ache was the same as mine. It was the absence of a child. Their smiles and the sheen of their eyes told that this moment was one they'd been waiting for.

"Your birthday present is here too," Barb announced.

Caleb opened a Lego set and squealed his delight.

"Do you want to put that together now?" Peter asked. "I'll help."

Caleb and Peter settled onto the floor and pieced together an airplane.

"Do you and Becky share custody now?" Barb asked in a hushed voice.

"Caleb's been living with us since August," Ben answered.

She crumpled her face. "I can't imagine why that was necessary. It must have been almost as big of an adjustment for you to wake up one day and have Caleb to take care of as us suddenly not having him after almost five years."

Ben nodded. "It was a bit of a 'sink or swim' moment," he admitted.

"At times, we swam better than others," I confessed. "But we're in a routine now."

"Does Becky have Caleb on the weekends then?"

Ben shook his head. "She's busy with working, and she's just about done with nursing school."

"That should have happened a long time ago. I'm sure with the clinic here, she'll be able to get a job. When she finishes, are you planning on having joint custody? We sure miss seeing Caleb."

Ben and I looked at each other awkwardly, trying to decide what to say and what not to say.

"We're going to be adopting Caleb," Ben told her.

"She's giving him up?" she hissed.

Ben lowered his voice. "It's an open adoption. She can see him whenever she wants."

"Why on earth would she do that?" Barb muttered.

"I think she wants a chance to do all the things she missed out on," I offered.

"That's just silly. Once you have a child, you put that behind you for the sake of the child."

"I guess if you don't have the desire to do that, you do the next best thing and find someone who will," I suggested.

"I just can't imagine."

"I hope you'll be able to patch things up with her," Ben proposed.

"We didn't walk away from her," Barb rebutted.

"But we haven't done a whole lot to let her know the door's still open," Peter stated.

"She still has the same phone number," Ben submitted. "You might think of giving her a call."

"I just don't understand," Barb said.

Peter and Caleb finished the airplane, and Peter walked us to the car.

"Barb and Becky don't see eye to eye," he told us once Caleb was in the backseat. "They never have. It's a constant battle for control, and usually, they both lose. We all do."

"I'm sorry to hear that," Ben said.

"Thank you for bringing him," Peter said. "Now at least we can take down the tree. By the way, who is Michael?"

"Becky's husband," Ben answered.

"Husband?" he exclaimed. "Well, that was fast."

Ben nodded and shook his hand and we drove away, sensing things were quite possibly worse than when we'd arrived. Eventually, they'd find out Becky was pregnant and that we'd be adopting that child too. When that happened, Barb just might need Pastor Gibbons.

"I've come to realize this isn't going to be pretty," Amanda said.

I was sorting a stack of papers from her dining room table.

"What do you mean?" I asked.

"Matt didn't come home from treatment suddenly being the husband and father I wanted."

"Oh?"

"He's lost his friend, Meg. Like your cigarettes."

"Don't worry. It's temporary. Eventually, he'll realize alcohol wasn't worth his affection."

"It's annoying to watch. It's like an affair. Not only that, but he's blaming me."

"Isn't that normal? I thought alcoholics usually blame someone else."

"Well, it's not a whole lot of fun, and I can assure you, I am not the sole reason he drank."

"I didn't think you were."

"I'll tell you something else. I think people put too much emphasis on having a clean house."

"You're probably right. There has to be a happy medium."

"I went too far one way, and I understand that, but Matt thinks we're going to have this perfect house now, and who's he kidding? We still have two small children. I'm not going to spend my every waking hour cleaning."

"I wouldn't want you to."

"Well, Matt does."

"You need to find your new normal. The house doesn't have to be spotless. It just has to be what you can both live with. If it were up to Ben, I'd see my friends about once a month. Maybe that is where we're headed, but in the middle of the chaos, I needed to see them more. He wanted me to do more of the parenting with Caleb. It happened, but not overnight. You need to be patient with each other and express your desires without expecting perfection or instantaneous change."

"And what if change doesn't come?"

"Are you talking about you or Matt?"

"He's just not dad material. He doesn't sit down and play with the kids. He's okay with me raising them."

"Then raise them."

"I can't do it all. I can't play with them and cook and clean and be the wife he wants me to be."

"Have him choose what is most important to him, and you do the same. That's what you work on."

"How do you know this?"

"Tons of counseling. Pastor Gibbons said it would pay dividends eventually. I guess you just cashed a check."

"It's going to take a mint for Matt and me to make it."

"Have you thought of counseling?"

"Matt's not interested."

"Ben wasn't too thrilled with me calling Professor Ambrose, but I was desperate, and I couldn't see us making it on our own."

"I know the feeling."

"Well, you're welcome to all I learned. Having a third party was nice. Pastor Gibbons was able to put both of us in our place. He did it nicely, of course, but …"

Chapter Fifteen

LIGHT ON THE HORIZON

February made its way to March, and March made its way into April. Tonya's baby arrived on schedule. Elijah had a brother whom they named Ezekiel, but they would call him Zeke for short.

I would not call him Zeke. Because I had a five-year-old and because we visited the Rochester Public Library often, and because Mr. Putter was fun for both Caleb and I, we had read many of the Mr. Putter books. Mr. Putter's friend and neighbor, Mrs. Teaberry, had a very ugly-looking dog called Zeke.

Tonya would someday know that, too, but I would not be the one to tell her. For the time being, I visited my ridiculously-perfect-looking-even-after-childbirth friend, her adorable newborn son, and her beaming husband. I held him and gave him snuggle toys, and all was well.

But all was not well. Becky was not well. Her blood pressure was the first sign, but now other parts of her body were retaliating, too, with a syndrome known as

HELLP. Decisions had to be made about inducing or sticking it out.

Adding to the drama, Becky required hospitalization, and it was nearing the end of the semester. Incredibly, Becky chose to stay in the hospital, giving the baby's lungs longer to develop, even as the doctors were giving Becky shots to facilitate that. We visited her daily, and she graciously showed us the latest ultrasounds. Every day, we prayed for Becky and the baby, and we waited.

Liz's last Bible study of the year met the third Sunday of April. Dora and Nora had been going with me, but neither of them were able to this time.

I wasn't sure I should go, but Ben assured me fifteen minutes wouldn't make a difference and he'd call me instantly if there was news. I made the trek alone, contemplating how life was about to change. By the time Bible study began again in the fall, I would hopefully have a five-month-old.

What kind of baby would she be? Amanda said she'd rather have a clingy baby than a colicky baby. What if I was like Matt after all, and parenthood was not my thing?

The parking lot to Christ Lutheran was abnormally full. I found a spot and sauntered in. As I stepped off the last step, I was bombarded with people yelling, "Surprise!" and ushered to a table. As I scanned the room, I saw faces from church, from Oronoco, and even Amanda and Tonya and Ezekiel were there.

Liz started with a prayer that God would bless our child with a healthy delivery and childhood, that the child would be a blessing to Ben and Caleb and me, and that God would provide Ben and me with all we needed to raise this baby and Caleb.

There were games, gifts, and a whole lot of food before the evening came to a close.

Amanda, Dora, Lexie, Liz, Nora,Tonya, and I were relishing the moments of the evening when Ben came in.

My heart sank when I saw him. Now, after all these gifts and blessings, I couldn't bear bad news.

"How'd it go?" he asked.

"Is everything okay?" I countered.

"I just came to help you bring everything home."

"Really?"

"No. Could you give your car keys to Amanda?" He turned to her. "Our house key is on the keychain too. Do you mind putting Caleb to bed tonight?"

I saw Caleb waiting by the steps.

"I don't mind," Amanda answered. "What's wrong?"

"Nothing. But Becky's water broke."

"She's in labor?" I cried.

"We have plenty of time."

The women huddled around me with squeals of delight. After handing off my keys and giving Caleb a hug and a reminder to be good, I followed Ben out the door, praying both Becky and the baby would be all right.

Epilogue

Dear Lily,

Thank you for your letters. It is always good to hear from you. I'm sorry I haven't had a chance to write until now.

On April 22 at 3:45 a.m., our baby girl was born. Ben and I were waiting outside the room and heard her first cries! We decided beforehand that we wanted Becky and Michael to have some time with her first and that we would not come in until the afterbirth was delivered and Becky was "decent."

Those first cries brought both Ben and I to tears. When we were ushered into the room and Michael placed her into my arms, I had to sit down, as I couldn't control the sobs. She looked at me with wide-open eyes right from the start. After seeing her and holding her, Michael and Becky signed the adoption papers. We were able to take her home after her shots and bath. She weighed seven pounds, four ounces and was eighteen inches long.

These days, I spend a lot of time holding her and praying God would forgive me for ever doubting I could love a child that didn't come from my body. She's up every two to four hours to eat, but I don't care in the least. I warm up her bottle and stare at the perfect miracle that she is.

We named her Hallie Elizabeth Martins. *Hallie* means "unexpected gift." *Elizabeth* means "consecrated to God," and *Martins* means she'll be raised in a godly family. It's taken me awhile to feel that way again, but Ben's mom reminded me that God weighs motives, not just actions. Thankfully, you and others kept reminding me Ben is a decent man.

I met another woman about your age here. Her name is Millie, just like Ben's mom. She crocheted the most beautiful pink-and-purple blanket for Hallie.

For Ben's installation, a member of the congregation gave me a Chronological Bible. I thought it was an odd gift (and to me!), but I've been reading it each night. I just read Psalm 78. It is all about Israel's rebellion, when they were in the desert, and how time after time, God gave them reason to trust him, but time after time, they found it easier to complain.

Verses 23-25 say, "Yet he gave a command to the skies above and opened the doors of the heavens; He rained down manna for the people to eat. He gave them the grain of heaven. Human beings ate the bread of angels."

Lily, I am eating the bread of angels. I have a gift so undeserved, so beyond what I could produce—a gift that fills me completely.

Thank you for walking me through my dark days, not just with all your encouraging cards and letters, but when I was at my lowest and popped in unexpectedly. Next time I stop for a visit, I will introduce you to Hallie.

Praying you are well and sending all my love,
Meghan

CPSIA information can be obtained
at www.ICGtesting.com
Printed in the USA
FFOW05n2107260116

9 781512 725742